FROM SHADOW AND SILENCE

AN ELEMENTS OF FIVE NOVEL

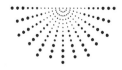

CARRIE ANN RYAN

FROM SHADOW AND SILENCE

An Elements of Five Novel
By
Carrie Ann Ryan

From Shadow and Silence
An Elements of Five Novel
By: Carrie Ann Ryan
© 2021 Carrie Ann Ryan
ISBN: 978-1-950443-03-1

For more information, please join Carrie Ann Ryan's MAILING LIST.
To interact with Carrie Ann Ryan, you can join her FAN CLUB

PRAISE FOR CARRIE ANN RYAN ....

"Carrie Ann Ryan knows how to pull your heartstrings and make your pulse pound! Her wonderful Redwood Pack series will draw you in and keep you reading long into the night. I can't wait to see what comes next with the new generation, the Talons. Keep them coming, Carrie Ann!" –Lara Adrian, New York Times bestselling author of CRAVE THE NIGHT

"Carrie Ann Ryan never fails to draw readers in with passion, raw sensuality, and characters that pop off the page. Any book by Carrie Ann is an absolute treat." – New York Times Bestselling Author J. Kenner

"With snarky humor, sizzling love scenes, and brilliant, imaginative worldbuilding, The Dante's Circle series reads as if Carrie Ann Ryan peeked at my personal wish list!" – NYT Bestselling Author, Larissa Ione

"Carrie Ann Ryan writes sexy shifters in a world full of passionate happily-ever-afters." – *New York Times* Bestselling Author Vivian Arend

Carrie Ann Ryan's books are wickedly funny and deliciously hot, with plenty of twists to keep you guessing. They'll keep you up all night!" USA Today Bestselling Author Cari Quinn

"Once again, Carrie Ann Ryan knocks the Dante's Circle series out of the park. The queen of hot, sexy, enthralling paranormal romance, Carrie Ann is an author not to miss!" *New York Times* bestselling Author Marie Harte

To those who believed.

FROM SHADOW AND SILENCE

The unforgettable conclusion to the epic fantasy Elements of Five series from NYT Bestselling author Carrie Ann Ryan.

The end of the centuries-long war is almost here, and the fate of the realm rests on one girl's shoulders. The Gray has gathered his forces—and has Lyric in his clutches. The enemy's plan to control the kingdoms has been revealed, but traitors from both sides might alter the course of fate.

Lyric must return to Easton and the others before all is lost. Battle lines must be forged, and surprising alliances cast. The prophecy has never altered, and life comes at an ultimate price. Not all who fight will survive, but in the end, it will come down to the choice of a Priestess and her soul.

CHAPTER ONE

LYRIC

I WASN'T DREAMING.

Odd, since I'd had this dream before. I'd felt these flames, this wind. I'd had this dirt under my feet; heard the sound of water hitting my ears from far off in the distance like I did now.

Only I knew this wasn't a dream.

It was a nightmare.

A living one.

I stood on the connecting points of five elements and four directions—the center of the abyss. But there was no real light, only shadow.

And I knew this wasn't a dream.

Wasn't where the world crept over my skin and seeped into my soul. It had to be real.

And I wasn't alone.

Braelynn stood near my shoulder, her wings tucked behind her, the right one brushing my hair.

She'd once been human, my best friend. Now, she was my Familiar, a cat with wings who could breathe fire. Recently, she'd found herself able to grow into the size of a panther, as well. Fortunately for my shoulder, she'd reverted to her original size—around the size of a house cat.

I knelt in the corner of a cave—at least it felt as if it could be a one—and tried to control my breathing. Braelynn nuzzled into the side of my face, and I reached up and tried to pet her, only I hit her wing instead, and cursed under my breath.

"I'm sorry," I whispered. I didn't know if anyone was listening, and I didn't want them to hear what I was saying. It wasn't as if the apology falling from my lips, issued to a cat on my shoulder, would matter in the end.

I let out a breath, tried to reach my Wielding, but I couldn't. I only felt a gaping void gnawing at my soul. Panic slid through me at the thought, and I tried again.

Nothing.

Again.

Nothing.

No Wielding.

I was the Spirit Priestess, one who could hold all five elements of the realm. Though I didn't know if I was *in* the Maison realm at the moment. Still, I should have been able to use Earth, Water, Air, and Fire. As well as Spirit.

When I was in the human realm, I wasn't able to use my Wielding to its full extent, but I could still feel the tendrils of power deep inside, spiraling through my body.

Others had sacrificed so much to help me get to the point where I could even unlock my elements. I had lost so much in my pursuit of them, and I was still learning to control my power. However, I should be able to feel them. Yet, I couldn't. It was as if something had blocked me; dampened my senses. And I couldn't understand why.

Was this the Shadow realm that Easton had talked about?

I swallowed hard and tried not to think about Easton. Because I missed him. He had been taken from me before. After enduring so much, after breaking the curse, finding him, and losing so many of our people along the way, now *I* had been taken.

I would get back to him.

I had to.

I would get Braelynn home. And I would find a way to protect the realm and bring the crystals back together.

There was nearly no light in the cave, shadows all around me. But the thin sliver of illumination I saw danced along my skin and shone brightly.

The sparkles within from the remnants of the two crystals—both the dark and the light—that had been embedded in my skin when they shattered.

The Obscurité and the Lumière fighting for so long, killing each other along the way, had destroyed their crystals, as well.

The crystals that kept the Maisons alive.

I didn't know what would happen now that they were gone.

Could I use them somehow? I didn't think so. They had only just shattered, finally losing their fight in the war. And, somehow, becoming a part of me.

Then The Gray, the Wielder of shadow, had taken me. Taken me to his realm, most likely—if that's where this was—and away from my friends. My new family. I had no other family left. The Gray had sent his lackey to kill my parents. They were gone, murdered in front of me, and that was how I ended up with the Spirit element in my body. The one I didn't quite understand.

It wasn't like it would help me now anyway.

Braelynn purred, and I wished she would grow and use that fire she could spew from her mouth.

It was a new talent, one I didn't understand, but everyone else seemed to. It was like a running joke for my friends to hide what Braelynn truly was and what being a Familiar entailed. I didn't mind. It was nice to have something fun, a mystery that couldn't hurt. Especially since I had so many secrets that had dug deep down into my skin, never to let go, their claws penetrating my flesh and taking part of my soul along the way.

"You seem so introspective," a deep, rumbling voice said from the doorway. I stood up, my knees shaking, my skin bloody. I swallowed hard.

"You've made a mistake by taking me," I said, my voice far stronger than I imagined. Good. Because I wasn't just going to lie down and take this. I wouldn't let him win.

I would find a way to access my Wielding, and I would break free. The others wouldn't have to come for me. They had other things to worry about. Namely, a realm that was being ripped apart at the very seams.

They needed to protect the territories, safeguard the innocent.

I would have to save myself.

"You seem to be full of words and false promises for someone locked in a cave with a cat." The Gray moved forward, his cowl over his head so I couldn't see his face. "But then again, that's not quite a cat, is it? A young Familiar? Interesting. Though one you don't seem to know how to harness the power of. Which makes sense. Despite the prophecy of the powerful Spirit Priestess, you seem to be nothing. No one. Of no consequence."

I swallowed hard and glared at him. I desperately wanted to pull from my Wielding like I'd been trained to, only I couldn't. I hoped it was only temporary. If not? No...I wouldn't think about that. I pulled my focus back to The Gray. "You're the one still talking, not me."

The Gray lifted his head, his cowl falling back. He glared. "Oh, I'm going to have fun with you, dear Lyric. Just like my friend had fun with your parents."

I glared, and Braelynn huffed smoke out through her nose as Garrik and another man moved up from behind The Gray. I didn't know who this other man was, but it had to be Durlan. The Gray's second, the one Easton hadn't been sure he killed. Evidently, Durlan was still alive, though he did look a little pale and sickly—probably because he'd had a knife in his gut. I hoped he died soon.

Not something I would have ever thought before I came to this place. After all, I had been born human. Or so I'd thought. I hadn't known the Maison realm lay upon the human realm. I didn't know there were even more realms, ones I didn't have names for yet, where others lived, and magic was wrought.

The territories of the Maison realm had been at war with each other for eons; the kingdoms split into two courts ages ago.

The Lumière, the light, held the Water and Air territories. While the Obscurité, the dark, held Fire and Earth. The Spirit territories lay between them, not of either court but of their own power. Until the Spirit Wielders were murdered, wiped out, and those who had survived hidden amongst the humans.

When the first kings fought for so long, they had turned their people against one another. Great battles and wars ensued and eventually created the Fall—a cataclysmic event that had forever and irrevocably altered the realm.

During the Fall, the realm had fractured, a large crack that had taken lives, including those of the kings. A new Queen of Obscurité and King of Lumière had risen, a daughter and son of their respective courts. They continued to fight, though not in the same fashion. Queen Cameo had done her best to keep the peace, though it hadn't looked as such. King Brokk, and his twin, Lord Durin, had broken the laws of the Maisons and sacrificed lives for their power. They'd used Bone magic and worse.

The crystals that kept the realms alive endured the most strain, the cost high. They bled power and thus created the Danes—former Wielders who had been stripped of their power but not their lives. They existed without Wielding in a world that required magic to thrive.

The fracture had also created the Negs, dark energy monsters that killed and worked for The Gray—a fact I hadn't known until recently. The Fall had created chaos and doom. And a demise that was sure to come.

However, the prophecy brought hope.

A foretelling that was me. The Spirit Priestess who could Wield all five elements and somehow seal the breach.

Only that wasn't happening.

Instead, the fracture had only gotten worse. The Gray had orchestrated more war, more battles. I had lost friends, family, and even a part of myself. It didn't matter that I had found my soulmate because I wasn't near him now, and the bond that we had created wasn't enough to save those we loved.

The Gray was winning.

He had used the king of the Lumière as well as his brother, the Lord of Water, to take down the Obscurité. We had lost, at significant cost to my friends, and had thus begun a new Fall.

Now, there was no Lumière and Obscurité. Just those against The Gray, and The Gray himself.

As I stood in the shadows and watched Durlan, the man who had tried to kill Easton—my soulmate, the king of the Obscurité Kingdom in title and one of our resistance leaders—I could only remember what the vile man had done. He had tortured Easton, and I knew he was here to do the same to me.

My anger was not for him alone. No, it was also for the Whisperer at his side.

Garrik was a Dane but held power in a way that wasn't of this realm. At least, that's what I thought. He could ferret out secrets, and had been spying on my friends within the Obscurité Court before he did the unthinkable.

He and The Gray had used each other and killed my parents right in front of me. It had shattered my soul into a thousand pieces, leaving me dust. Somehow, I was still standing, looking at the man who had killed my family. And while I knew I had no Wielding here, I wasn't powerless.

I couldn't be, not with the rage inside my soul.

"Ah, I see you remember me. How is my old friend?" Garrik asked, grinning. He ducked his shoulders, lowered his head, and gave me what I thought might be puppy-dog eyes. All I saw was death. "The Prince of Obscurité was never much for strength. 'Oh, help me, I'm just sad, and I hate being part of this. They always hurt me, and nobody likes me. Won't you like me?'" He started to laugh. I moved forward, my hands outstretched. No Wielding came, but Braelynn growled on my shoulder. The Gray simply laughed.

He laughed.

"Stop trying to use your Wielding, Priestess. You are amusing, though." The Gray flicked his fingers, and shadows slid around me, ropes of darkness coiling around my stomach and my arms. They shackled me to the walls, arms outstretched, feet tethered to the floor. Braelynn was still on my shoulder, and it was like The Gray didn't even bother worrying about her.

For that, I was grateful. He could hurt me if he wanted. I would find a way out. But if he hurt Braelynn…?

I would never forgive myself.

And he would scream in agony as I killed him.

The shadow ropes around my wrists tightened, and my fingers splayed, trying to get blood to flow through them. It felt as if the bonds were burning as they dug into my flesh. Blood trickled down, and I let out a slow breath. I could survive this.

I would.

The others wouldn't need to come for me.

I could do this.

The Gray looked at Braelynn on my shoulder and flicked his fingers again. Suddenly, she was floating in the air right above my head, wrapped in a protective smoke cage. She beat at the wispy bars and growled, but she seemed unharmed.

Pain radiated through my arms and legs, but I didn't care. He couldn't hurt me. I was going to survive this. I had to.

The Gray smiled, and Durlan moved forward, a knife in his hand. I let fear slide into me. Just a trickle of trepidation.

But I knew something he didn't.

I knew The Gray couldn't hold back my powers forever.

Easton might have been able to make it out with someone's help, and for that, I'd be forever grateful. But I could feel some of my Wielding coming back. It was as if my powers were trapped behind a wall. If I kept digging, using whatever mental strength I could muster, I could get to them. And I could get myself out of this.

I had to.

Because I was the Spirit Priestess, and I would not let anyone else die for me.

"The Maison realm will be mine, and we'll no longer be locked within this Shadow realm for long stretches of time. You'll remain here as my power, my source. And I will rule as I should have long ago." He took a step forward and then another. "Because you should know who I am, dear Lyric. You should know a Spirit Wielder when you see one."

My eyes widened. I shook my head, shock and shame sliding through me. "No, the Spirit Wielders are dead." He couldn't be of the lost people.

"Not all of them. Some hid, and others were chained. For, of course, not all Spirit Wielders were on the side of the Obscurité."

I frowned. "What are you saying?"

"The King of Lumière, the old one, the one who died in the Fall, used bone magic and the Spirit Wielders to create his power. He was the one who started all of this. And I was his knight." The Gray grinned, even as realization dawned.

I had always known it hadn't been balanced. The Lumière hadn't always been right, and the Obscurité hadn't always been cast in shadow. The histories weren't always of truth. They were written by those in power.

I hadn't known a Spirit Wielder had been on the side of the mad king, though. The Spirit Wielders were often tortured and had almost been eradicated.

They touched souls and kept the living free.

And *he* had been one of them.

But one of darkness. And yet, he'd worked for the Lumière. The light.

"I am a Spirit Wielder, Lyric. And that means I can take your soul. I can touch it. I can wrap it in shadow. I can twist it. I can do whatever I need to."

"You'll never win," I spat, fear laying on itself within me.

"You think your perfect little boyfriend will be able to find you? Or is that two boyfriends? I never can quite keep up with teenagers and their sordid affairs."

"No one needs to save me. I'm the Spirit Priestess. I can save myself."

The Gray smiled, a flash of teeth. "Well, that should be interesting. You have no power here. I am the one with the Wielding, and have a Whisperer and a man with a knife besides."

Durlan took another step forward. The flash of light was quick, and I screamed.

CHAPTER TWO

EASTON

I TRIED TO CATCH MY BREATH, BUT I COULDN'T. THERE WAS ONLY rage and the absence of anything pure. I thought I had lost my soul once, but I had been wrong.

As I stood in the field where Lyric had once been before the shadow took her, I knew I had lost my soul again. Not like a tragedy where I could dig myself out after I found a way to heal. This was all-encompassing. Pure terror that ripped me limb from limb as I begged for a salvation that would never come.

"Easton. We don't have time for this."

I looked over at Wyn, one of my best friends, my fellow warrior, and wanted to rip her throat out. "Don't have time for what?" I asked, my voice calm. *Too* calm. Thankfully, she seemed to realize what that meant. Fire slid up my arms, but I tamped it down, not wanting to use my Wielding. I was exhausted, bleeding, and broken. My Wielding reserves were almost depleted. But I had enough to scream.

To vent.

To purge.

Tears filled Wyn's eyes for a moment—only an instant before she quickly blinked them away.

I cursed under my breath. I knew she wasn't cold, wasn't heartless. No, that was all me.

Had always been and would always be. The only flame that could melt the ice was that of the woman who was no longer in front of me.

Vanished within smoke.

Wyn raised her chin. "I'm sorry, but we need to gather our forces, our dead, and figure out exactly what the hell is going on. And who took Lyric. *How* they took Lyric."

"I know who took Lyric." My voice was cold, precise. "You know, too."

She nodded, her face covered in dirt and blood. "Okay, I do. But we can't fix that right now. We can't go after her. Not until we know what we're facing. If you leave right now, you are leaving *everyone*—your people. And you don't have much else. We need your help, Easton. We all do." She paused. "*I* do."

She looked down at her hands, Water sliding from her fingertips, and I held back another curse. She had lost her Wielding during one of the dark crystal's many power surges during our new Fall. Somehow, after Lyric had connected with the crystal, Wyn had gained her powers back. But instead of being only an Earth Wielder like she had been for centuries, she was now an Earth Wielder...*and* a Water Wielder. I didn't know of any other person over the past thousand years who had held those two powers.

It had always been Earth and Fire or Water and Air. Obscurité and Lumière. Spirit had been lost to death, cast in mystery.

The two factions outside of Spirit didn't meet, not after the realm had eventually been carved into two separate kingdoms. When the old kings began the wars for more territory, more power, or whatever other fabled explanations the histories gave, the two kingdoms didn't mix powers.

It was unheard of.

There had been stories of long-lost loves and those who secreted themselves away to hide in the Spirit territories or even the human realm. Those Lumière and Obscurité who'd shared a forbidden love. Even their children never had more than one power. One element.

Most Wielders only had one Wielding to begin with. Two elements within a single Wielder was not uncommon, but those who had it weren't in abundance, either. A dual Wielder with the powers of both kingdoms running through their veins?

I had never heard of such a thing after the Fall, and it was only myth and legend *before* that time.

And now, here Wyn was, standing in front of me with power I knew she couldn't handle—at least, not yet—and that was just the beginning of it.

The realm was shattering around us, breaking into pieces, and holes in our very universe were rupturing. People were crying, healers trying to work their magic. *Literally.* Doing their best to keep others alive, and still others finding their places as they gathered themselves and tried to breathe.

"Okay, okay. I get it. We'll figure it out. Do what needs to be done." I paused, lowering my brows. "I'm going after her as soon as I can. I'm going."

"We wouldn't have it any other way," Wyn said quickly. "We're going to find her. And not just because of who she is. Not because of *what* she is. Because she's Lyric. And she's ours."

I understood that. The realm needed Lyric because of her powers, because of the prophecy. Our friends and family needed her because she was Lyric.

I needed her because she was the other half of my soul.

My heart, my future. And I was supposed to die for her, not the other way around. I'd be damned if I let The Gray have her.

"Any other updates?" I asked as we began moving through the ranks, looking over the people who had fought for freedom by our sides. There were warriors, bakers, teachers, those who had never fought before but were powerful in their own right. They were trained, and once we were able, they would be taught more. They had dropped everything to keep our people alive, and I would never forget that.

"Lanya is with Delphine. She's helping the other woman."

I sighed. "Will Delphine survive?"

Wyn nodded as Teagan came up when we stopped near a bluff. My other best friend stood silent, his jaw tense, soot covering his face.

I didn't know what to say to him, though I didn't think there were words. He had watched his mother burn to ash and had fought alongside his grieving father to protect the realm. But it almost felt as if it hadn't been enough. I couldn't help them.

"Delphine will never see again." Wyn let out a shaky breath as she continued. "She saved my life." Teagan reached out and gripped her shoulder, squeezing it, but Wyn shook off his hand.

That surprised me, but it shouldn't have. The two had always had a rocky relationship, but they were pulling away from each other more and more. There was nothing I could do about that. There was nothing I could do about so much.

"And Lanya. How is she faring?" I asked after the Lady of Air—a title I wasn't sure she wanted anymore.

"My grandmother's whole. Unharmed but for a few bruises," Rhodes said as he made his way over to our group.

I looked at the other man, his dark hair pulled back, his silver eyes shadowed. I had once hated him. After all, I had grown up believing that he was the opposite of who I was and everything I stood for.

The *actual* Prince of Lumière, the late Eitri, had been my opposite, but I had never thought much about him. He had been nearly powerless until he used The Gray to try and kill us. He died painfully because of it.

Rhodes, however? Rhodes had always been similar to me in power. He had searched for the fabled Spirit Priestess just like I did. When I was forced to stop hunting because my kingdom was dying, and there were only so many people who could protect it, Rhodes had been the one to look for her.

He had found Lyric, and thought she was his soulmate—not mine. We had all been wrong, and I had been a jealous asshole.

In the end, Rhodes left his home and found her, but he hadn't known the true decay lurking within his kingdom. None of us had.

"I'm glad she's okay," I said honestly.

"She'll be with Delphine until the former Queen of Lumière can fight again. She will, even if she has to learn to Wield differently."

"Are you sure?"

"She can fight alongside your uncle and help heal."

My uncle, Ridley, was a healer. One I had once thought belonged to the Obscurité. Instead, I'd found out he was a spy for the Lumière and was actually a Water Wielder. However, no one had the time to go through the exact ramifications of that. He had married my Uncle Justise, our blacksmith and the son of the old king. The line of succession went to me after my mother died while saving Lyric's life. Now, I was the king of the Obscurité Kingdom—or what remained of it.

Looking down at the burned remains of the battlefield, I wondered what type of kingdom I had left to rule. I pulled myself from my thoughts, knowing I needed to focus. Only I couldn't when Lyric was gone. She had been taken from me. From all of us.

"And you're okay? Rosamond?" I asked him, speaking of Rhodes' sister, a Seer.

"We're both well enough. She's with Emory, helping Ridley and Justise with the wounded."

I held back a flinch at the mention of Emory. Not because she was Lyric's ex-girlfriend, but because I still didn't trust her. She was a siphon, one the late king of the Lumière had created. She could siphon Wielding from others, and it was only because of the bracelets she wore that Justise had made for her that she could stand amongst the Wielders now and not pull their magic and their life right from them.

She had changed since the king's attack, at least from what I had seen. She wasn't so angry all the time now. However, with so much uncertainty amongst us, it was hard to trust anyone.

"It seems like we're running out of lords and ladies," Wyn said, her voice soft. Both Rhodes and Teagan winced, but Wyn held her chin high. Her father was dead, the former Lord of Earth, and her mother had been outed as a traitor. If she needed to get angry, we'd let her. The others would understand.

"We'll rebuild," I said. "But I don't know if we can truly have lords, ladies, or even kings and queens anymore. The wards are down, and there are no more separate kingdoms. There can't be, not when there are no crystals." A fact that still shocked me. The wards had come down between the two courts, and now, nothing separated the two kingdoms but land and armies. Armies that were now mixed between the four territories. "There are only people who need to survive, and an enemy we have to face."

"Well, my mother's going to be on the enemy lines," Wyn said, her voice revealing that she clearly fought back tears...or perhaps anger. "She wasn't my father's soulmate, after all. She used him as a shield and let him burn to a crisp in front of us all. And yet, she survived." Tears slid down her cheeks now, but she didn't brush them away. There was no need. We all felt what she did.

"What's the next step?" Rhodes asked, looking directly at me.

"We need to recruit, train, and take the wounded back to a place where they are safe. And keep everybody under guard. We don't know when The Gray will come for us, or what forces he'll have. But we know it's not Obscurité or Lumière anymore."

"No. Therefore, don't you dare start calling me the king of the Lumière," Rhodes rasped out.

I laughed. I couldn't help it. So much pain, anger, and anxiety whirled through me, yet I smiled. "You never did want to be king, did you?" I asked.

"Neither did you. But it doesn't seem like we have a choice." He swallowed hard and looked around with this piercing silver eyes. "We're going after Lyric, right?" he asked, his voice hollow. I understood the feeling well.

"Of course, we are," I snapped.

"Our people need a king," Justise barked, his tone unyielding as he walked towards us. It seemed as if we were having a full court meeting right in the open. Good.

Let the others know who was in charge.

Show them who would fix this.

And I will know that I am not alone.

I turned on my uncle. "And they need their Priestess."

Justise didn't back down. The man was big, battle-weary, a machine. "They do, and the others can find her. You need to be here. We need to strategize, come up with plans. Because when The Gray comes again, he's going to know we are weakened."

"We have some of their forces, those that Lanya already helped us determine are directly on our side." Lanya and her granddaughter, Rosamond, had used some type of Wielding to figure out if they were telling the truth. It was good magic, not borne of darkness like bone magic, which was created out of death and unwilling sacrifice.

I still didn't know the power behind what these two were doing. It wasn't something I held or fully understood, but I trusted Lanya and Rosamond with my life. What I did know was that the magic tasted of ancient hope and power. But of peace, as well.

"I'm not going to let others find her, Uncle. I need to go."

Justise shook his head, and it felt like a thousand knives sliding into my skin. "She will be found. We will defeat The Gray, but you are needed here, with your people."

"*She* needs me." I let out a breath, knowing that my uncle was right. And I hated the fact that he was. I fisted my hands at my sides, and flame danced along my knuckles while the earth rumbled under my feet.

My two elements warred inside me, each wanting control. But I was the dominant one. I always had been.

While Lyric still needed to focus on the elements inside her and learn how to rein in that control, I had always known the truth of who I was deep in my bones. I'd held these powers my entire life. I'd been forced to learn dominance with the amount of Fire in my veins—the hardest element to Wield. I'd found that power deep within myself and nurtured it. I'd taught Lyric what I could about it and had trained her to control hers, as well. At least I had been trying. Between the curse that had kept me from her initially, The Gray attempting to control me, and the war that threatened all of us, I hadn't been able to help her as much as I should have.

Now, I didn't know if she had enough training to protect herself. She had enough power, but it was unwieldy.

I shoved those thoughts from my mind. No, she would be fine. We would find her, and she would be able to protect herself until we did. She was so much stronger than she gave herself credit for, so much stronger than anyone else I knew.

There was no way The Gray would defeat her.

There couldn't be.

"You're right," I said into the silence. Wyn and Teagan blinked at me. I didn't blame them for their surprise.

Rhodes spoke first. "I'll go. I can help find her. You need to be here for your people, to show them their leader. I might confuse others with my presence since they'll likely be looking for another king to name."

At any other time, or if I were still the person I was even a month ago, I would've shouted and made some snarky reply. I'd have been jealous. However, I couldn't afford that reaction anymore. Not when so many more important things were before us.

"Go. Take Alura with you." I spoke of the secretive Wielder who had lived in the human realm for as long as I could remember. She had watched over Lyric but kept her secrets, hid her Wielding. However, I thought that perhaps she was a Seer like Rosamond. She had trained Lyric during her year away from the realm, but she had so many secrets that I sometimes thought she knew more than she was letting on. I wanted someone that could find Lyric, and Rhodes and Alura had found her before. They could find her again.

"I can do that. I'll find her," Rhodes vowed.

"Keep her safe. And bring her back. We will prepare for battle." I was dying inside, and the other man knew it. There wasn't anything I could do about it, though. Not when the weight of our world rested on my shoulders. However, if Rhodes didn't find Lyric soon, I'd throw it all away for her.

And everyone in this circle knew it.

"W—" Rhodes' words were cut off as a growl sounded from behind us. My Fire stretched out.

Negs.

They were the absence of light, made of darkness and cruelty. Negs were dark monsters with sharp fangs and even sharper claws. They worked for The Gray, had once worked for the knight of the Obscurité, Lore. The man who had tortured me and killed my mother.

And, as it turned out, my father.

Lore had wanted more power, and he had helped to create the Negs along with The Gray.

But Lore was gone. The Gray, unfortunately, was still here. And he was the one who controlled the Negs now.

"Protect the wounded," I shouted and let out my Fire, singeing one of the Negs as it jumped at us.

Rhodes pushed at the ground. He used his Air Wielding to fly up, a trick I hadn't seen him do in person before. He slammed back to the ground, his Air pushing at the Neg as he did. It crushed the beast, burying it beneath the Earth that Wyn Wielded.

I hadn't seen them work together like this before, but it was interesting.

I counted seven Negs, and knew I needed to fight, had to burn off some anger. This was just the beginning. War was here. It was no longer on the horizon.

We were in the trenches, and without a Priestess. Without a land to call our own, in a realm that shuddered along the crack in its power.

As a Neg bared down on me, I let my Fire out, burning it to ash. I was suddenly afraid we weren't going to win. Not without help.

Not without Lyric.

CHAPTER THREE

LYRIC

I LET OUT A DEEP BREATH AND TUGGED AT MY BONDS AGAIN. IT WAS no use. They weren't going to budge, but my Wielding was growing. I could feel it deep inside of me, stretching, wanting to come back.

I knew as long as I waited for the right moment, as long as I did my best to keep alive and stay sane, I would get my Wielding back. And I would break free.

I would set us both free.

I looked up at Braelynn, who now lay curled in a ball inside the smoky cage. I wished she could get out.

But no, she couldn't. Instead, she remained the size of a small house cat and looked as if she were conserving her strength.

I didn't know how long we had been here, but it had to be at least a couple of days. The Gray and his men had been in and out of the room and the cave multiple times, each time leaving me exhausted, bloody, but with my soul intact. The Gray hadn't used his Spirit Wielding on me yet. I was grateful for that.

Because I didn't know what he was going to do. Wasn't sure if he could do anything. After all, he had been locked in this pocket realm for how long now? Maybe he didn't have access to his Spirit Wielding anymore.

Or perhaps I was only fooling myself. I didn't know. What I did know was that I was exhausted, and I knew that Braelynn had to be, too. Neither of us had truly slept. We were both too afraid. I could feel her anxiety like my own. The emotions wrapped around each other, but at least we were together.

My best friend was here, the girl I had watched die. And I wasn't about to do it again. Least of all not at the hands of The Gray and his people.

In a perfect world, my Wielding would come back, and I would rip these shadows from my body. I would burn my way through this realm. I'd end the world right here, and then I'd walk through whatever portal I could find and make my way back to the Maison realm and to Easton. In these wonderful fantasies, Braelynn would be by my side, unhurt, and even in her human form.

But she would never have that again. And this wasn't a perfect world. This was the end.

Not my ending, though. I refused to allow that to happen.

I was tired, beaten. I had cuts on my arms and my belly, but they were shallow. *"Just a taste,"* Durlan had said.

But I was relatively unscathed. I was still whole.

I wouldn't let them beat me.

"You're truly not very good at keeping your thoughts to yourself, are you?" Garrik asked as he prowled into the room, his chin high, a smirk on his face.

Easton smirked often, and I loved it when it came from him. Even though the King of Obscurité annoyed me, the first time I saw him, he had smirked over his shoulder while playing with the Fire dancing across his fingertips. But then we had used the fire flower together to take out some Negs as if we had done it all our lives. It hadn't felt as if we were meeting for the first time in that moment.

And, over time, the smirk had grown on me. When I learned more about him and became *part* of him, I realized that expression was his defense. Something so others would see that he was whole and happy and confident. An indication that he knew he could protect his people and keep everyone alive and safe.

They didn't need to know that he was breaking down and worried inside.

Garrik did not have *that* smirk.

The fact that Garrik's expression had even reminded me of Easton at all was almost another nail in the coffin.

The Whisperer in front of me looked nothing like he had when I first saw him. He had been weak, cowering, almost afraid of the world.

But…it had all been an act. We had all known that something was likely up, so we watched, and we listened.

But he had spied more. He could listen in on the whispers of those around him and gain their secrets. He could also get into people's heads, something I hadn't known was possible.

"Are you that bored that you have to listen to my thoughts while I'm chained up in a cave?" I asked, sending out curse words and other horrible images to him in case he was actually listening. I imagined everything that I could do to him, everything I wanted to level upon him for what he had done to my parents. I was pleased to see that he blanched ever so slightly under his already putrid pallor.

Good.

Because I'd do it all.

The girl I'd been before this might not have even had those thoughts. Now, however, I'd do all of it and more, without regret.

Especially after what he'd done.

What he still might do.

"My my. Don't you have an imagination? I thought you were supposed to be the beloved and pure Spirit Priestess. But there's nothing pure about you, is there?"

"You're a murderer. And I'm going to enjoy it when you finally get what you deserve."

Garrik spat in my face, but I kept my chin held high. Braelynn hissed, and I just grinned, despite having no humor in my body. He *would* get what was coming to him.

Because I refused to believe anything else.

"I always wondered what would happen to your sad little realm once you realized the truth. That you don't deserve to be there. That you were wrong. But now, I don't care. How am I supposed to care when you are nothing? Just a figment for those who thought they had hope. Those in power have taken far too much. They are the ones who stole the magic that broke down their societies. Now, they're crying out for help, when they were the ones that did it. Why should we feel sorry for them when they did it to themselves? They do not have the strength nor the power to survive. Why should we allow them to think they deserve anything better?"

"You are a piece of work," I said, my voice low. I needed to keep up my strength, but I would not give up.

"And you are nothing but a fabled liar—a failure. When The Gray has his due, you will be propped up as a pawn, a symbol of everything they've lost. You wonder why Durlan hasn't cut deeper? Because you don't get to die. The rest of the world needs to see you lose. They get to see their last chance of hope and their savior bend a knee before The Gray and beg for salvation. But you will never find that reprieve. Because you are nothing. Just like your precious king and your prince. The greatest plans...*so* many plans for you. And we've only touched the tip of the iceberg of what they could possibly be."

"Now, now, Garrik. Don't tell the Priestess too much of what we have planned for her," The Gray said as he moved into the room.

Durlan was behind him, a silver dagger in his palm.

I held back a flinch at the sight.

I didn't want to be cut again. I could still feel my skin tugging around the cuts from before, the ones that nobody had healed and were still bleeding.

They weren't deep enough to kill me, but they did hurt. And that's precisely what The Gray wanted.

To make me suffer.

"She knows nothing. Just like always." Garrik rolled his eyes and went back to stand on the other side of The Gray.

These men were The Gray's fourth and his second.

"Why did you call Easton your third?" I asked, wondering again why The Gray would even think that.

The Gray tilted his head, studying me with piercing eyes and sunken cheekbones. He looked like death. All he was missing was the scythe.

"He tells you so much, even though you still don't know whether I can control him."

I smiled then, showing teeth. "We broke his curse."

"Ah, I see you did. He saved your life and broke the curse. Pity. Although the king was never supposed to kill you. You were meant to be mine." He snarled the last word, and I was a little glad to know that he could lose his temper. That meant he didn't have as much control as he thought.

That was good.

I'd be able to figure out how to use that.

Maybe.

"He's my king. He's mine. Of course, he told me."

"So interesting. As for why I called him my third? Because he was destined to be mine. I took Durlan first, brought him under my wing. And when Lore found the boy, Easton was to be my third. Only we needed him to remain within the Obscurité castle walls for longer. So, he stayed, able to be pulled under my direction whenever I wanted. But I waited."

I didn't know if that was the case or not. If The Gray had absolute control over Easton, he would have done something with it. I thought he probably only had the ability to take him and use his memories. But he hadn't been able to control my soulmate completely. No, Easton was too strong for that. And that had to grate on The Gray.

"Garrik came to me next. Hence why he is my fourth."

"For now," Garrik said, and The Gray just smiled.

That smile sent shivers down my spine, but I did my best to hide my reaction.

"I will have a fifth and a sixth. There is already one who could be my fifth soon."

I froze. "Who?" He wouldn't have mentioned it if I didn't know who it was.

"I should tell you a story. Would you like that, Lyric? Would you like to hear a story?"

"I don't think I have a choice," I said dryly and held back a scream as Durlan moved forward and sliced my arm. Icy pain seared my flesh, and I let out a breath, pretending that I wasn't screaming inside.

Blood welled, and Braelynn hissed again.

But The Gray didn't tell his little minion to stop.

Thankfully, though, Durlan didn't cut me again.

As blood dripped to the floor, I held back tears. It was only a slight pain now, no bigger than a papercut, but I didn't want any more.

I hadn't been prepared for any of this.

I had been stabbed, burned, killed, and nearly killed again, and yet...this was worse.

Because I was alone. Alone with Braelynn.

And I couldn't protect her.

I was afraid I wouldn't be able to save myself either.

Garrik grinned from behind The Gray, and I knew he was reading my thoughts.

So, I imagined him burning at the stake, using my Fire Wielding to do it. Sadly, he didn't wince this time.

I'd have to have more vivid thoughts next time.

Come up with new ways to torture him as I was being tortured.

"I was not always The Gray. I had a name once. It was so long ago that the name my parents gave to me—my poor, weakling parents—doesn't matter. I earned my title, and I am now The Gray." He began to pace, and Durlan and Garrik took a step back as if guarding their ruler.

But The Gray was no king.

"I have spent most of my life within this realm, a pocket inside of the Maison realm."

"This is a jail for you, isn't it?" I asked.

"Don't interrupt." He held out a hand as Durlan took a step forward.

"She won't listen if she's bleeding to death. Allow her to heal a bit more, and then you can cut again."

"Whatever you say, my liege."

I wanted to kick Durlan in the nuts, but I didn't have that option.

"When I was named, another—the king of the Lumière—found me. He knew of my talents, not just of Spirit, but also of shadow and bone." He smiled, and I felt bile rise up into my throat. "I helped kill the other Spirit Wielders, using all three of my Wieldings, my magics, to keep the King of Lumière healthy and more powerful than any could imagine. The King of Obscurité tried to stop me, but he was never enough. But when the Fall occurred, and the kings died, the powers that be didn't want me where I had once been."

"Who are these so-called powers that be?" I asked, wincing as my cuts tore anew.

"The twelve Spirit Wielders, of course. They created their touchstone long before you were even a glimpse in a prophecy. And they shoved me into this pocket realm. My cage. But I was able to get out. For the past five hundred years, I've spent time in the Maison realm, waiting and plotting. Whispering secrets into the ears of those in power. I tried to get to the Obscurité, for I had already worked with the Lumière. But the king and the queen refused to listen to my whispers. Their knight, however, listened. And I got to their son, even with the curse." He started to pace again, and sweat broke out over my body, my incisions bleeding once more.

"I met someone. Someone who understood me. She didn't know my name, didn't know who I was, didn't know who I could be. But I saw within her a power I could have. And with her, I produced a son. An heir of power and strength. Yet I couldn't raise him myself." He waved his hand in the air as if the idea that he'd had a son meant nothing.

My pulse raced, and I couldn't help but wonder who it was. The Gray had a son out there somewhere? Who could it possibly be within the realm? Was he alive? Was he still there, waiting?

"Others took him from his mother, and when she found out exactly who I was, she tried to kill me. It didn't work, as you can see. But I haven't forgiven her for that. She's still within the realm. Has always been within reach. She'll do what I say because she knows I'll take her son if she doesn't. The whelp was raised not knowing who his parents were and shamed. Shamed because nobody knew what power could be within him. And when I'm finally able to claim him as mine, my son, the one of light, he will come to me. Because he will know what blood runs in his veins. He will be mine."

A thousand thoughts and possibilities ran through my mind, but I couldn't be sure of any of them.

"Who are you talking about?"

"It's not your precious prince or your king. But it is someone close. After all, his mate is your Familiar, is she not?"

I froze, blood now pooling at my feet. Braelynn hissed, fire spewing from her mouth but not reaching any of the others.

Luken.

Luken, *the bastard* as others whispered about him in hushed tones, was the son of The Gray.

And I knew deep in my heart that he had no idea.

The Gray wanted him. And what The Gray wanted, he got.

As Durlan moved forward again, The Gray talking some more, I tuned all of it out, holding back my screams. Even though the cuts went deeper this time, my flesh parting with ease around the steel of the blade, I remained silent.

Braelynn hissed again, but she couldn't help me. Her fire couldn't penetrate whatever wards The Gray had put up.

Luken was The Gray's son.

And my friend's mother?

His mother was out there, as well.

CHAPTER FOUR

LYRIC

CHAINED TO THE FLOOR, MY BODY SHOOK, BUT MY MIND WAS STILL alert. It had to be. Because if it wasn't... I was afraid what would happen. I refused to break here. I would not allow The Gray and his ilk to do this. I had to get home. I needed to get to the others. But what if I couldn't? What if this was the end, and the others died because I wasn't strong enough?

I let out a shaky breath, and Braelynn meowed above me, a little puff of smoke wafting through the shadow cage and hitting my face. I leaned into the warmth and tried not to sigh. It had been so long since I had been warm, even though I didn't know how much time had passed.

Had the others fought a war without me? Had they fallen?

Perhaps the beginning of the fracture, the new Fall, had already ended and they had won. Maybe I was left here alone, chained in the Shadow realm, never to find an ending. Never to find salvation.

"You seem to have lost it all, haven't you?"

That voice. I hated that voice.

I loathed it more than the blade the other brandished.

Durlan cut. He made me bleed. He grinned as he did it, clearly enjoying it. But he had the face of the enemy. He was precisely who he said he was. A brute who liked to torture. One who wanted to kill. He worked directly for The Gray and enjoyed his job. I knew what he would do and how I would hurt as a result. Durlan wasn't who I feared. He wasn't who I hated.

The Gray should have been whom I hated the most. For what he had done. For how he helped to orchestrate the Fall and was now helping to cause the second. But he wasn't who lay across my heart as a scar. A symbol of shame and regret and horror.

The Gray was a horror to me, sure. A representation of evil and terror. Not a mere symbol, though. No, he *was* those atrocities. He scared me more than I cared to admit because of what he could do to the others. Because of what he *was* doing to them. However, he wasn't the only one to fear.

The one who crept across my dreams whenever I got to sleep scared me beyond reason.

And that was the voice in front of me. The one who made my spine stiffen and scared me more than anything.

The Whisperer. The man who'd killed my parents.

The wretch who lied.

"You," I rasped, my voice dry from screaming, hoarse from having no water.

I could do nothing to ease the pain.

Not yet. They weren't feeding me, weren't giving me liquids. Still, somehow, I was supposed to survive.

My elements were coming back, though. I could feel them, moving in inch by inch, day by day. I just didn't know if it would be enough.

What would ever be enough?

"You're not going to speak to me? Really? You just say my name like you're in pain, like the little trash bunny you are, and I'm supposed to feel sorry for you? You could have had everything. You could have had power beyond recognition. And what did you do? You used it to get in bed with a king and pretend to be the people's savior. You are a waste of space. A desecration of that power. You're lucky The Gray doesn't just kill you now. But he needs you. Needs you for something. I don't care what. It means nothing. *You* are nothing. Just a sad excuse for a power you could have had. Power you could never be strong enough to truly understand or hope to possess."

I forced myself to sit up. Chains rattled. Even though my bonds were made of shadow, they still made the same sounds as those forged of steel. Apparently, The Gray liked the effect.

Braelynn hissed from her cage above me, and while Garrik glared at her, he didn't do anything else. Good, because I would have found a way to kill him for that.

She started to shake even more, and I looked up at her, risking a glance as she began to grow ever so slightly. I didn't think Garrik noticed, but maybe this was good. Perhaps she'd be able to break free of her cage. As long as she didn't hurt herself, I was fine with whatever she did. Together, we would find a way out of this.

It was odd. Just moments before I had been lamenting that perhaps I might die, that maybe I had been forgotten and everything was lost.

But the idea of Brae and I coming together to kill this man? To find a way to end him? That changed everything.

It was an ending I could put a face to and was one that gave me the strength to keep going. In the back of my mind, I knew it wasn't just him. It was the others, too. It was Easton. But thinking of him hurt. Just thinking his name hurt my soul. So, I pushed those thoughts away. I could only work on the tangible. On those I hoped were looking for me. Although part of me didn't want them to. They needed to protect the realm—not only its Priestess.

I held my shoulders back, my bones aching, my stomach growling. I couldn't remember the last time I had eaten. It had been before the battle, I knew that much. And that seemed like ages ago.

I knew who I was, who I needed to be. I would not feed on my anger, my pain.

I would not become bitter. I would not become cruel. I would not allow this man to take everything from me—everything I had left anyway. He had already taken so much. Had literally ripped my soul into a thousand tiny pieces. I had somehow glued them back together. I wasn't going to let him do it again.

"You look so angry for someone without power. You don't even have your Wielding. Your precious magic that was supposed to protect the realms. And yet, The Gray snapped his fingers, and you have nothing. You are chained, restrained. You were never supposed to be anything. Were you, Lyric?"

My Wielding took that moment to slowly slide through my body. Not a rush, not with mighty force, but as a trickle. I could feel the Earth beneath my feet, the Air dancing in my hair, the Water trickling behind me as it edged ever closer. I could feel the Fire of the burning lamps on the other side of the iron gate. And I could feel my soul wavering on the edge of an abyss. One that could change my destiny or keep me on the path of truth and wholeness.

I didn't know where that would lead, but I could feel my Wielding coming back. And that was enough for now.

I just needed to wait him out a little bit longer. I let him continue talking, rambling on, trying to torture me with his snide remarks.

"You talk a lot for a man who's fourth in command," I taunted. I had to keep him talking because my magic *was* coming back. And the closer I got to having the ability to use my Wielding, the closer I was to escape. At least, that was my hope. I didn't have a plan beyond one step at a time. But Easton had gotten out of this realm before. I would do the same. I risked another glance up at Braelynn. I saw that she was once again growing. Not so much that anyone who didn't know her well would notice, but still...

That was good. It meant she was planning to try and help me. At least, that's what I hoped.

I didn't understand fully what a Familiar was, or what she could do. But if she had the ability to spew fire, that was a weapon we could use. She'd be able to protect herself when we escaped this place.

"I'm not the fourth. Not with Easton no longer a part of us. I'm the third."

"Are you sure?" I asked, letting the Wielding grow within me. It burned, the tingles sharp like pinpricks of ice. It was almost as if my limbs had been asleep for far too long and were just now waking up.

"You know nothing. You're just chained here. You're nothing."

"I know that The Gray has a son. Wouldn't he make his son the second? Push Durlan to third? That would still make you fourth. Always last."

I expected the slap, but my head still shot back, and my cheek stung as the hand hit my face. I spat out blood, annoyed with myself for letting him hurt me. But I needed him to remain here, distracted, to not notice that I was slowly regaining my Wielding. I needed to keep him from seeing that Braelynn was steadily working on her bindings.

I needed him to focus solely on himself and his plans. If he did, he wouldn't notice that he was losing.

At least, that was my goal.

"You're nothing. Just a bitch."

"Maybe. But there's a reason The Gray wants me bound. Is he scared of me? Maybe he has to be. It would only make sense. That's why he continues to keep me alive. He has uses for me. What good are you? The Gray already knows all the secrets that he can ferret out. There's nothing left for him to uncover. To be worried about. And yet, he keeps you around. For what? To torture me? No, that's his second's job. Maybe you're just here because he doesn't know what to do with you. He pulled you back from the Maison realm into this shadow dimension. You might be a Whisperer, but there are no secrets left for you to find."

"I'm going to enjoy when Durlan slices you into a thousand little pieces, and you scream for your king. The one who hasn't even tried to find you. It seems you weren't that special, after all. He's probably already replaced you with that other Wielder. The one with the dark hair and darker eyes. You always were replaceable. Nothing special. You weren't even the real Spirit Priestess, were you? You are just an abomination. Not strong enough to do anything. To be anything to anyone."

"Go to hell," I snapped, not letting the words hurt me but needing to make him think they did. They didn't. Honestly. I didn't believe a word Garrik said. He was using whatever fake stories he had to keep me angry, to elevate himself. But it wasn't going to work. Brae and I *would* get out of here.

I looked up again as the Whisperer began to pace back and forth, seemingly not paying attention to me.

I met Braelynn's gaze, and she growled at me, a low sound. I knew it was time.

I tugged on my Wielding, and it sliced through me, causing agonizing pain as it slammed into my pores and ran through my body.

Fire licked my extremities, Water sliced through me, creating steam amongst the shadows. Earth trembled, and Air slid around, pulsating.

Garrik froze. Stared at me wide-eyed.

"How? How did you—?"

"I am the Spirit Priestess. I hold more power in my pinky than you could ever imagine. You might have thought you could harm me, to take everything. But you used lies and deceit to make that happen. You utilized the worst of humanity, the depravity of what you could have had, to try and take everything from me. You'll never do that again."

"You're nothing. Nothing," he said. But I knew he didn't believe it. There was too much fear in his eyes.

"You are the one who believes in falsehoods and lies. You're the one who killed my parents."

"And they screamed, didn't they? You couldn't save them. You weren't strong enough then, and you aren't strong enough now. Not in *my* realm."

He emphasized the word *my*, and I narrowed my eyes.

"Is it truly your realm? Or is it that of The Gray, and he just allows you to live here? You have nowhere else to go. No one wants you."

"No one's coming for you," he said quickly. "I don't know what you think you're going to accomplish by this stunt you're trying to pull. You can't escape. The only reason Easton left before was because of me. It was my plan. What I wanted. He wasn't strong enough, wasn't smart enough to realize that he had been played."

I just shook my head. "Easton always knew there was something wrong with you."

"Well, his *knowledge* wasn't enough to save your parents, was it?"

As he said that, the last tether of my bonds broke, and the shadow chains around me snapped into pieces. I watched as Garrik's eyes widened with fear.

Part of me relished this, the bit that had tried to take control every time I gained a new element. It wanted to savor his pain. Wanted to force him to feel the agony I did.

The other part of me knew that if I focused too much on making him hurt, I'd be no better than the others who had tried to kill us—the ones who had tried to take everything.

I couldn't allow that to happen.

Instead, I tamped down my agony, and knew that this was how it was going to be. This was how it would end.

The shadow chains disappeared, turning into smoke. Finally, I was free.

"Are you ready?"

Garrik's eyes widened as I said that. "Ready for what?"

"I wasn't talking to you," I said softly.

Braelynn let out a growl, one so loud I knew she wasn't a mere house cat anymore.

The shadowed cage disappeared, and Braelynn, now the size of a panther, stood proud next to me, her claws tapping on the cave floor.

"What? How?"

"Once again, I am a Spirit Priestess. This is my Familiar. You killed my parents. You murdered so many. You don't get to tear another family apart."

"So...what? You're going to kill me? I thought you were supposed to be better than that."

He threw a knife, a dagger I hadn't seen, but not at me. Not towards my heart.

Instead, the blade shot towards Braelynn, and I slammed out my Earth Wielding, smashing the weapon into pieces as it fell harmlessly to the rocks below.

The Whisperer blinked at me, calmly, then threw another dagger—this time towards me. I used my Air Wielding and flipped the blade. I pushed harder, knowing that a part of me, something deep inside, would die because of this. I didn't want to kill him, but I couldn't let him live. Not only because of what he had done to my family but because of what he could do to so many others if he continued on his current path.

Spirit within me slid around my heart and squeezed, and the dagger slammed into Garrik's chest. The sound of flesh tearing, of blood pouring, filled my ears. It didn't make any sense. I shouldn't be able to hear every little nuance of his death, but as the Spirit Wielding slid through me and towards him, I knew that what was happening was for a reason. I needed to remember every action, every death that lay on my soul and on my conscience.

Because I couldn't become callous. I might now be a warrior, but I couldn't let death after death make me numb.

Garrik fell to the floor, and Braelynn let out a puff of fire so hot even my Fire Wielding shuddered under its strength. Garrik let out one final breath as the flames slid over him. And then, he was ash. I knew we had to do it. I knew that if we left him here alive, others would know what we had done far sooner than we wanted.

"We need to go," I said, pushing away my thoughts. "Quickly." Braelynn gave me a nod, then ran towards the door, her body seeming to get stronger as we moved.

I swallowed hard and followed her, my Wielding at the ready. I wasn't at full strength yet, and I didn't think I would ever be within this little pocket Shadow realm. But I at least had something.

I didn't hear anyone. I didn't know if anyone else was here. For all I knew, only Garrik, Durlan, and The Gray lived here. And perhaps The Gray and his second were somewhere else.

Brae and I made it to the edge of the cave system, and I looked down, worried.

There was a portal. I could feel it with my Spirit Wielding. I just didn't know how to use it.

"How are we going to get out of here? The portal could go anywhere, and I don't know if we have the kind of time we need to figure it out."

Braelynn looked at me then, and I wondered if she understood what I was saying. This was my best friend, and I missed how she had once been. I missed her laugh, her smile. I missed the way she made me feel. The way she made Luken feel.

Luken.

The Gray's son.

How were we going to tell him?

And was I supposed to tell him at all?

I didn't know, but I didn't have time to worry about that now.

Braelynn looked at me, and suddenly it was if the world around her sparkled and shimmered.

And she shifted.

I staggered back a step.

Oh.

"So that's why they were laughing at me. You weren't ready earlier."

Braelynn looked at me, her body now so much larger than before. She nodded, a knowing look in her eyes. She had known. She had known what a Familiar was and who and what she could be.

But I hadn't.

As I looked at the black and silver dragon in front of me, her scales glistening even in the dim light, I knew that this was her other form. And she was beautiful.

"You're a fricking dragon, Braelynn," I said, laughing. I hadn't even known I could laugh anymore. But here I was, laughing because my best friend was a fricking dragon.

Braelynn lowered her head, and I swallowed hard. "You want me to ride you?"

Braelynn tilted her head and gave me a look.

"Okay. Apparently, I'm going to ride a dragon out of here."

I paused.

"My life is truly different, isn't it?"

I could have sworn she smiled, but I couldn't tell for sure with her new dragon face. Honestly, I was a little scared.

As I slid on top of Braelynn's back and held on, I realized that while I might be the Spirit Priestess, my best friend was a dragon.

And that meant more changes were likely coming.

There was a shout behind me, and I noticed Durlan coming, his blade ready.

"Ready?" I called out, and Braelynn nodded before lifting into the air, her large wings spread wide, her body strong.

I knew that she had never flown like this before. I would have known if she had ever turned into her dragon form. Wouldn't I?

I held on to my best friend as we flew, a scream in my throat at the surrealness of it all.

As we slid through the portal into the Maison realm, the wind in my hair, and my body close to hers as we soared, I knew that this was only the beginning. The beginning of the end, most likely. But we had power. And secrets. We could be the start of change.

I only hoped that was enough.

CHAPTER FIVE

LYRIC

I WANTED TO SCREAM, TO LET OUT A SHOUT OF BOTH GLEE AND FEAR with everything flowing through me. Instead, I lowered my body closer to Braelynn's back, her scales hard yet smooth beneath my palms. Perhaps it just felt soothing? I wasn't sure, but I held on tightly, not wanting to startle her. I could practically feel her fear mixing with exhilaration. She flew across the skies, high up in the air where we were probably only a spot of darkness to anyone who may see us. And not everybody tended to look up.

We had exited the Shadow realm with relative ease, though I was exhausted, starving, and in pain. Blood had seeped into my clothes, my wounds still not fully healed from Durlan's ministrations. Braelynn was likely just as exhausted and hungry as I was.

We wouldn't last long in the sky, and I knew it. But we had to get closer to where Easton and the others were. I couldn't call it the Obscurité Court anymore because it was now attached to the Lumière Court without the wards. Besides, I didn't know if there was Lumière or Obscurité at all. All I knew was that I needed to get back to the castle I called home and return to the man I called mine.

From what I could tell, we were somewhere over the southern Spirit territory. Considering we had been taken from the Lumière Court, I wasn't sure how the geography of the Shadow realm worked.

Perhaps like the Maison realm lay on top of the human realm, the Shadow realm was a pocket that didn't land on any territory. Maybe it floated on top of it all. Reasonably, it could have pockets within pockets that hid anywhere around the realm itself.

My head hurt. I was thinking far too hard and yet not linearly at all. I pushed thoughts of exactly how all of it worked out of my head and hoped that we were getting closer to our destination. Or at least to a point where we could rest. Braelynn needed it.

"Do you know where you're going?" I asked, hoping she could hear me over the wind.

She made a purring sound, which was kind of part growl, as well. She wasn't in her cat form, but rather this newfound dragon form that scared me as much as it excited me. I wanted to take the noise as an agreement. However, since I couldn't know for sure, I was simply grateful that it looked as if we were about to land.

Again, I thought of how I missed my best friend in her human form. We used to talk all the time, figure out what each other needed. And just listen. But with her in any of her Familiar forms, I couldn't understand what she wanted or needed. And I always felt like I was two steps behind in making sure she was okay.

After going over a barren mountain, we finally landed on one of the foothills. Leafless trees surrounded us, and everything looked a little sun-bleached. But that was the Spirit territory for you. Everything always had a slight sepia tone, too, as if I had on glasses that I hadn't cleaned correctly.

Braelynn settled on the ground, her chest heaving. She lowered her head as I moved off her. I moved to the front of her and rubbed my hand between her eyes. She pushed into me, clearly needing the touch.

"You're beautiful," I whispered.

Her tongue slipped out, catching my arm, and I laughed at the touch.

"You are. I can't believe you're a dragon, and you didn't tell me. That nobody told me."

Her eyes danced with merriment, even though I could see the exhaustion in them.

"I guess you were just waiting to see what would happen, huh?"

She seemed to almost shrug, and I hoped we were genuinely communicating.

None of this was easy, and I missed being able to read her expressions and hear her voice. I had just started to figure out exactly what she wanted while in cat form—even though that form had bat wings. Now, it was like starting all over. And this dragon form of hers was nothing batlike *or* catlike. No, this was a whole other version of Braelynn.

And she was magnificent.

"Are you up for more of the journey? Or should you shift back to your cat form? I can carry you. After all, you did carry me for a while."

She didn't answer, though I didn't really expect her to. I looked around, hoping there was something to eat or at least some water.

I closed my eyes and listened, and then let out a sigh.

"I hear a stream. We can at least hydrate. But I think we may have to go hungry for a bit longer."

Technology didn't work in the Maison realm, so it wasn't as if I could call Easton and the others and tell them where we were. We would have to get there on our own and hope for the best.

I just didn't know if us returning was for the best.

What would happen when we got there? Would I tell Luken what I had learned?

And would we be enough, even all together, to take down The Gray? He had so much power, even though I should have it, too. Or at least a version of it.

I didn't feel like I was enough, and that worried me. I needed to be. I had to understand what to do about Luken, and learn who The Gray's spy was.

I had been thinking those things repeatedly as we flew over the landscape. The only thing comforting me was my thoughts.

Braelynn nuzzled into me, still in dragon form as we made our way through the foothills and found the stream. There were no animals here. No other Wielders. The area had clearly been deserted after the Fall.

We took our drinks, both of us on high alert. For all I knew, the League, the Creed, or The Gray himself were waiting for us.

We wouldn't be safe. Maybe not ever. I wanted to think that I would be sheltered, that both of us would be secure once we got back to the Obscurité Court, but I couldn't think that way. Not when there was a spy in our midst, a traitor. And given the idea that The Gray could come at any moment.

But perhaps now that I knew that, I could stop him.

I closed my eyes and let my Wielding slide through me, the Water and the Earth mixing, the Air and the Fire dancing. The Spirit Wielding within me coasted over my body as if it were waiting for the right moment or some kind of feeling.

I wasn't sure what any of that meant, but I knew I would eventually figure it out. I had with the other elements, and I hadn't fractured in so doing. I hadn't broken apart like I thought I would when I entered the Lumière Kingdom all those months ago. Was it months? Or was it days? Years? I didn't know anymore. Time seemed to stand still and yet moved far too quickly all at the same time.

And here I was, standing back, hoping for an answer.

"Are you ready to start again? Tell me what you need." I paused. "Or at least show me. I wish you could talk to me." I leaned forward and rubbed my head against hers.

I met her large eyes. In answer, she lowered her head, and I climbed onto her back once more. We weren't nearly where we needed to be, but we were out of the Shadow realm, at least, and I had to hope that would be enough for now.

"We'll go for however long you can. Okay? Then we'll walk, and I'll carry you. I promise. We're in this together." She used her wing to rub my thigh, and I leaned forward, kissing the top of her head.

I missed my best friend more and more with each passing day, but we had this, at least. I had to believe that counted for something. It was more than some people got.

Brae leapt into the sky, and I held on tightly, Braelynn's dragon form moving as if she had been doing this for lifetimes rather than for the first time today. We were still near the mountain range that would lead us towards the Obscurité Court, which meant we were closer to the ground. I was grateful because even with my Fire

Wielding helping me stay warm, it was still far too cold up in the sky without warmer clothes.

I winced, risking my handholds to press my free hand to my side, hoping the blood had stopped flowing. It had seeped into what little of my shirt remained, and I was covered in stains, but it didn't feel like I was losing any more blood. That honestly had to count for progress at this point. I would take it as a win.

Braelynn flew even closer to the ground about an hour into our journey, and I knew her wings must be hurting. We'd flown for too long. I was about to tell her to land when I caught sight of something in the distance. I froze, wanting to scream or shout out a warning. Only I didn't need to. Braelynn had seen it, too.

The giant snake whipped its tail at us from below, its scales bright green with tan and purple diamonds along its back. It looked so out of place here within the Spirit territory that I knew it must have been locked away, kept dormant for eons. Perhaps long ago, it had once matched and blended into the area when the Spirit Wielders had thrived within the territory's borders, and larger mythical creatures had roamed free.

However, those creatures had turned to dust or gone into hibernation long before the Fall. With the broken magic and the fractured warding of the realm itself, things had unraveled to the point where these creatures were now waking. They were hungry, angry, and they lashed out at anything in their path. What was worse, the enemy had learned of their revival and were *using* the creatures in their armies.

I didn't see any other beings around this snake...a *basilisk* now that I got a good look at it. I hoped it was alone and wasn't being controlled by anyone.

I didn't think Braelynn and I were strong enough to fight more than what we were seeing...and, honestly, I wasn't sure we were strong enough for that.

I thought of all of this while holding onto Braelynn for dear life as she tumbled from the sky, turning over onto her back for a moment as I screamed in panic, and she sprayed fire at the basilisk. She righted herself, flapping her wings harder, but the snake lashed out with its tail again, slamming it into her side.

I shrieked, though not because I'd lost my hold or because there was only open air beneath me, or the earth coming at me at an alarming speed. No, I yelled because Braelynn was beside me in the sky, plummeting to the ground, her side covered in blood as she tried to make her wings work correctly.

I could *not* lose my best friend again. Hearing the agonized, painful sounds from her chest brought tears to my eyes and caused rage to run through my veins. I pushed out my Wielding, using Earth to bring the dirt and soil up towards us as I made my Air buffer us and slow our fall so we both ended up on our feet.

Braelynn stood next to me. Her breathing labored as she faced the basilisk. I held out my hands, ready to use anything I could within my arsenal to protect us both.

Then I remembered what the texts had said a basilisk could do.

"Don't look into its eyes!" I shouted, and Braelynn lowered her head. A basilisk could cause death by a single glance. Only we'd looked directly into its eyes already, the green slits bright with poison.

How was that possible?

"Your Spirit Wielding will protect you and your Familiar," a voice whispered on the wind, and I shivered where I stood. I knew that voice.

Seven.

One of the Spirit Wielders not of this time but of the past, the present, and the future. She was one of those who'd tried to help me, even if she spoke in riddles half the time.

However, I was glad for her voice. Because it meant that Braelynn and I could meet the basilisk's gaze and survive. My Spirit Wielding was the only element I still hadn't gotten a firm grasp of, but it seemed it had a hold of me.

That was good enough for now.

The basilisk, seemingly annoyed that it couldn't kill us with a single glance, lunged. Braelynn shot fire at it while I pushed my Fire Wielding towards its face. It screeched, spitting poison at us. Both Braelynn and I ducked out of the way, separating enough that I was fearful my Spirit Wielding wouldn't be able to help her. I moved closer, shaking the earth beneath my feet. The basilisk's massive body shuddered, and I was grateful that my Wielding was finally back.

I threw Fire at the snake as Braelynn opened her mouth and shot flames, as well. The basilisk hissed and tried to come at us again, but it couldn't make it through the wall of fire. Soon, the acrid scent of burnt flesh filled my nostrils, and I almost gagged. The basilisk fell to the ground with such force that the rocks and soil shook beneath our feet.

"Hell," I whispered and made my way to Braelynn. "I can't believe that worked. Are you okay?"

My best friend turned to me with pain-filled eyes before shifting back to her much smaller cat form. I went to my knees, my body aching, my soul damaged, and held out my arms.

"I think...I think I can try to heal this." I let out a breath. "It'll take my Water *and* Spirit Wielding, but Ridley taught me a few things. I'm not a natural-born healer, but I might be able to work with this." I was almost out of my power reserves, but Braelynn was hurting, and I had to try.

Besides, the Spirit Wielding within me wouldn't let me do anything less.

I *had* to heal my best friend.

Braelynn settled her head in my palm, lying her body across my lap as I looked down at the damage. She had a massive cut on her side and possible bruising, but I couldn't tell with her dark fur. I closed my eyes and tugged on my Wielding. Warmth and pinpricks of sensation slid over me as I did.

I didn't know if this would work, but I had to try. I pushed everything I had into Braelynn, imagining her flesh repairing itself, and her body becoming whole again. Ridley had mentioned that was how he did it, and though he couldn't tell me everything, I had to hope this would be enough.

Time passed, and I grew weaker, but I didn't care. Braelynn needed to be whole. After everything that had happened already, she needed to be okay.

When she licked my palm, I slowly opened my heavy-lidded eyes. My mouth was dry, but I felt a smile form on my face.

"Braelynn," I whispered, my voice cracking. "You're okay."

She leaned into me, and I held her close, praying that we'd get home soon.

I didn't think either of us could face another beast, but the road to our new home was long and full of terrible things. If we didn't find an answer soon, this could be it for us.

I couldn't let myself dwell on that. Instead, I let out a breath and pulled away from Braelynn, who seemed to be thinking along the same lines as I was.

It was time to get going again, no matter that we were running on empty.

Braelynn turned back into her dragon form, and I reached for her. I hated that she had to shoulder the responsibility, but I knew I was too tired to walk very far.

But then the world turned gray, and I *screamed.*

CHAPTER SIX

LYRIC

"The Spirit Priestess will come of five, yet of none
     at all.
She will be strength of light, of darkness, and choice.
You will lose what you had.
You will lose what you want.
You will lose what you will.
You will lose what you sow.
Then you will find the will.
Find the fortune.
And then you will make a choice.
A choice above all.
A sacrifice above will.
A fate left denied.
And a loss meant to soothe.
You will make the choice. You will fight your fate.
And once you find the one you choose, you will have
     more to lose.
When the crystals fall, the end is near.
When the crystals shatter, you will fear.

Then you will fade, you will choose, and the crystal
    will shine.
Though the world cries, and the one you love is in
    shadow,
The world will burn.
The world will live.
And you will know the end.
The end of all, the end of nowhere.
But the end."

THE OTHERS FINISHED SPEAKING THE PROPHECY, AND I DID MY BEST
to come back to the present.

To feel. To breathe. To *be*.

Fire coasted over my skin, Water dousing the flames before it
could burn. Air whirled in my hair, and the ground beneath me
shook. My body warmed, the Spirit within me reaching out to
whatever souls it could.

I pushed at my Wielding, forced myself to control it. I wasn't
strong enough yet to do it all, but I was learning. I wasn't the girl I
had been before. The one who hadn't been ready. The one who
hadn't known.

I hadn't been that girl for a long time.

If I faced her now, the teen with the long, blond hair, wide eyes,
and a penchant for wonderment, I wasn't sure I'd recognize her.

Although, I should.

I wished I could. Perhaps then I would be able to fully face what
was in front of me, rather than retreating to my mind so I could
catch up.

"Lyric, we're sorry to bring you here as we did. We know the
journey can be quite jolting."

I looked up at the sound of Seven's voice and let out a harsh
breath.

"I don't remember it always being this painful," I said, rubbing
the back of my neck. As I regained control of my Wielding, I looked
around me. Panic washed over me, and I shook.

"Where's Braelynn?" I asked, my Fire in my palms, ready to
fight. "Where is she?"

"It would have been hard on her after her healing to bring her
here," Seven said, and I finally got a look at my surroundings.

I was in the center of the circle like I had been in my dreams from long ago.

There were different elements and seasons all around me. Spring on one side, winter on the other. Fall and summer fighting each other on the other cardinal directions.

The place seemed to be something out of my fantasies rather than somewhere real, but I could never be sure when it came to the Spirit Wielders. They had been forced into this captivity, into this plane of existence that didn't make much sense.

This place felt as if it had always been part of my life, yet I didn't understand it.

And because I was at the center of the four seasons, the middle of those five elements, I also felt like I was at the nexus of a clock, with each of the numbers along the outside replaced by a Spirit Wielder.

Sometimes, I could see their faces. Most of the time, I couldn't.

I thought I had met one of these Spirit Wielders in person, though I wasn't quite sure if I had.

But Seven was the female voice that whispered in my head and seemed to be the closest to me. She judged me, sure, but she'd also saved me.

Or maybe she had just given me reasons to save myself.

I didn't know anymore. I was so tired. So over all of this.

"I want to go home," I whispered, not realizing that I was going to say the words aloud until they were already out.

I turned to Seven, who tilted her head and studied me, a maternal look on her face that I hadn't seen from her before.

It made me miss my mom. Pain clutched at my heart, and my stomach clenched. I held back tears. It hurt so much that Mom wasn't here. That she never would be. When my Spirit Wielding unlocked, exploding out of me with such intensity that I thought I would die, I had reached out to try and take her soul, and my father's...to bring them to my side and back to their bodies. To do *something* to save them.

But that was not what a Spirit Wielder did.

No, that's what The Gray would have done.

"I know you want to go home, Lyric. And you will. I promise. You will get home, and you will fulfill your destiny. We are here to remind you of that."

I whirled on the others, but they didn't say anything, so I turned back to her.

"That prophecy is the only thing that ever goes through my head. I'm losing everything because of it, and I don't even understand it."

"You were supposed to lose much. You know this. The world will burn, but the world will live, and you will know the end. The end of all, the end of nowhere. But the end."

I shook my head at her words. "Are you saying I have to die? Or that the world does? And which world. The one I came from? Or the one that I was destined to be in?"

"You will know when the time is right."

I threw my hands up into the air. "I hate riddles. It's always riddles with you."

"Perhaps it needs to be." She paused. "Your home is with Easton," Seven continued, and my head shot up.

"Yes. With the family I have made. Because this war and this prophecy took all the other family I had." Emotion twisted me up, but I pushed it back.

I still had the flames in my palms, but I didn't extinguish them. I wasn't going to hurt the beings in front of me, but they couldn't see me as weak, either. Although I was pretty sure they could read my thoughts, so it wasn't as if they didn't know me inside and out regardless.

"The prophecy said you would lose what you loved most. And you have lost. For that, I am sorry," Seven said.

It wasn't lost on me that she had used *we* when discussing what they knew but being sorry came from her alone.

So she didn't speak for all of them when she talked about her feelings. That made sense. Especially since I didn't know the others.

I felt like I knew Seven, but I didn't trust her. I didn't trust anyone anymore.

No, that wasn't right. I trusted my core group. The people I was going back for.

"Can you help me make it back to where the others are? I can't even say the Obscurité Kingdom anymore because, without the wards, is it truly two separate kingdoms?"

Seven just stared at me and blinked as if I wasn't making any sense. I didn't blame her. My entire body hurt, as did my soul. I needed time—the one thing we didn't have.

Seven finally answered. "No, we are nearing the end. Where it will either fall completely, or there will be a new kingdom to rise. A new leader to follow."

More riddles.

"And what am I supposed to do now?"

"You have the path, and you will follow it. Or, you will not. It is all up to you and what you decide. But just know that the world relies on you."

I let out a harsh laugh. "I think I've got that by now. That's all anyone's been telling me. That I'm the Spirit Priestess, the one who's supposed to unite everyone. How am I supposed to do that with people who hate us? That isn't what's happening, is it? Do I only unite the good? Or do I unite those who have fought against us and bled for what they believed in?"

"That's a choice you and the court will have to make."

"What court?"

"That's a question you will have to ask."

I threw my hands into the air. "I honestly have no idea what I'm doing." Tears slid down my cheeks, and I was embarrassed that I had let them fall. "I've chosen to stay. That's what the prophecy said. I made a choice to come back. I made a choice with Easton. And I've watched so many of those I love get hurt or die. We're in the middle of a war, not against the kings or the queens. But because of a Spirit Wielder. Do you understand that? The Gray was one of you."

"He was never one of us," one of those behind me snapped, but I didn't turn to look at him. He was just a faceless voice that never answered my questions.

"But he was, wasn't he? Maybe not in this circle, but he *was* a Spirit Wielder." Amongst other things.

"Yes, and he went too far. Was swayed by hate and death. And when the courts fell, and the new ones were built, he was sent to his personal dimension, the Shadow realm. But we were never able to keep him there for long. And that is where you came in."

So, the Shadow realm *was* a jail for The Gray.

"And the crystals fell. They shattered. So now I have to fade? What choice do I have to make now?"

"Time will tell."

"And you can't get me there any faster?"

"You must continue on this journey. But fear not, Lyric. You will not be alone for long."

At that cryptic comment, the elements slammed into me again, and I found myself on my knees, the sepia tone of the southern Spirit territory surrounding me once more. Braelynn hovered over me, her wings outstretched as she protected me. I looked up at her, her warm scales shining as her claws dug into the ground. She snarled at whatever faced her. I shook myself out of the daze I was in and rolled to my stomach and then rose to my knees. Braelynn didn't even look at me, even though I knew she felt me there. Could tell I was moving. She had protected me when my soul was in that other place. Though she hadn't been alone for long it seemed.

I had hoped the first person or creatures we met along this path would be friends, not foe.

I looked forward and cursed.

Of course, it was the League. Water Wielders, who had been on the side of the King of Lumière at one point. Assassins who didn't care about anything but profit and wreaking havoc.

Some members of the Creed of Wings and the League had come to our side after the last battle, but not all.

No, it seemed these were either anarchists or were now on the side of The Gray. Or maybe they *wanted* to be on the side of The Gray.

And killing me and my Familiar, my best friend, was their way of getting it done.

I didn't have answers, but I wasn't going to waste time questioning.

I would protect my friend and myself.

A large wall of Water came at me, and I wondered where they had gotten it to Wield. Most Water Wielders, just like Fire and Earth Wielders, couldn't create elements out of nothing. They had to have access to the medium to use it. And since I *knew* that not all the League members in front of me were those special Wielders that could *create*, they must have had a storage basin of Water somewhere and were using it to fight. I slammed my hands against the ground as I rolled out from under Braelynn, a wall of Earth separating us from the League.

Braelynn spewed fire, searing the tops of the Earth wall so no League member could make it over.

They shouted on the other side, and I grinned, looking at my best friend. Braelynn winked, and I smiled. There she was. She wasn't gone. Though it didn't feel like it sometimes, she was still in there. I had to remember that, even if it broke me a little inside to think about it.

I kept moving, using my Wielding as the League tried to get around the wall of Earth. They slammed Water into it again, this time shaking it to its core. I used Air to push down on the assassins.

Braelynn flew up, scorching them. They screamed and used Water fashioned as daggers to come at us.

I didn't care, I kept moving, kept fighting, eliminating one after the other.

I threw Earth at them. Water slammed into us. Another wall of Water seemingly coming from nowhere created a tornado. Apparently, one of them was a dual Wielder, using both Air and Water to attack. A funnel with single-minded focus. Knowing this, I used Fire and Earth together, creating a cyclone of my own. It smashed into theirs, shouts of wonder sounding around us. The cones were long, five stories high, at least, as they tangled with one another, our Wielding taking form of another as they fought, rather than with pure power from me or the other Wielder.

They slammed into each other again, separating into the four elements before pulling back and coming together once more. My fingers ached, my hands shaking as I use my Wielding against them. But I was stronger. I didn't only have two powers, I had five. So, I pushed the other three into my funnel, creating one giant vortex that could take over everything.

The tornado slammed into the League, and they screamed. Some ran for cover, fleeing, running for their lives. The others didn't make it.

Their existence was extinguished as the flames faded to dust. I knew I should feel horror. I should feel...something. But I felt nothing. How could I when all I had was the person next to me, the person who wasn't even a person anymore? I ached. The loss burned within me, but there was nothing I could do about it.

Perhaps there was nothing I could have ever done.

Braelynn landed beside me. I looked at her and pulled her close.

She wrapped her wing around me, tucking me against her side, and I sank into the warmth of her scales, letting out a deep breath.

"Well, then," I whispered. "I suppose we need to keep going."

"Since when do you have a dragon?" a familiar voice said from behind me. I whirled, Fire in my palms that I quickly extinguished.

"Rhodes!" I screamed and ran to him. He stretched out his arms, his silver eyes focused on mine as he searched for wounds most likely. I jumped and landed on him, holding him tightly as tears slid down my face. He held me even closer. My whole body shook, as did his, and relief poured through me.

My friend. Rhodes. The one I had thought I could have a deeper connection with. We had realized almost too late that it was only a friendship bond in the purest form.

He kissed my cheek, then my temple, before he pulled back and searched my body. "You're hurt?"

I was covered in blood, and the goddess knew what else. But I was alive. I was as whole as I was going to be. "I'm fine," I whispered.

Suddenly, Braelynn was behind me, nudging him with her head. Rhodes' eyes widened.

"I see Braelynn has found her second form."

I reached back and punched him hard on the shoulder.

His eyes widened more, and he rubbed at the spot I'd hit. "What was that for?" he asked.

"You didn't tell me about this form. You all thought her being my Familiar was a joke. It would have been nice to know that she could turn into a dragon."

Braelynn sat on her haunches and wiggled her shoulders, letting her neck elongate just a bit.

"She's gorgeous. And we didn't think it would happen for a while yet. Plus, you had other things on your plate."

I glared at him. "No, you liked making fun of me. Or at least you liked having something to smile about. Since there isn't much these days, I can't blame you."

I searched his face, trying to see what I couldn't at first. Beneath his light brown skin, I saw the pallor that spoke of weariness and exhaustion. His hair was unruly, and perhaps a little too long. But I didn't mention that. He looked healthy, whole, if a bit distraught.

He had lost everyone, just like I had.

I wasn't alone. I knew I had Easton. Still, the three of us had lost so much. We now had each other, though not in the way I had thought I would have Rhodes.

Easton was my other half, my soulmate, the one I was running to.

Rhodes was the one who had found me and brought me to this realm. There would always be a connection between us, an emotion I could never hold back.

And, thankfully, the guys seemed to realize that. They still fought, still grumbled, but I figured it was so they could turn a corner and find a connection that would always be there between them, too. And to let off some steam.

"How are you here?" I whispered.

"We've been searching, using our magic to find your path. When we saw the League running to fight, we figured we'd follow and see exactly who they were after."

"We?" I asked and turned to see a familiar yet weary face.

"Alura," I whispered. "You're here."

"Yeah, I am." She looked at me then, her eyes dark, and I wondered what she saw. She had helped me so much when I was in the human realm, but then she hadn't been around enough after for me to get a real feel for who she could be.

I didn't know her, but she had saved my life before. And I felt like I should trust her.

I still didn't know who I could trust completely, not with The Gray having spies everywhere.

But if I kept wondering who I could trust and ended up trusting nobody, I would wind up hurting myself more in the end.

"Thank you. Thank you for saving me."

"It looked like you were doing a fine job on your own," Alura said, looking around. "Your powers have strengthened since I last saw you," Alura said.

"Seriously, they've strengthened since The Gray had you," Rhodes whispered.

His hands were on my cheeks, and I leaned into his touch mostly because I missed warmth. "Are you hurting?"

I was bloody, covered in wounds, my soul scarred beyond redemption in some cases. But in the end, I nodded. "I'm okay. But I want to go home."

Rhodes smiled, but it didn't reach his eyes. "Home is a relative term these days," he whispered.

"I know, but let's get our people. Our friends. I have so much to tell them," I whispered. "Only I don't know where to start."

"You escaped The Gray, let's begin with that," he said and took my hands. We both looked over at the dragon, at Brae, then we turned towards home.

It wasn't a court, it wasn't a castle, but it did have our people. They were our home.

And I was so ready to be there.

CHAPTER SEVEN

EASTON

My hands inched along the stone as I leaned against the wall, trying to slow my breaths.

It hadn't always been difficult for me to calm down. Just the opposite, really. The others might think I could smirk and laugh and act the brooding prince without a care for others, but that was just a façade. And those closest to me knew the truth.

Before all of this, I was always calm. I had to be. There hadn't been another option. My family—my mother—needed me. So, I had been the calm one with the mask that spoke of something else. But that had been what was needed at the time.

Then I met Lyric, and everything changed. Although I hadn't realized that it'd changed until it was almost too late.

Until I nearly lost her.

And now, it seemed I had.

The Gray had taken me and cursed me with thanks to Lore's reach, but The Gray now had Lyric. I had to be here to help my people. I couldn't go to help her.

Heavy is the head that wears the crown?

Those words might be uttered with contempt, even in my head, but those who spoke them never really understood. How could they when I barely did?

"Are you sulking again?" I glanced over my shoulder at Wyn, who stood in the doorway to the throne room, leaning against the doorjamb, her arms folded over her chest, feet crossed.

"I'm not sulking," I said, my voice quite sulky.

"I don't believe that at all."

"We're going to get news soon," she said, and I turned fully, rolling my shoulders back as I tried to cast off the rest of my bad mood. I wasn't a fan of sulking, but it was apparent that was what I was doing today.

Something I would have to refrain from doing again if I wanted whoever was left in our realm to see me as a competent leader.

"Of course, we are. That's why we sent Rhodes and Alura, two of my best warriors. Oh, wait, neither of them is mine."

"Now you're just looking for something to growl about," Wyn said, rolling her eyes. She pushed off the wall and made her way to me. Wyn had always been a good friend. We had grown up together. She understood my moods more than most did. The only one who understood me better was Lyric. The fact that she got me, after such a short time, meant more to me than anything.

"Rhodes will find her. We both know that prince—or is he the king now?—whatever he is, he won't leave a stone unturned. After all, he found her the first time. He and Alura. They'll find her again."

I ground my teeth and let out a breath. "Of course, *he* found her."

"Stop it. You're not actually jealous, are you?"

I gave her a look and then shook my head. "No, I'm not. It's just habit to growl about him."

"Because pretty boy prince has always been your rival because he had to be."

That put a smile on my face as my lips tipped up. "I love that you call him that. And so many other things."

She shrugged and tossed her long, curly brown hair over her shoulder. "What can I say? He annoys me. So, I enjoy making fun of him."

I studied her face and frowned again. "Why does Rhodes annoy you?"

Some expression crossed her face, but I couldn't tell what it was. I moved forward. "Wyn?"

"It's not important." She shook her head. But I still studied her.

"Wyn."

"It's fine."

"If it was fine, you wouldn't be changing the subject."

"There's nothing going on. Pretty boy prince just annoys me. I don't know why he always gets under my skin. However, all I can see now is when he almost died." She shuddered, and I reached for her. I gripped her shoulder, giving it a squeeze before I let go.

"That was hard for all of us." And that was the truth. Although we had grown up on different sides of the war, I had always respected Rhodes in many ways. He had never been cruel or callous like the rest of his people. Mostly, he annoyed me back then because he had a family—one who seemed to care about him. I hadn't realized at the time that they were broken just as much as my family was. And maybe I was jealous, but I would never tell the man that. I had principles, after all. But no, the thing that made me the most jealous was that he had found Lyric first. The person I was supposed to be with, though I hadn't been able to tell for too long because of the curse.

I fisted my hands at my sides.

As long as we get her back.

"We're going to get her back," Wyn whispered, echoing my thoughts. I raised a single brow and turned away from her.

"We will, but there's a reason I didn't go. Our people need us."

"They still call you king," she whispered.

"They still think of me as one, but it doesn't mean I deserve the title. After all, the Obscurité Kingdom is gone, just like the Lumière Kingdom."

"But we're still at the Obscurité Court. They still see you standing near your throne, where the crystal once was before it shattered."

"You're right. Because that's what the people need to see. They don't see us in the war room. They don't see Rhodes' aunt, the former Queen of Lumière, healing because she lost her sight in the last battle. They don't see you learning your new element. They don't see that our family, our people, are struggling on the inside. Because we have to show them that we are strong."

"That's our job. To be the strong ones."

"But it all seems like a lie, doesn't it?" I asked.

"Maybe. So, perhaps it's precisely what it needs to be. We can't decide on titles and who should rule until we get rid of The Gray. Once we do that, the right answers will be in front of us. Hopefully."

"I never wanted to rule," I said honestly, surprising myself.

"We all knew that," Wyn said softly.

"You did?" I asked, letting out a harsh laugh that was anything but humor-filled.

"Of course, we did. If you were to rule, that meant your mother was no longer with us. And we loved your mom, even though she kept secrets from us."

I ignored the familiar pang I felt at that.

"We all keep secrets. That's what royalty does, it seems."

"Yet what are you going to do when we find Lyric and defeat The Gray? When we all survive the war and are forced to make plans for a new world. Do you know what you're going to do?"

Dread crawled through me, and I shook my head. "One thing at a time." One thing I did know, Lyric would not be queen. She was a Spirit Priestess. And that meant, in order for us to be together, I couldn't be king. And I could handle that. I could walk away. I'd never wanted to be king. I'd never really wanted to be a prince. I only wanted to help my people. And so, I had done it in the best way possible. I stood back and let the Lumière find the Spirit Priestess so she could help our entire realm. Because I had known they'd be there to help my dying kingdom, even as they helped theirs. And now, I was the ruler of a lost society.

Or maybe just a ruler in name. Because we all worked together as one. My uncles, Luken, and Teagan. Wyn and the former queen and lady. We worked together to find a way to heal those who were injured, to train those who were able, and to find The Gray.

But all of it would be for naught without the rest of the prophecy. Without my soulmate. Without Lyric.

The ground shuddered, and Wyn's brows rose.

"Hold back your Earth Wielding, Easton."

"I'm fine," I snapped.

"You might be, but you're still growling."

"It's what I do. I sulk. I growl. I don't get shit done."

"Now you're talking like Lore. Or any of the old Lumière that didn't come to our side. Or anyone who's ever talked about you behind your back or even to your face to say that you weren't good enough. Don't be that person."

"I'm not. I'm just waiting. As always."

"Easton."

"What do you expect me to do? People are starving, and we are trying to find the food that wasn't tainted in the war to feed them. People are dying because we don't have enough healers. Rhodes and Rosamond's grandma is trying to ferret out the deserters and those Lumière who aren't on our side. They're using magic that isn't bone magic, isn't death, but it's something I don't understand, nor can I Wield. They are doing so much for this realm, and all I can do is stand back and organize it all."

"Stand back? No, that's not true. That's not you. When was the last time you had a full night's sleep? When's the last time you sat down and ate with your family?"

"There's no time for that," I rasped.

"There needs to be. You have to put yourself first, even if for a moment."

"Not until Lyric is back."

"And what happens if she doesn't come back?" Wyn asked, and I turned to her. Fire erupted from my fingers. She blocked it with her Water Wielding, even though I hadn't sent it her way. I had that much control, at least. Still, I staggered back, my hand over my chest as I tried to shove my emotions down again.

"Easton. What are you going to do if she doesn't come back?"

"If she doesn't come back, if we lose the Spirit Priestess, then we will fight The Gray with our dying breaths. And we will piece our realm back together. We don't have the crystals anymore. We don't have our conduit anymore. Our realm can't use its own power to push Wielding and health through the crystals to keep our people alive. We will find another way. I refuse to believe there's nothing else we can do."

"Then make sure the others see that. Know that. You're doing an excellent job, but you're starting to fray around the edges, and those who love you can see that."

"Then don't needle me," I growled. "Let me be."

"You know she's never going to let you be," Teagan said from behind Wyn, and I let out a sigh as my best friend walked into the room, Luken, the Air Wielder, right behind him.

"You know, I should take offense to that," Wyn retorted. "But somebody needs to keep us on our toes. To keep us looking forward."

"Maybe, dear Wyn. Or perhaps we could all just use a break. You asked when Easton slept last. When's the last time *you* slept?"

"I'll sleep when I need to," Wyn said, rolling her shoulders back.

"Afraid Rhodes won't come back?" Luken asked, and everyone looked at him. I knew there was surprise on my features, and saw the same on Teagan's face. However, Wyn simply glared.

"I have no idea what you're talking about," she said.

Everyone just blinked and then looked away. Well, that was interesting.

"Either way, he's going to come back. Same with Alura. Same with Lyric and Braelynn," Luken said, and I met the man's gaze then nodded quickly.

I had to believe that Lyric would be okay, and I had to tell myself that at least I was in a better position than Luken was.

Luken's mate was now a Familiar. She was lost to him, and there was no coming back from that.

I was about to say something when my chest warmed. I rubbed it and felt the connection that had previously been dulled. My eyes widened, and I ran past the others, my feet slapping the floor. They quickly followed me.

"What is it, Easton? Do we need to sound the alarm?" my uncle, Justise, asked as he came around the corner, his husband by his side.

"No, no, I don't think so."

Suddenly, I was out in the courtyard, my eyes wide as a shadow blocked part of the moon.

A very large shadow.

"Is that a...is that a dragon?" Wyn asked.

The smile on my face widened, even as my heart raced. "I do believe our Familiar has found her second form."

"My goddess," Luken whispered. Teagan whispered something to Wyn, but I didn't hear what was said.

I looked at the blond-haired woman riding atop the dragon, two others behind her holding tightly as well. Relief soared through my veins. It was almost too much, and I nearly fell to my knees. But I didn't. Because others were watching. They saw the power of their Spirit Priestess.

They didn't need to see me being weak.

When the dragon landed, Alura hopped off and moved to the side, that familiar odd breeze that wasn't a breeze in her hair. But I didn't pay much attention to her. Instead, I focused on Rhodes, who hopped down second, his hand outstretched. Lyric took the proffered palm, and I realized there wasn't a single ounce of jealousy in me. I couldn't feel that. Not when them being together meant she was here. I peered at her more closely. Blood coated her, and she looked exhausted. She was probably in pain, but she was here.

I ran towards her, not caring who saw. When my arms were finally around her, Rhodes stepped to the side, and Braelynn nuzzled both of us with her massive head. I cupped my mate's face, then ran my hands down Lyric's back.

"You're here," I whispered, my voice cracking.

I could feel her warmth against me, even as her knees shook. I held her up, knowing she would likely pass out soon.

"I'm back," she whispered. She looked at me then, her eyes wide, gaze piercing.

"I knew you would come back," I whispered.

"I had to. I had to come back to you." She paused. "And everyone else."

In a blink, my mouth was on hers, tasting her, needing her.

Her arms wrapped around me, and there were cheers and shouts as everyone moved around, welcoming Alura and Rhodes and Braelynn back home. I felt a rush of warmth beside me, and then a small cat jumped into Luken's arms, purring as he ran his hands down her back, checking for injuries.

When Ridley came up, ready to heal, it was hard for me to let Lyric go, but I did.

Because Lyric was back, the Spirit Priestess of the realm had returned.

And now the war could truly begin.

And the battle within myself could finally calm.

I could breathe again.

CHAPTER EIGHT

LYRIC

I WASN'T SURE IF MY HEAD RANG BECAUSE OF THE TORTURE I HAD JUST endured, or the yelling in front of me. As Teagan's and Wyn's shouts increased, and the Lord of Fire's voice boomed, I rubbed my temples..

I let out a sigh and sat back against Easton's throne as I had during the last meeting we'd had in this room, when we'd tried to come up with a plan to save our realm—only to have it shatter around us, along with the crystals that held it together.

Our circumstances were far different now. We might be back in the Obscurité castle, but only because we needed a place to regroup. No wards protected us from the other kingdom. I didn't think there ever would be again. There was no more Lumière Kingdom. No king or queen or even court to come at us with death in their eyes and revenge in their hearts.

The only people with a claim to the Lumière throne were in this room with us, and they weren't taking up the mantle. Instead, they were by our sides, working to fight The Gray.

Lanya, the Lady of Air, leaned against the back of her seat, listening patiently as the people in front of her yelled and shouted at one another as they tried to devise a plan to protect our people. Her two grandchildren, the next in line to the throne, Rhodes and Rosamond, were in the middle of an argument, as well. They were trying to maneuver the chess pieces that were our armies, our Wielders.

Nobody had stepped up to take control of the Lumière Court, and I understood that. There wasn't time for that, and it wasn't necessary, not when we all needed to unite under one banner anyway.

However, that wasn't going to happen. Nor were we going to decide on a king or a ruler or anything like that until we defeated The Gray.

We needed to come together. But adding politics to everything that was already happening was just confusing everyone.

There would be time to appoint a true king or queen to oversee the Maison realm. But I wanted nothing to do with that.

I felt it within me, the Spirit that came with being the Priestess.

My job was not to rule, but rather to *unite*. Soon, we'd have to find answers as to who *could* rule...to aid in the advancement to the next stage of our new realm. For now, we followed each other's paths, a coalition of rulers until we could form the new government.

At the moment, however, our group didn't look very much like a ruling coalition.

No. Instead, it was just a large room with a bunch of loud personalities, each trying to decide what to do.

"We have to take care of the eastern flanks," Luken said, pointing to the map in front of us on the large table. On it were clay, metal, and wooden pieces to represent our armies, the enemies we were aware of, and other factions we were trying to find. "We've been ignoring them for too long."

"The only ones attacking the eastern flanks are the Creed of Wings, who are trying to get through to find Lyric," the Lord of Fire snapped. "We are fortified."

"Not enough," Luken rebuffed.

"We don't know where The Gray will attack next," Teagan said, keeping his voice calm. Frankly, I was surprised. He usually shot off first, but since his father was the one doing it today, perhaps he figured he should be the calm one. I wasn't exactly sure. What I did know was that I had a headache, and I wasn't sure how this fighting was going to help anyone. But they all needed to get this agression out of their system so that I would let them.

"Of course, we don't know what The Gray's going to do. We never have."

"So what do you suggest?" Wyn asked. "If you say that we've never known what he's going to do, then what are we supposed to do now? Are we supposed to fortify what we have? Or are we supposed to go out and find him?"

"You won't find him until he's ready to be found," I said, and everyone turned to me. I shrugged, not caring about the odd looks being leveled at me.

"Lyric—" Rhodes began, and I held up my hand to stop him.

"He is the ruler of his little Shadow realm and he governs that space and has more power than we give him credit for."

"I don't know, he was always the bogeyman of our childhoods. I assumed he had great power," Teagan grumbled, and I nodded.

"Perhaps you're correct, but not everyone here believed he was real until it was almost too late." I met Easton's gaze, and he gave me a sad look, but not one anyone else could see. And that was fine. It was just for me. No one else needed to know what we truly felt when it came to The Gray.

After I had returned from the Shadow realm with Rhodes and Alura, all of us riding on Braelynn's back, I had hugged Easton tightly, trying to tell him without words that I was home. I was safe. That we'd find a way to heal. And I hadn't been able to talk to him since.

I hadn't even had time to rest. Instead, Ridley had done what he could for me, healing up the cuts on my body, the bruises, the aches and pains. But he couldn't get all of them. That would take time; time we might not have.

After, we'd entered this room and had been closed off since, fighting with each other as we tried to plan our next steps for protecting our people.

"So The Gray is going to come to us. We know that much. He's been behind this all along," Rhodes said.

"Exactly. He's had people on his side since the beginning when he was a Spirit Wielder and walked through our lands, even before the Fall."

"I still can't believe the kind of power he holds. And none of us knew," Rosamond said. She pinched the bridge of her nose, and Emory leaned closer to her, rubbing her back.

"You might be a Seer, but you can't know everything," Emory said, and I wanted to reach out and hug them both.

"I know. But I should know more than I do. Maybe if I had seen what The Gray was up to, we wouldn't have lost so many people." She paused. "We wouldn't have lost the crystals."

Everybody did a terrible job of trying not to look at me as she said those words. But I glanced at my skin, at the iridescent sparkles that still shone in the firelight.

Underneath the onslaught of power, it had dug into my skin, protecting itself the only way it could: by coming to me. And I didn't know how to fix it.

Had it been part of the prophecy? Were the crystals supposed to somehow help me defeat The Gray? Or was this just the beginning of the end?

I didn't like that train of thought, so I pushed it from my mind and looked back at the others as they started to fight again over what to do about our enemy. The problem was we didn't know where the next fight would originate. We could protect our people in only so many ways. For instance, we could worry about the borders, such as they were. Still, without true wards to safeguard the kingdom, anybody could get in—and anywhere.

On top of that, even though the Lady of Air was using her powers to figure out who was on our side and who was on the side of The Gray, we weren't actually sure if she was getting it right every single time.

An error of such magnitude could be the end for all of us, but Easton and I refused to allow the innocent to be turned away. So, we were taking a chance, but we also needed to formulate a plan.

"We need representatives from every faction," I said suddenly, and everyone turned to me.

"We are those representatives, my Priestess," the Lord of Fire said. Teagan winced from where he stood behind his father.

My lips quirked at the lord's patronizing tone. "You're right, but not all of them. What we have now is a Lord of Fire and your son. You two represent that element. We have Rhodes and Rosamond to represent Water and Air, but Lanya represents Air, as well.

Delphine, who is still in bed resting, could represent Water, but I'm not sure everybody would trust her—at least outside this room."

"And I'm not sure we should trust her *inside* the room," Teagan said.

"Agreed." I held back a sigh when the others started to speak again. "That's Air, Fire, and Water. But Earth?"

"I guess there isn't going to be a representative from there," Wyn said, looking down at her hands.

I didn't blame her for her sadness, or even her anger. Her parents had been traitors, the worst kind. Her father was dead, and while her mother still lived, she was hurt. The fact that neither of them had suffered from each other's wounds told us they hadn't been true soulmates. They had lied about it the entire time.

That had to be difficult for everybody, Wyn, most of all. Because they had come into their power not only through familiar lines, but with a hope for the masses that true soulmates could exist. Not everyone was fortunate enough to find theirs. The idea could have been a beacon. Though now, we all knew it to be a lie.

"You can be the representative for Earth," I said casually, and Wyn raised a brow.

"Even though I'm also a Water Wielder now?" she asked, Water in one hand, Earth shaking beneath her feet as she turned her other palm to face the floor.

"Maybe."

"They're going to need you," Easton said. "I'm an Earth Wielder as well, and I can help, but Lyric is right, we need reliable sources from each of the sectors."

"There's another Earth Wielder we could use," I said, and everyone looked at me. "What about Slavik?"

Easton's eyes narrowed, and Rhodes snorted before he spoke. "The Earth pirate? You want to use the Earth pirate as a symbol?"

"No, not as a symbol, as a warrior." I paused. "Don't look at me like that," I said to Easton and the others. "We're running out of lords and ladies," I said bitterly. "We don't have the crystals anymore. The Gray can come at us at any time, and if we have to use the Underkings and queens and everyone else who has been shunned by those too hungry for power, then so be it."

I knew I was talking to the same people that I was admonishing, but I didn't care. Not right then.

"Slavik has power, and the Underkings follow him. Plus, he protects those under his care."

The Underkings were the men and women who worked the underworld of the realm yet still knelt for the king or queen of the kingdoms.

"And his second almost killed you," Rhodes said.

"Yes, and that man is dead. There have to be others out there who can help us. We've already said that the courts don't truly exist anymore. The kingdoms aren't separate. Let's go and find those who have been rebuffed in the past. Those who aren't evil but toe the line of what is good."

"It could work," Rosamond said, her eyes glassy. She was in the middle of a vision, and Rhodes and Emory sat on either side of her, holding her steady.

"If we go to each of the forgotten factions' leaders, we could formulate a plan."

"That's good," I said, my palms damp. "We need everybody we can get. There are Creed and League warriors that want to be on our side. While they fought for the wrong kings, they never wanted to back true evil. There have to be others out there in hiding that could help. Those who have been forgotten and buried beneath statutes and the kings and queens that didn't see them."

"Our uncle hurt a lot of people," Rhodes said.

I couldn't deny that. "Yes. And there must be other Wielders who hid from him."

Rhodes nodded. "Perhaps. If there are, we'll find them."

"My mother never went after Slavik," Easton said, his voice harsh. "She knew, just like I did, that he would be useful."

I went to him then, not caring that the others were looking at me. I put my hands on his chest, rose to my tiptoes, and kissed his chin. "You were fighting to save your people from The Gray, and battling against Lore. We all understand that. And Slavik *isn't* the most law-abiding citizen."

"And yet you want to use him in your war." Easton's brows rose, and I wanted to both knock and kiss the expression off his face.

"Don't get snippy. And it's not just my war. The Gray started this. But we're going to finish it. However, we need everybody. Even those who are a little sketchy when it comes to the right side of the law."

"That doesn't seem like something a Spirit Priestess should say," Easton said softly, tucking a piece of hair behind my ear. "I like it."

"Well, I'm the first Spirit Priestess, so I guess I should forge my own way."

The others around us mumbled and talked plans. And that was good. The things I'd said had gotten them thinking.

But I was so exhausted. I just needed time to breathe.

The real battles were still coming. Not just in this room, but also in the world where The Gray could get to us. Where innocents might die if we weren't strong enough.

As I leaned into Easton, I breathed in his scent and tried to calm myself.

We could make this work. We would fight.

But first, we needed a plan.

CHAPTER NINE

EASTON

I SHUT THE DOOR FIRMLY BEHIND US AND RESTED MY FOREHEAD against the cool wood for a moment to catch my breath.

As small hands touched the place between my shoulder blades, I smiled, knowing exactly who it was, especially since I had just locked her in the room with me.

"Are you okay?" Lyric asked from behind me. I turned, pulling her in to hold her close without replying.

I wasn't sure how I could answer that question. How could I be okay? The shattered realm surrounding us screamed, people were dying, and we didn't have clear answers yet. The Gray was pure smoke, sliding between our fingertips. We had to find him. Somehow.

Everybody still fought amongst themselves and with those on the other side of the line, and there wasn't a clear way to rally the troops and the civilians to explain that we would find a way to make everything work.

And because of that, I worried.

So, no, I wasn't okay. But I wasn't going to tell her that.

I pulled away slightly and looked down at her face.

Maybe she was the person I needed to tell.

"I'm as okay as I'm going to be," I finally said, looking down at the eyes I would never get enough of.

I slid my hands through her hair and scowled at the length of it.

"Why are you growling at me like that? Is my hair that horrible this length?" Lyric asked, self-consciousness in her voice. She pulled back slightly, running her hands over her now shorter blond hair.

I could have kicked myself. Instead, I leaned down to kiss her hard on the mouth.

"I'm scowling because I remembered that a sword was so close to your neck that it slid through your hair and cut it. If this were a hairstyle you picked on your own, that would be one thing. But the fact that a weapon did this during the heat of battle makes me want to hit something."

"Well, I don't mind the hair that much anymore." Lyric slipped her hands through her shorn locks, and I leaned forward and kissed her on her nose, her forehead, then her lips again, my hands following hers through her hair.

"I love the way it looks on you. And hopefully, the next time you get a haircut, it'll be of your choosing."

"That sounds like a plan to me," she said, searching my face.

"I would ask what's bothering you, but I feel like it's so much."

"You're right, it is a lot," I said finally, running my hands over her hair again. My uncle might have healed her, but I could still see the bruises and the cuts. I wanted to find The Gray and everyone who worked for him and hurt them. I wanted to take them away from this world. But there was nothing I could do. At least, not yet. But when the time came, they would scream for what they had done to her.

That might make me a tyrant—though some already thought I was—but I didn't care.

They had hurt her, and they would beg for mercy.

"I'm just happy you're here. That they found you."

"I think Braelynn and I would have made it back here no matter what eventually, but we *were* tired. And after fighting the League once we returned to this realm, it was a lot."

My hands fisted on either side of her hips, and I leaned forward, resting my forehead against hers.

"It helps that you had a dragon on your side."

"Especially with the basilisk."

I closed my eyes and let out a breath through my nose, trying to calm down. "You were alone up there with Braelynn, trying to save yourself. And I was here, in meetings, trying to form a plan. I should have been out there looking for you." I pulled away from her and started to pace, my Fire sliding over my fingers as Earth rumbled under my feet. I knew the others would be able to feel my Wielding, my temper. But I figured...screw it. I was tired of holding everything back for fear they would think I was a king of no kingdom who couldn't control my emotions.

They could deal with me later. Right now, I needed to make sure that Lyric was whole, and I had nowhere else to focus my anger, not when we couldn't fight our enemies head-on.

"You couldn't leave our people behind," Lyric said, her voice stern, but my brain locked onto one word.

Our. She'd said our people.

So weird to think that I wasn't completely alone in this anymore. That I could feel her within my soul, her own heart beating beside mine. I never thought to find my soulmate, and in some respects, I hadn't been sure I possessed one to begin with.

I had been cursed, had lost most of those I loved and was forced into a life that I hadn't chosen for myself. People had hated me, the prince of the dark court, at least during the time when light had to be good, and dark must be evil. We had been set on the paths of our fates long before we were even born. Yet, somehow, I ended up with the other half of my soul.

It didn't seem like I deserved her. It didn't seem fair that I should have this moment of peace and happiness when others had nothing.

Maybe it'd be better if I walked away. If I gave her a chance to thrive without me. But I wasn't that kind of man. Plus, I had walked away before. I wouldn't do it again.

She was mine, just like I was hers, and the world and the fates would have to deal with it.

"Why are you staring at me like that?" Lyric asked, her tone cautious.

"I know you told us what happened with The Gray, but I also know you left some things out," I said after a moment, studying her face.

Her eyes turned dark, and part of me hated myself for bringing it up, though I had to know.

"You're right. There are some things I couldn't tell the others."

"You can tell me."

She searched my face and smiled, even though it didn't reach her eyes. I reached out and traced her cheek with my fingertips, loving how her eyes closed, and she leaned into me.

"I know I can tell you anything. It's so weird that I can."

I let out a laugh. "Really? Weird?"

She blushed a pretty pink that covered her cheeks and descended down her neck.

"I meant it's weird that I have somebody I can tell things to. I didn't know that I ever would. It feels like I've known you my entire life instead of however long I have."

"It does feel like so much longer, doesn't it? But I guess that's what it means to be soulmates."

"I suppose that's what it means to have that word be real," she countered, and I nodded, knowing she was taking the long way around to the subject. That was fine. I could wait. But I hoped she would tell me everything eventually.

Not only because I needed to know, but also because I knew she needed to get it off her chest.

"You know it wasn't just The Gray who hurt me, right?"

"Yes, I know," I growled out. The flames in the hearth beside us grew, the white tips of each flicker so bright and hot it could sear flesh in an instant. She narrowed her eyes at me, and I shrugged.

"You know this is going to make me angry, no matter what you say, and my Wielding needs to go somewhere."

"I do know that, but please don't burn down the castle."

"I can't promise anything, but I'll do my best," I said dryly.

"At least that's a start." She let out a sigh.

"It was The Gray, but he had Durlan cut me. He was always the one with the knife."

A single crack appeared in the wall beside us, my Earth Wielding growing intense as the Fire raged in the hearth. Suddenly,

Lyric's hands were on my face, caressing my skin and then moving down my chest as she soothed me. "Stop it. I'm fine. He didn't even scar me. There's nothing left of him on me."

"I'll gut him."

"You might have to stand in line because I want to gut him first," she growled.

I kissed her. She'd never been so damn hot to me before.

"He's still out there, but I killed Garrik," she said without a hint of remorse in her tone. I was grateful for that. If she had felt bad about his death, I would have done everything in my power to make her understand she shouldn't feel remorse for what she had been forced to do. Not given what Garrik had done to us.

"I'm sorry that I couldn't be the one to do it for you," I said honestly.

"There are some things I need to do for myself, and not just because I'm the Spirit Priestess."

"Maybe. But if I could shield you from the bad ones, I would."

"That would be nice, but not truly feasible." She let out a breath and pulled away before she began pacing.

"What is it?"

"The Gray said something to me, and I know I should take it with a grain of salt, but I'm anxious to know if it's the truth."

"What?" I asked, uneasy now.

"He said there are others on his side. People within our ranks."

"I wouldn't put it past him," I growled, anger surging within me once again.

"He said that he has a son."

I froze, blinking, my mind whirling. "The Gray has a son?"

"Yes, and he told me his name," she whispered, her hands shaking now. I moved forward, holding her close.

"Who is it?" I asked, my voice barely above a murmur.

"Luken," she whispered.

I froze and cursed under my breath.

"The bastard of the Lumière is The Gray's son?"

"Don't call him that," she snapped.

"That's the title they gave him, it's not what I call him myself."

I pulled away so I could look down at her. "Luken has no idea, does he?" I asked, knowing that had to be the case.

"No. And that's why I know he's on our side. He would do anything for Rhodes and Rosamond and Braelynn. He's not truly The Gray's. But I don't want anyone else to know because I don't want them to look at him differently. I don't want distrust to slide through the ranks. If it does, we'll become weaker than we already are. Plus, I don't want Luken to hate himself even more than he already does because he couldn't protect Braelynn."

"He'll need to know eventually," I said, hating myself for even mentioning it.

"I know. But first, we need to figure out who his mother is."

My brows rose. "Wasn't he raised by his mother?" I asked, trying to remember some of what I remembered about Luken's past.

"He was raised by a woman he *thought* was his mother, but The Gray said that his mom is someone we can't trust and a person we may know." Lyric looked at me then, her throat working as she swallowed hard. "His mother is someone we must worry about, though I don't know where to start looking for her."

As I listened to her tell me more about what had happened with The Gray, I nodded and leaned forward, holding her close as I tried to get my mind back on track.

We had a traitor in our midst, one who had been with The Gray. Who had a son by him. Had she chosen her direction? Or was she just another on the path The Gray had laid out for us?

I wasn't sure, but I knew we needed answers.

"I don't want to talk about this anymore," Lyric said softly. I looked down at her, saw the heat in her gaze. I kissed her gently, then a little harder, and then even harder.

"Make me forget, just for tonight," Lyric asked, and I nodded before kissing her again and leading her to the bed. We had done this before, the two of us, and I knew that what we had was more than anything I could have imagined.

As we loved one another, hands against skin, a gentle brush of lips, I knew that this break in the chaos, this moment of peace where we could have one another might be our last.

Because even as we both fell over the edge of bliss, taking one another in both passion and heat, I knew the outside world was waiting for us.

We were at war, and sacrifices would be made. But the woman

in my arms, the Priestess in my bed who clung to me as I did her, wasn't a dream.

This wouldn't be our ending.

As we connected once more, aching for each other, I knew this might be our last time together.

Even though in a perfect world, it would only be our beginning.

CHAPTER TEN

Lyric

The stones above my head rattled, and my eyes shot open. Easton had left my side before I even had a chance to jump out of bed.

"We're under attack! Wielders, to your positions!" Easton called out, his voice and the meaning bringing me to full awareness in a jolt.

We dressed quickly, not bothering to speak, our footsteps echoing against the stone as we ran down the hall.

"How? How did they get so close?" I asked, turning the corner and heading towards the throne room where we had all said we would meet in case of emergency.

"That's what I want to figure out. But first, we need to see what the hell is going on," Easton said. Suddenly, the others joined us, all of us going to the balcony to see what was happening. It was an easy path to the courtyard or any other part of the estate where we could fight, but this was the best view to see what was coming.

As I took in what was happening in front of me, my blood chilled, and my magics wavered just a touch, enough for me to shake. How in the hell had this happened?

Rows and rows of Wielders stood in front of us as if they had been waiting on what had been the Lumière side. Lying in wait for just the right moment to come at us. I could see the colors of their uniforms and knew they were former Creed and League members —ones that had stayed on the side of The Gray. There were Wielders from all territories, brandishing all types of elements. Those who had not come to the side of light, but rather stayed on the side of shadow and The Gray.

I didn't know why they were doing this. I didn't know every single reason for their betrayal or understand what they saw as right. But I knew they were against us.

Were they against change? Were they against those in power?

Or were they solely against me?

I didn't know. However, at the moment, it didn't matter. Not really. Their actions would speak louder and be far more deadly than their motivations.

There were hundreds, *hundreds* of Wielders, and as another Fire wave slammed into the side of the castle, I knew we didn't have time to stand around and come up with a plan.

"Rhodes, take your team and go west. Justise, go east," Easton began. They nodded as he issued orders, and everybody spread out. There was no time to say goodbye, to wish anyone luck or hope that everyone made it out of this.

We *had* to make it out of this. There was no other choice.

I followed Easton because we fought well together, and our Wieldings complemented one another. But when he took my hand and crushed his mouth to mine, I let myself sink into him for just the barest of moments. A breath where I could almost believe that we would all be okay, that whoever was coming at us wouldn't hurt us too badly, and we would find a way to make this work.

While we had been on the defensive, trying to protect our people and keep them fed and whole, The Gray and the others had been training their army even harder—which was never more evident than now.

"Be safe. Got it?" Easton said, his forehead against mine.

"Always. You need to be safe, too."

"It's what I live for, pet," he said and then kissed me hard again. After that, we were off.

As we reached the courtyard that led into the field, there was no more time for talk.

My Wielding slipped through my fingertips, every element rolling around in my body, readying me to fight.

Two Creed members stood in front of me, their Air Wielding strong, practically pushing against me. And I knew they weren't even really trying. They were that powerful and were merely testing me.

They pushed harder, two funnels of wind coming straight at me as if they had been looking for the Spirit Priestess and were happy to find her.

I stomped one foot on the ground and shoved my palms out straight in front of me, pushing at the Creed Wielders. Earth slammed into the wall of Air while Fire danced at the top, singeing any magic that came at us.

I let my right arm fall and then ducked as another Wielder came at me, his Fire coming so close to my face that the Air Wielding that separated us burned.

They had Fire Wielders, Earth Wielders, and Danes with weapons—and so many others.

The conflict that had destroyed the realm had started as a war between the kingdoms, but now it was a realm of shattered promises and broken ideals.

There were no barriers between the kingdoms now. Every Wielder could belong to the realm, rather than a part of the whole.

We were all against each other now, and it didn't matter that he was a Fire Wielder and should have been with the Obscurité.

There were no titles anymore.

Instead, we were simply enemies.

I shot Air Wielding towards the Fire Wielder and then moved closer to another group.

They came at us, another stream of warriors, another fight, but I had to keep going.

I rolled on the ground when a fireball shot over us but quickly got to my feet again. Easton shouted at me, even though he was fighting four Wielders on his own.

I gave him a nod and went back to it.

Luken and Braelynn fought to the left of me, Braelynn in her cat form since her body was too tired to take her dragon form after our long trip across the Spirit territory from the Shadow realm. I knew she wanted to do more, I could feel it in my bones, but I was glad she was with Luken. She remained in her pouch on his back and shoulders as he used his sword to direct his Air Wielding, slicing through one enemy after another. Braelynn beat her wings and pushed air currents towards the fire erupting from her mouth, singeing those that got too close.

I ran to Easton's side, and we fought back to back, another row of Wielders coming at us. There was no time for words, only fighting. I pushed my Air Wielding under Easton's Fire, and it shot out farther than before, a giant maelstrom of flame and heat as it slammed into the other Wielders. They screamed, jumped out of the way, and pushed Air and Water towards us.

We each moved our arms to the sides, Earth Wielding deep within us as it created a wall of dirt to protect the Wielders near us.

Justise and Ridley were together, Ridley doing his best to heal those who were hurt as they went, and Justise in charge of the battlements.

He had created weapons for those who didn't have magic, for those Maisons who could only fight with steel and might.

"Give us the Spirit Priestess, and we'll let you all live," one of the League Wielders shouted above the din of battle.

I didn't even hesitate to throw out a burst of Fire, while Easton and Teagan did the same, our three flames combining. The League member who had shouted ducked out of the way and shot Water at us.

Wyn moved forward, pushed her forearms together, and created a wall of mud—Earth and Water blended together to demolish anyone in front of her.

I had never seen her perform that trick before. Someone had been teaching her.

Rhodes? Or maybe Ridley. After all, he was a Water Wielder, though he used his powers to heal rather than to fight. Sadly, we would need him now more than ever. There was more to this than using offensive and defensive talents.

Rhodes moved to the right of us, the Wielders behind him those he had trained before he even met me. He pushed a wall of Water towards the enemy, shouting out orders as his Air and Water Wielders moved as one, a unit fighting with grace.

Rosamond used her Wielding, as well, Emory at her side. I didn't understand why Emory was here, nor did I know everything she could do with the powers she had now. But it seemed she wasn't truly fighting the entire time anyway. I could see that Rosamond's eyes were wide, the surface slightly glassy. Every few moments or so, she'd shake as if being slapped hard with another vision. Emory braced Rosamond's body each time, and when Rosamond whispered, Emory moved to the side to fight, using the sword that Justise had given her. She still wore the cuffs to hold back her siphon abilities, but I didn't know how long those would last.

Would we need her to use that power in the future? I wasn't sure, but at the moment, they were fighting as a team, Emory moving with a finesse I had never seen from her before.

Easton tugged on my arm, and I brought myself back into the fight, slamming my palms together in a whoosh of Air before pushing it forward towards the Wielders in front of us. Easton stomped his foot on the ground, a large boulder hovering in the air before shooting towards the enemy.

I followed his movements, using methods I hadn't been trained in, but I could feel the Wielding inside of me.

Wyn appeared, doing the same with a dozen other Earth Wielders. We stomped on the ground, boulders rising into the air before being shot off into the distance, reminding me of the pirates and Slavik. Rocks came back at us from the other side, some doused with Fire, and I knew the Earth and Fire Wielders working for The Gray were collaborating, so we did our best, as well.

The Lord of Fire had such control over his element. I couldn't forget how he had danced with his wife, a burning ache that had sent tears to my eyes at its beauty.

He had lost his soulmate, that much was clear. Because he was only a shell of a man.

I knew that anger and agony were the only things keeping him going, along with his son. Still, he was here with Teagan, pushing Fire at the enemy.

Alura danced along the battle lines, using her sword to fight. I still didn't know what her Wielding was, but it didn't matter because she was on our side, and she was fighting.

The factions that had once been our enemies surprised me the most, though.

Creed and League warriors fought against our brethren but fought for us.

They had been disenchanted by the king of the Lumière, had been lied to for decades. Now, they were here, battling against those they had once called their own. Wielders they had called their brothers and sisters.

Water against Water, Air against Air.

But it wouldn't be enough; I could feel that.

We had our armies too spread out over the kingdom, protecting innocents and doing what The Gray wasn't. He wasn't helping any of the people fighting for him. The Gray's forces were coming at us full force, and here we were, in an old castle, trying to fight without the crystals' help.

Thanks to Lore and the damage he'd done to the crystals, we had fewer Wielders on our side than they did. That was just fact.

Before the crystals had shattered into a million pieces and settled into my skin, they had pulsated with power and destruction, removing the Wielding from people one by one.

Many of the fighters battling near us were Danes or Maisons that were losing their power and Wielding. And because Lore had used the crystal for personal gain, we had more Danes than the other side.

The Lumière had used bone magic, and even blood magic to strengthen their base. We hadn't.

And now, The Gray had more power than we did, at least in this battle.

But we would not die. It wouldn't end like this.

The Gray wasn't even here.

I kept looking. Every time I pushed out with my Wielding, I searched for him.

But he wasn't here.

Was this all a distraction? Or was this only the beginning?

As the enemy began to close in on us, working together with swift and deliberate movements, I was afraid we were about to discover the answer.

There were so many of them. As Fire came at us, the flames licking as it burned, I pushed with all my Wielding and hoped to hell we would find a way out of this.

CHAPTER ELEVEN

EASTON

I THREW MY HANDS INTO THE AIR, FIRE GLIDING THROUGH MY fingertips as I created a wall, blocking the heat from the Wielders in front of us.

I let out a curse, looked to my left, and allowed a relieved breath to slide from my body as I saw Lyric standing there, her hands outstretched, all five of her Wieldings pushing forward into a chasm of bliss and power.

Somehow, she had mixed the five elements, something I hadn't seen her do before, and it was stunning.

The Wielders that had come at us had strength in their veins, using any and all Wielding they possessed. There were more of them than us because we had separated our forces into groups to protect the innocent and those weaker than we were.

I wouldn't regret that. I couldn't. But as I heard the dying screams of those who weren't going to make it because we weren't strong enough to protect them, I knew those echoes would haunt me until the end of time.

I had to push those thoughts away, bury them deep. I would

think about it later. I needed to keep the rest of us alive so I *could* mourn those we'd lost.

I didn't know what Lyric's Spirit Wielding could do, but as people fell to their knees in front of her, their whole bodies shaking, I had to wonder if she was touching their spirits somehow. As if she heard my thoughts, she shook her head.

"The Spirit Wielding only increases my other Wielding at this point. I'm not stealing souls," she said. I moved closer, my hands outstretched, Wielding still flowing. Then I kissed her again. I just needed a touch. Her eyes widened a bit, but there wasn't time to talk. We had to fight.

They came at us with Fire, Earth, Air, and Water.

Sweat poured down my back as I pushed my Wielding to its limits. Even my reserves were almost depleted.

I had spent my life training to fight, to protect my world, my kingdom, and my people. Now, I feared I wouldn't be enough. I worried none of us were going to be enough.

Wyn fell to her knees, the ground shaking beneath her touch, and Water spewing from her hands as flames arced across her shoulders, a breath away from singeing her. Teagan and his father sent Fire in an arc, damaging a whole swath of Wielders and covering Wyn in the process.

Rhodes stood on the other side of Lyric, pushing his Air out with hers, slamming it into the bodies of the Wielders who came at us over and over again.

Luken and Braelynn worked alongside Emory and Rosamond. Sword against sword, weapons clashing.

And I still didn't think it was going to be enough.

Alura battled, too, Justise and Ridley at her side. Delphine and Lanya fought, as well. The former Queen of Lumière floated above a crest on the sea as she made wave after wave surge into our enemies, her long hair floating in the air, practically flying next to Lanya. The Lady of Air used her Wielding much like her grandson had and hovered near Delphine, taking down warrior after warrior with a kind of grace that took my breath away.

It was magnificent, something I had never seen before in my lifetime. Yet I *still* didn't think it would be enough.

A dragon form filled my vision at that moment, however, and shattered any illusion that we might be winning.

I cursed under my breath, and Lyric approached.

"What is that?" She panted.

"It's not a Familiar. It's a dragon. A *real* one."

When shouts rang out, I threw myself over the nearest Dane with no power to protect himself, and thrust my hand up into the air, blocking the fire that came down at us with my own Fire Wielding.

Lyric covered another Dane who had been fighting with a sword and didn't have the Wielding to protect herself from what was coming.

I wasn't sure we would have enough power to save ourselves, let alone others.

"Get back!" I shouted. "Get the wounded!"

As the earth rattled, the dragon slamming its claws into the ground and spewing more fire, I felt like everything slipped through my fingers, the absence of light shocking in the shadow and darkness.

I looked over at my uncle. There was an Air Wielder matched with a Water Wielder in front of us. As one, they sent an ice blade towards Ridley. I opened my mouth to scream with nothing coming out just as Justise threw Ridley down and put up a wall of flame to stop the blades.

Only he wasn't fast enough.

Another blade came at him. I slammed my feet into the ground, sending Earth Wielding into the dirt below me, one stomp after another, trying to get close, attempting to stop the onslaught of power heading toward Justise and Ridley. But I knew I wasn't going to be fast enough.

The Creed and the League were working together, but this wasn't a random attack.

No, this was an assassination. They were too singularly focused on Justise, the lost son of a dead king.

I ran as fast as I could, sweat beading on my brow. Lyric ran up beside me, but everything played out in slow motion in front of me.

Another blade came at Justise, and he wasn't fast enough.

Ridley stood up, just enough to push Justise partially out of the way.

The ice blade tore into Justise's arm, so precise it was like a surgeon's scalpel, but at least it wasn't in his chest. Blood spurted, spraying everything, and we screamed as the appendage fell. Fire and Earth erupted from me. A wall of mud and dirt and boulders cobbled together with fire shoved into the assassins, killing them instantly. Somehow, I was suddenly at my uncle's feet, trying to stanch the blood. Ridley pushed me away, his hands coated in his husband's lifeforce as Justise's brown skin paled to an unhealthy gray.

"No, you do not get to do this. No." Ridley just kept saying *no* repeatedly as he used his healing, as people still fought all around us, some dying, others screaming. We weren't going to be enough.

The Fire kept coming, and when it started to torch the castle, the grounds now burning, I knew we needed to leave. We had to retreat. This battle wasn't ours to win.

"Your uncle's going to be fine. We're going to save him," Ridley said.

But as I looked at Justise's arm, at the fact that it was no longer attached to him, I didn't know if that was the case. I met my uncle's gaze, saw how glassy it was, but gave him a tight nod anyway. Then I pushed up to stand. Lyric had been near me the entire time, protecting us using her Wielding, but she was swaying on her feet. Even the power of the Spirit Priestess was waning.

"We need to go. Tell everyone to retreat."

Lyric met my gaze and nodded, her face pale, her features drawn.

"We weren't going to be enough," I whispered to myself.

As the castle burned, the home that I had called mine for centuries, I knew that I couldn't say that this changed things. Because as the days passed, there *was* no home anymore. Everything had changed with a blink. Nowhere was safe any longer.

Rhodes picked up Wyn, Teagan dragged his father, and the others kept moving, leaving one by one, keeping the pace as they helped those weaker than them.

We were all covered in blood, soot, and ash. This was the end.

The Obscurité Court had fallen long ago, perhaps even with my mother's death. But now I was a king with no castle and no kingdom, just a people who needed a leader. However, I didn't think there was anything left to lead.

The others on the Lumière side, on The Gray's side, had started to move back, not bothering to kill any more of us.

The Gray wasn't here.

This had been a test. That much was clear. A test we had failed. One where The Gray had shown his power. Power he didn't even have to use. Just his people's.

They had come at us, and I could only hope our people were safe. We had separated to keep the weak sheltered, and that meant our castle and everyone in it was in danger.

The bricks burned, smoke billowing out of the royal room where the crystal had once been housed, where my mother had died. Where I had found my soulmate and watched her die the first time before coming back to me despite my curse.

There was nothing left for me.

It was all gone, turned to ash and death and nothingness.

As Lyric slipped her hand into mine, we began to retreat. I knew I would use this rage, this nothingness later. Because I would not let this be the end. The castle might be gone, the home I had known for my entire life turned to ash, but we had survived. And we would win.

I would not allow The Gray to become the victor.

No matter what I had to do to make that happen.

CHAPTER TWELVE

Lyric

I HAD VAGUE RECOLLECTIONS OF MOVING MANY OF OUR PEOPLE TO the Fire Estate. It wasn't as if I had been able to sleep or concentrate beyond keeping us alive on the journey.

Our group knew we needed to focus, to finish our plans, and to make hard decisions. But I hadn't thought we would lose our home as we did. That was on me. I should have realized we would lose at least part of who we were along the way. After all, I had already done so while on the path laid out before me.

Some of our warriors were scattered along the roads leading from the former castle of the Obscurité to the Fire Estate. Many of them had come with us, the weak and the injured, being forced to travel long distances to stay safe.

We weren't safe in our former castle, though I didn't know if we were safe at the Fire Estate either. Still, other wards and magics that the Lord of Fire had put in place long ago at the estate had once been part of the court itself even though they had worn away after decades of war.

It was also closer than the Earth Estate by days, and since we didn't know what the Lady of Earth was doing, her treacherous ways only somewhat uncovered, we didn't want to travel there.

At least, not yet.

We had lost so many people. Although, thankfully, no one new along the way. People had died at the hands of The Gray's forces, and there was nothing I could do about it. Spirit Wielding didn't bring them back to life. That was the one main thing I couldn't do, the forbidden thing that I promised myself I would never do. After all, I had watched my parents die, had seen their souls float away into wherever the hereafter was. I was never going to bring anyone back. The Spirit Wielders had forbidden it. I understood that I would only be delaying the inevitable, twisting fate and becoming far worse than The Gray ever was.

It had been two weeks since the battle and our defeat. We were healing and consoling those we could. There wasn't much we could do outside of that, and it hurt me deep down in my soul.

"Lyric?" Easton asked from the doorway. I turned from the window where I had been staring outside and pulled myself out of my thoughts.

I hadn't had too much time to myself since we had arrived, nor had I had any time to be alone with Easton. We had both led this charge, trying to do whatever we could while planning for the inevitable.

Strong hands slid around my waist, and I rested my head on his chest, just for an instant before pulling away.

I saw uncertainty in his eyes when I looked at him. I tried to smile, but I knew he likely knew it wasn't real.

"We're starting the meeting."

"I figured, I'm on my way."

"I'd say you could rest a bit more, but we both know you don't sleep any more than I do."

"I wish that wasn't the case. Let's get this over with."

"They're just going to keep yelling about the same gripes over and over. Every plan we make gets thrown out the window with each of the Gray's movements."

He was right, but I was trying really hard not to think about that.

Over the past two weeks, we had waited for The Gray, had fought in small skirmishes, and not just the primary battle that had taken so many. Only we weren't getting anywhere with any of it. The Gray was hiding in the Shadow realm, and we had to find a way to lure him out.

That's what today's meeting was about.

"I love you," I whispered.

Easton blinked as if startled by my words. He leaned down, brushed a kiss on my lips, and then squeezed my shoulders.

"I love you, too, Priestess."

"So, let's figure out how to save the world."

"Again," he said, winking. He looked almost like the man I had met at the Fire and Earth border all those months ago.

It almost seemed trivial now what that wink and smirk did to me.

Because despite that, it now felt as if there was no hope.

And that was something I needed to push from my mind.

When we made our way to the war room, I realized the fighting had already begun.

Teagan and his father were at each other's throats, yelling about something or another, and I knew it was something they needed to get out of their system. They were grieving the Lady of Fire, and there was nothing we could do about it.

But it was exhausting.

They seemed to notice that we were standing in the doorway and, thankfully, stopped bickering for a second.

"Any updates?" Easton asked, and Justise shook his head. He sat near the back of the room, his stump bandaged and what remained of his arm in a sling. Ridley had done what he could to heal the scarred flesh, but no one could regrow a limb, not even with magic.

Justise was now a Wielder with one arm. Not the first. But as the blacksmith of the people, one who was the most talented weapons maker anyone had ever seen, I knew it likely hurt him more than just the physical pain. He would figure it out, though.

We all would.

I had to keep that thread of optimism alive because if I didn't, I wouldn't last long.

"There was another attack on one of our camps," Rhodes said, his hair messier than I'd ever seen it. It appeared as if he'd run his hands through it over and over again. His silver eyes looked dull, and I saw lines of strain at the sides of his mouth and bracketing his eyes.

We had all aged over the past months, but I didn't think Rhodes had slept since we arrived at the Fire Estate.

I only slept the little I did because I was so exhausted after the meetings, and fighting, and healing of each day. I could barely keep my eyes open. Honestly, if I didn't fall asleep next to Easton, his warm body near mine as he told me I would be okay even if neither of us believed it, I didn't think I would go to sleep at all.

"Any casualties?" Easton asked, and I could hear the anger and fear in his tone. Even though he sounded so crisp, so cold and calculating, that I wasn't sure the others would be able to hear what I did.

Maybe it was because I could feel him inside my soul, the bond that neither of us knew what to do with pulsating.

"Four," Luken gritted out. "All Danes that couldn't fight against the onslaught of power."

I closed my eyes, let out a breath, and sent a prayer up to the sky, hoping that whoever might be listening could send us some help.

Only I didn't think that would happen. I was the foretold savior, after all.

"We need to go to him," I said, and everyone looked at me.

"To the Shadow realm?" Easton asked.

"You know we do. The Gray won't come out. Why would he? He doesn't have to. He has so many people on his side that he's either brainwashed or who think they're disenfranchised and agreed to fight us. And some believe the lies and think that it's still Obscurité versus the Lumière."

"And what about those who went to his side?" Teagan asked, his voice stern.

"They did that because there was no hope," Wyn said, and I saw Easton flinch, but nobody said anything for a moment.

"Because of Lore?" Easton asked. "Or because of me?"

"Stop it," I snapped. Everyone looked at me. "Lore used the crystals and stole people's Wielding. Innocents died because of him. Not because of you."

"You know that's not the case," Easton said, his voice so low that it sent shivers down my spine, but everybody else heard him anyway.

"We don't know what's coming. Nobody does," Wyn said, her voice slow. "So, I guess we need to go to the Shadow realm."

I looked at her and let out a long breath. "It's the only way to get him to fight on our terms. He's not going to come out here, and his people won't stop while he's their leader, even if some of them might know who's pulling the strings."

"That is the worry, isn't it?" Luken said, frowning as he scratched Braelynn behind her ears. She purred, and my heart broke just a little more.

"It doesn't matter. Because the Obscurité members who went over to The Gray's side left because they thought they had no choice. But that's not on us. At least, not completely." Wyn raised her chin.

Easton shook his head. "You say that, but I don't know if I quite believe it. We're all at fault here. But we don't have time to keep flagellating each other. It's time to figure out exactly how we're going to get our armies to the Shadow realm."

"I think they need to stay here to fight those that stay back," I countered. "And I think only a few of us need to get to the Shadow realm."

Easton's gaze narrowed. "Please tell me you're not thinking of facing him by yourself."

I threw my hands into the air. "No. Didn't I just say that we needed to take a few of us? There needs to be people here to train and to lead the armies, but I'm the Spirit Priestess. I need to fight The Gray. It's been foretold. So, here I am. I need to go to him. Besides, he still has people on his side, and however many he has within his realm now."

"I thought he only had his second and fourth," Luken said, and I did my best not to look at him directly. We still hadn't told him about his father. And, honestly, I wasn't sure how to. Everybody stood at the edge of a precipice, where one shove in any direction would make us all falter.

It was wrong of me to keep the secret, and we would tell him soon. I just didn't know how to yet.

"I killed the Whisperer. But his second is still there. And there might be others he's pulled into the realm by now. The fact that we don't know for sure is a major roadblock. Meaning, we need to go to him." I rolled my shoulders back. "That's not the only thing we need to do.

"You want to go find Slavik," Rhodes said.

I nodded. "And anyone else that hasn't come to us yet."

"If they haven't come," Rhodes continued, "is there a reason for that?"

"Many of the underground leaders have been in hiding, keeping their people safe. If they're at least against The Gray, we need help. We've lost too much," I said, doing my best not to look at Justise or anyone else who had lost someone or something dear. Though that touched every single person in this room if I was honest with myself.

"We need every faction we can find to protect our people and to bring the realm together. The crystals are gone," I said, looking down at my skin. "I don't know how to bring them back, but parts of them are within me. You in this room know this, though no one else does."

Everyone nodded, and I continued. "We need to get the crystals back—somehow, some way. We need to defeat The Gray, and we have to protect our people. And to do that, we need all hands on deck. That includes the pirate king and anyone else who has been hiding since the last battle."

Easton looked at me then, his expression grave, but he nodded. "You're right. We need everybody. So, we'll find them. And we'll discover a way into the Shadow realm."

"We let The Gray come to us last time. We can't do that again," I said. "We'll go to him. We'll take the war to his door. And we'll win. Because while the realm might be fracturing, we won't let it fall into ruin. Not completely. We won't lose our people."

As everyone started talking at once, making plans for who else they could contact, I turned away. I looked out across the unfamiliar landscape of the Fire territory, firedrakes dancing along the edges, fire erupting from a volcano miles away, and I wondered what a plan could be without an actual ending. I knew the prophecy. I knew what it entailed, even if some of it was still vague.

The crystals were now in me. I knew this. And for them to come out, something needed to give.

A sacrifice had to be made.

Suddenly, I had the feeling that once we reached the Shadow realm, I wouldn't be coming back.

I had left the human realm long ago. And even if we defeated The Gray, a part of me knew I wouldn't be returning to the Maison realm either.

CHAPTER THIRTEEN

LYRIC

THE ROAD TO THE OTHERS WAS LONG AND VERY DIFFERENT FROM THE last time I had been on this path. When I had come this way before, I had been hurt. We were sometimes in wagons, other times being dragged, all the way from the Earth territory up through the borders and then towards the Fire territory.

Then, I had been with Luken and Braelynn and Rhodes.

I had met Easton in the borderlands. Had learned how to use my Air Wielding with his Fire Wielding, and had fallen just a little for that smirk, even though I hadn't realized it at the time.

He had been a prince of no name then, even while Rhodes had been the same.

None of us were who we used to be.

Today, we were on our way to find Slavik and his people, and recruit any underground leaders we could get our hands on.

Having us stick together might not be the smartest plan, but The Gray wouldn't come after the others without Easton or me or Rhodes present. He hadn't yet, not after how many times we had been away. It had always been an attack on at least one of the three of us. So now, we were staying together, heading to gather more people.

Rhodes, Lanya, and the others had stayed behind. As had the former Queen of Lumière.

Easton's uncles were training, although Justise was taking a longer road back to recovery than we had hoped. He had lost his arm in battle, and for now, it seemed he was ignoring anything past his initial healing. He wasn't using the Fire Estate's furnace to make weapons. He was only using his Wielding to train others to fight. Other blacksmiths could pick up the slack and were doing so with clear understanding. Only I didn't know what was best for Justise. It was his decision, however, no matter what he decided—something we all recognized.

I wasn't sure what would happen when we returned. I had to trust that Ridley would know how to help Justise. He knew his husband better than anyone and had had to overcome *his* abilities. After all, he'd had to hide his Water Wielding for centuries. *And* he'd had to learn to be a warrior and a healer.

Hopefully, he would be able to help Justise now.

So many had stayed behind, our armies gathering. We had met smaller camps of warriors along the way, ones who had stayed to protect their small towns and villages rather than meeting up with the king.

We all understood that but had done our best to persuade those who *could* leave to go and join the other armies to fight as one. Most had agreed, simply taking their families with them. We understood that, as well. If they didn't, there would be no one left to protect them.

Because we all knew that not everybody was safe. Not everyone was on the side of good.

We had all learned that the hard way more than once already.

And now, without the wards, it was hard to know who was friend or foe. Not that it had ever been easy to determine that.

This was the seventh village we had visited, and we were exhausted, but I knew this was only the start. We used carrier hawks to get messages back and forth to and from the uncles, hoping each time that they weren't intercepted. Easton used some of the magic he had learned from his mother to keep it all secret, but I was still worried that the enemy would intervene. We didn't know exactly how powerful The Gray was, after all.

Braelynn and Luken traveled together, with Braelynn in her cat form. We didn't know if she could willingly shift into her dragon form, but it had taken a lot out of her when she did, so we were all glad that she was saving her energy for another fight.

Because there *would* be another fight.

Teagan and Wyn were with us, too, Wyn wanting to see her former home, the Earth Estate. I imagined Teagan had come to get away from his father—at least partly.

We had left the Lord of Fire behind to train the Fire Wielders in combat, those new to the power that had popped up after I pumped more magic into the crystals before they shattered.

Although the entire kingdom—the realm itself, really—was breaking down, creatures escaping from wherever they had been hiding, earthquakes and other natural disasters taking over, the Danes were actually fewer in number than ever.

Whatever I had done, had forced what had happened to Wyn hundreds of times over.

Some of the former Danes had gotten their Wielding back, while others got Wielding they never had before.

I hadn't seen any other dual Wielders quite like Wyn yet, but I was sure they were out there.

And all Wielders, new and seasoned alike, needed training.

If we survived this, we would do our best to make sure they all had a place to belong: a place to feel safe, a place to use their powers however they needed.

A home.

A sanctuary.

But first, we needed to defeat The Gray.

I walked between Easton and Rhodes, all of us exhausted and silent. We walked up front, with Luken and Braelynn behind us as Wyn and Teagan pulled up the rear. We switched positions over time, but right now, I was between the two former princes, who were not talking to me or each other. Not because they were fighting, simply because there was just too much on everyone's plate.

"You sure this is where we're going to find that pirate king?" Easton asked, derision in his tone.

I held back a sigh as Rhodes answered. "He was this way last time we saw him. However, we know he has an actual ship that drones over the hills."

"I've seen it. I still don't believe he's going to end up on our side. He never wanted to listen to what my mother had to say before. I don't even think he sees me as a king." Easton frowned and kept moving. "Not that I see myself as a king."

"We can worry about titles later," I whispered, trying to keep the peace. "I just need a united force against The Gray."

"And behind you," Rhodes said.

I frowned at him. "What do you mean by that?"

"I'm not saying anything rude. We will all fight with you. And when we defeat The Gray—because we will, damn it—then we can see what happens and acknowledge titles and royalty, if that's even needed."

"It would be nice if I didn't have to be king," Easton said offhandedly, and Rhodes and I shared a look.

I knew that Easton didn't want the power and responsibility that came with being a king. He would shoulder it, but having all those lives in his hands? I knew the kind of weight he felt because I felt it, too.

And neither of us wanted our shoulders to break under the pressure. But we would do it. There was no other choice.

"We will find him," I said.

"And hope he doesn't kill us?" Easton asked, that smirk on his face again.

It almost reached his eyes this time, and I gripped his hand, smiling. "Yes. He's going to be our little pirate king. And he'll use his very fancy Earth Wielders to go against The Gray. They have powers I've never seen outside of their group."

Rhodes nodded. "It's true. They're quite powerful."

"And he never went against the throne, so Mother let them live." Easton shrugged. "Frankly, they kept the peace amongst those who tried to prey on the weak, except for a few within their ranks."

"The pirate who killed all those innocents is dead. We made sure of that," I said, my voice shaking.

I still remembered the sight of that woman who had died for me. The one who had been a Seer, who had known she would die for me. That she would give me her power so I could break free.

I would not let her sacrifice be in vain.

I would not let the memory of so many deaths be in vain.

I opened my mouth to say something, not even sure what, when a screech echoed in the air. We all went on high alert, our Wielding in our hands, Luken's sword at the ready.

"What the hell is that?" Rhodes asked.

"That…is a chimera," Easton snapped. "Long extinct. Or so we thought."

"That means the rift between the worlds is opening even more," I said.

"And we don't know what else came out of it."

"How do you kill a chimera?" Wyn asked. She paused as another screech echoed in the air. "How do we kill *multiple* chimeras?"

Easton growled. "You have to cut off their heads, but their hide isn't easily penetrated."

I looked at the giant mass flying towards us and swallowed hard. It had the head of a dragon, not unlike Braelynn's in her other form, but that was the only similar thing about them.

The chimera's body was that of a lion, and it had talons on its feet, and falcon-like wings.

The realm was genuinely shattering. The horrors of ages past were coming forth.

And if we didn't defeat The Gray soon and find a way to unite the realm and make it whole, it would bleed over into the human realm.

And more than one race and people would die.

"I count seven," Teagan shouted over the screeching.

"Okay. Then we do this. Watch your backs."

"Everyone take down one, and help those near you," Rhodes said, each of us spreading out to confront the chimeras surrounding us.

I heard a deep growl and looked over my shoulder as Braelynn turned into her dragon form, fire slipping between her fangs.

I had already lost her once. I'd be damned if I did it again.

Honestly, I had already lost most of the people in this group *more* than once. We would not die today. None of us. Not by a chimera. Not even by many chimeras.

Everyone split off as the beasts lunged. I stomped my right foot on the ground, a wall of Earth rising into the air. It slammed into the lead chimera's throat, but it did a barrel roll in the air and came at me, trying to slash me with its talons. I pushed myself back with my Air Wielding, flying backwards and then rolling to my feet, the claw coming at me missing my face by mere millimeters.

I shot Fire from my left hand, Water from my right, pulling from a nearby stream. The Wieldings pummeled the chimera, and its screams echoed in my ears, along with the cries of the others.

There were grunts, sounds of Water and Air and Earth and Fire all around me. My friends were on the ground, then back up again, blood coating most of us as the chimeras' talons got too close, or if we hit the ground too hard.

But we were stronger than these creatures. We had beaten things worse than them.

And we would prevail here, too.

I dropped to my knees, slammed my hands into the ground, and moved them upward to pull a disc of Earth into the air. I spun it in the sky repeatedly until it created a sharp disc, and then used my Air Wielding to push it towards the chimera in front of me, flames licking the outside rim of the coin-shaped weapon. It sliced into the chimera, and the beast screeched so loudly, my ears felt as if they might bleed.

Its head fell off and dropped to the ground, its body following a second later. As it shriveled to ash, I turned towards Teagan, who was trying to use Fire to lash out at it. It wasn't enough, not when he couldn't cut through the beast's head. I did the same, using my reserves to slice through the chimera's head. Those with Earth Wielding were able to follow our lead, and Luken and Braelynn took down both of their foes—Luken using his sword, Braelynn using her dragon jaws.

As I turned to see the last one, I noticed that Easton was riding atop it, Rhodes using Air to move it up. And then Easton made a swishing motion with his hands, Earth strangling the chimera. I screamed as Easton slammed into the ground along with the chimera, the beast's head rolling off as Easton landed on his feet as if he hadn't just been riding a giant mythical creature.

I ran up to him and threw my arms around his neck.

"What in the realms possessed you to do that?" I asked, slamming my mouth onto his.

He held me, kissed me back harder, and then smiled, looking so much younger than he had over these past few weeks.

"Well, he tried to eat me. So, I had to take care of business."

We all started laughing, the carnage around us now smoldering. The smell of burnt chimera tickled my nose, but I ignored it.

We had won another battle and had been strong enough to do it ourselves.

We were going to survive this. I had to have hope.

The air shifted around me, and I froze before letting my Fire out again. All of us stilled for a second before turning around in a circle, our backs to one another. Braelynn had returned to her cat form and now stood on Luken's shoulder.

Men and women in black robes emerged, each with a silver raven logo on their shoulders, the stitching prominent in the light.

They surrounded us, Fire at their fingertips, so hot it burned bright blue.

I had only seen Easton do that, and he rarely did it since it used up so much energy. It seemed this group wanted to put on a show.

Everybody was on edge, and I had no idea who these people were. If they were part of The Gray's army, we would defeat them. I'd had enough.

"Spirit Priestess," a man said. Before I could answer, Easton took a step forward.

"You were supposed to be dead," Easton said. I swallowed hard, confusion and a feeling almost close to betrayal sliding over me. Who were these people? And how did Easton know them?

"Easton?"

"These people are the Unkindness of Fire."

Rhodes and Teagan and Wyn all sucked in breaths, while Luken and I looked confused.

"Hello, King. We are sorry for hiding so long, but we needed to keep our numbers intact. To find those who were lost amongst the ruins so long ago."

A man stepped forward, the one who had spoken. He pulled back the hood of his robe.

He looked almost like Teagan, but not really. I wasn't quite sure who this guy was, but he seemed to be the spokesperson for this group, this Unkindness of Fire.

"Spirit Priestess, kings, those of the court. We are the Unkindness of Fire, as King Easton has said. We are an old, nearly lost society. We have not been needed for centuries because of Queen

Cameo and our King Easton. But when Lore began his scheme, and The Gray started to move again, our ancestors were called forth, and we knew we needed to train. We are only now back to this realm, but we are ready for you."

They all dropped to a knee around me, and I froze. I wanted to reach out for Easton but I didn't want to look weak.

"We vow our allegiance to the realm, not to a kingdom or a territory or an element. To the realm itself. And to you, dear Spirit Priestess. To the one who will unite us all. We, the Unkindness of Fire, come to you. We will fight for you."

I didn't look at the others, but I knew they were turning to me, wondering what I would do next. So, I bowed my head and took a step forward, knowing that my friends trusted me.

"Thank you. All of you. We have been searching for those who can aid us. And it seems as if your ancestors are right on time."

Actually, I thought they were a little late, but I didn't say that out loud.

"What will you have us do, Spirit Priestess."

I looked at Easton and gave him a tight nod before looking at the new group. "Rise, and let us make plans. You will be needed to train the others we send to our armies spread across this former kingdom. War is coming, and you are desperately needed."

"For the realm, for the Priestess, and for our future."

At their words, every member of the Unkindness of Fire speaking as one, their blue flames shot into the air. I looked up, knowing this had to mean we had hope.

We had more fighters for our army now, more people who could save our realm and our innocents.

Or, we would have more cannon fodder if The Gray got what he wanted.

We just had to ensure that he didn't win.

For the survival of everything.

For the revival of hope.

CHAPTER FOURTEEN

LYRIC

THAT NIGHT, WE CAMPED NEAR WHERE WE HAD KILLED THE CHIMERAS.

I was exhausted, but I couldn't sleep. My mind whirled in a thousand different directions as I tried to figure out exactly what our next step should be.

I sat cross-legged near a small fire and rolled my shoulders back, just trying to breathe. To focus. If I couldn't sleep, I might as well work to soothe my aching nerves.

The others were either on patrol or resting—a smarter choice than mine since they were saving their energy. But I couldn't do it. My brain needed a bit to slow down. Only I couldn't focus long enough to make that happen.

"Talk to me, Priestess," Easton said as he sat next to me, his thigh brushing mine. He leaned into me, his arm on the other side of my hips. I inhaled his scent, the Fire and Earth that was so much a part of him. It wrapped around me as if it had always been meant to do so. My soul reached out for his, aching for more, a confirmation that we were together in truth. We didn't have time for such desires or needs right now, though.

"I should be sleeping," I whispered, aware that the others might be able to hear us. We were all close enough that they would probably be able to listen to us just fine.

Wyn and Teagan slept near the edge of the camp. Luken and Rhodes were out on patrol, each taking their turn. Braelynn lay on the other side of the fire, curled into a ball with little snores coming out of her nose every once in a while. She had started on my lap at one point but had moved to the other side of the flames, giving me the space I needed.

"Let's get inside the tent and get some sleep."

I looked over at Easton, then kissed his jaw and rested my head on his shoulder. "I don't think I can sleep."

"That's not the smartest thing."

"So says you, who isn't sleeping either."

I looked down as Braelynn made her way to my lap once more, kneading my thigh before curling back into a ball. She yawned widely and went back to sleep.

I held back a laugh and ran my hand down between her wings, scratching her fur. She arched into my touch for just a moment before settling back in.

"Well, if we're not going to sleep, what should we do?"

I gave Easton a look as he tried his best to look innocent. There was nothing innocent in those eyes, but I just smiled and shook my head.

"Not today, my king."

"I was afraid you were going to say that." He kissed my temple before leaning against me, and we sat there staring at the fire.

I wondered how Drake was doing—the little firedrake that had followed me home last time. We had left him back at the Fire Estate with the others, and I hadn't seen him. He'd gone to stay with the other firedrakes on the estate. He didn't answer to me or need to stay with us. After all, he wasn't a pet.

Then again, neither was Braelynn.

I had met so many on this journey that were now either gone or apart from us, their paths tangling with mine in a twisted way that nearly sent me over the edge in a frenzy of frustration and worry.

"I can see your brow furrowing," Easton whispered. "Tell me your troubles."

"I'm just thinking about Drake. And everyone else we've met. Even the new Unkindness of Fire, or the small groups of people who came together because of a common purpose and have now bowed before me. How am I supposed to use their promises to defeat The Gray when it could mean their lives? What have I done to deserve this?"

"You have fought and bled on the battlefield. You died once, nearly died again. And yet, you still ask this question?"

"I've only done things others have. I have all these powers, yet they don't seem to be enough when pitted against someone who doesn't follow any rule known to man or Maison."

"You have the crystals within you. They shattered, and their power drained and broke because of what our realm did before you even stepped foot into it. You will save them. You will save us all."

"That kind of pressure doesn't help," I said honestly.

"I know. That's why I try not to say things like that too often. But it's still the truth. And I will be by your side helping you, no matter what. The Gray may not follow any set rules, but there has to be some type of code or magical rules he does follow. He can't bend and break every law out there and remain whole."

"I'm not sure that's the case anymore." I leaned into Easton for a bit, my eyes drooping as he ran his hand down my back. Braelynn purred in my lap. I could almost pretend that this was all a dream. That we were sitting at home and living a pleasant and soothing life. An existence where we weren't scared to leave our homes or scared of what was coming.

That wasn't really the truth, was it?

For the moment, I could pretend that we were safe.

My eyes had just drifted shut when a shout came from behind us. Easton and I were on our feet in an instant, Braelynn right by my side, growing into the size of a panther, her wings back as if ready to attack.

She growled, and I looked up to see Luken coming towards us, his sword covered in black blood, a gash on his side.

"Negs," he growled out.

One word, and horror filled me.

The Negs. They had been working for Lore, now they were working for The Gray. Though, in essence, they always had been, hadn't they?

"Everybody stick together!" I shouted.

Easton smashed his mouth to mine, a quick kiss that spoke of all the things we couldn't say. In an instant, we were fighting, back to back, the Negs coming at us with such intensity that I almost stood there in silence, just staring at them. I had never seen so many in one place before. They kept spilling out of the trees as if there were an endless supply, all waiting to tear us limb from limb. They were the absence of magic, the lack of life and light.

They were the result of a fractured realm.

And they were controlled by chaos himself.

Dozens poured out of the tree line as Teagan and Wyn and Rhodes came to our sides, each ready to Wield. I didn't think it would be enough.

Not with how many we were facing.

Suddenly, there was no more time to think. The Neg closest to me jumped on top of me. I pushed out my Air Wielding, and it slammed into him, but he kept coming. I let out a curse.

"These are stronger than the last ones," Rhodes called out, echoing my thoughts.

"That means Lyric's Wielding won't be as effective," Easton added.

"I can see that," I said, slamming my Fire Wielding into the next Neg, but it wasn't good enough. I had to use more and more power, and my energy reserves were already drained from having to use so much against the chimeras earlier.

There was no time to think, no chance for us to shout out directions to help each other.

We were all fighting as hard as we could, but it didn't look like it was going to be enough. The closest Neg bit into my calf, and I screamed. Easton's gaze shot towards me, and I yelled, trying to warn him, but it was too late. Another Neg jumped on him, clawing at his shoulder. He punched it with his Earth Wielding, burying the Neg in the ground before slowly staggering to his feet, blood pouring from his wound. I limped away from my now-dead Neg, cursing all the while. Easton had been distracted because of me; because I wasn't fast enough.

I shot out more Water Wielding, and then Earth Wielding, taking out another Neg, and then another. Blood poured from my wound, and I saw that the others were bleeding and screaming all around me.

There had to be at least sixty Negs around us, and they were far stronger than I had ever seen before. Far stronger than us, even with us fighting as a unit.

Energy pulsed within me, and I started shaking, punching a Neg in the face using my Fire Wielding as it came closer.

I didn't recognize this energy. It was new to me, foreign.

The dark and the light crystal reached out to me as one, yanking me to something. But I didn't know what.

It spiked energy within me, pulled at my skin, my muscles, and my ligaments as if trying to escape. I didn't understand how or why.

The crystals within me slid through my body as if trying to merge, attempting to do something. I really didn't understand it.

Then I reached out towards the next Neg, and some power that wasn't mine seeped out of my skin, drawing blood.

I could hear Wyn's shocked gasp from beside me as I fell to my knees, blood pouring out of my pores as the crystals' magic tried to escape, attempted to attack the Negs.

I dug my fingers into the ground, the soil rich and intoxicating as I pulled at my Earth Wielding. The water particles in the air attached to my Water Wielding, the same with my Air magic. Fire leapt at my skin, singeing the blood the crystals had awakened and making it hiss.

I could hear my friends screaming my name, but I couldn't focus. Instead, I pulsated along some phantom edge of agony and bliss as the crystals burst from within me, moving just a short distance. I threw my head back, power erupting from my eyes, ears, nose, and mouth. Everywhere. Then there were screams, the Negs' bellows as they burned to ash, falling dead at our feet.

I couldn't breathe, couldn't think.

I fell onto my side, felt the others coming near me, and then Easton's hands on my shoulder. He screamed my name with his face pressed to mine.

"What?" I asked, my throat dry and feeling as if it had been rubbed raw by sandpaper.

"What the hell was that?" he asked, holding me close. His hands and his chest were covered in blood, but I didn't think it was all his. No, some of it was mine.

I looked down at myself and saw that I was coated in red—the lifeblood that had seeped out through my skin.

"The crystals wanted to help."

"Never again," he snapped. "You are never doing that again."

"You would have died."

"Then we fucking die. You do not get to do that. Ever again."

I looked up at the others. They were all shaking, their eyes wide with fear—fear for me, or fear of me, I wasn't sure.

"Never do that again," Wyn said, running her Water Wielding down my face. I didn't know how she was doing it with such ease. When I looked at her eyes, I saw the strain there. She was in pain, yes, but she was also learning how to use her new Wielding. Water slowly cascaded over my face, washing the blood away.

"If you do that again, I'll lock you in the tallest tower I can find and never let you out."

I leaned away from Easton, looking down at our wounds and knowing that it would take time to heal these, though we couldn't stay here for long.

"I'm going to do what I have to, to protect everybody. And you can't stop me."

"Watch me," Easton snapped.

The others were suspiciously silent, but I understood. I had scared them. I had scared myself.

But Easton wouldn't always be able to protect me. And we both knew it. That was the fear I saw in his eyes. Not the fact that I had used the crystals—or rather, they had used me.

No, it was because we all knew what would happen when I met The Gray again.

There was only one way we could win. One way the prophecy had foretold.

And that meant I wasn't coming back to him.

This wouldn't be the only time I would be covered in my blood.

This wouldn't be the last time that Easton held me while the others looked on in helplessness.

It was only the first.

CHAPTER FIFTEEN

LYRIC

I KNEW ANGER SIMMERED BENEATH EASTON'S SKIN ON MOST DAYS, but I'd never seen it boil like this before. The idea that the anger was directed at me and what I'd done didn't help.

The only way I could ensure that I would never get that look again was to promise that I would not risk my life for my people and friends. That I wouldn't risk my soul to save those I loved. And that was something I would never do.

I would always put them first. That was my destiny, to save those I loved, even if I risked everything I had.

And the fact that I had scared my soulmate? That was something I would have to learn to deal with. Something Easton needed to live with, as well. Because I would do anything to protect him.

Even if he hated me for doing it.

"We're almost there," Rhodes said suddenly, breaking into the silence that had become deafening between us all.

"Should be interesting," Easton grumbled, and I pulled at his arm for a second, meeting Rhodes' gaze. Rhodes lifted his chin and directed the others to keep going. Thankfully, Easton stopped moving.

He needed to give in for me to stop him, and the fact that he did, told me that maybe we hadn't hurt each other too much.

"Stop acting like this," I said softly, hoping the others couldn't hear.

"I'm not acting any differently, Lyric. This is the same man I've always been."

"You say that, and yet I see the anger in your gaze. Don't hate me."

Easton glared at me. "I could never hate you, pet." He cupped my face with his hands and leaned forward, resting his forehead against mine.

"Then why do I feel like you're disappointed in me?"

"Because I was," he said, the word slashing at me. "Only I was more disappointed in myself. I hate to see you in pain. Especially when I can't damn well do anything about it. And I know what you're supposed to do, what your new destiny is—at least what we both know you might have to do. But I hate the idea of you constantly putting yourself on the line to protect us with powers that we don't understand."

"I don't understand them either."

"You were part of that 'we' I just mentioned, Lyric. You're always part of that."

That warmed me, even if I was still confused.

"This is all scary. Everything is unknown. And the fact that you have the crystals inside you now freaks me out a little. I don't know what's going to happen next, but every time I turn around, it seems you are throwing yourself into the fray to protect us. It scares me. It terrifies me so much, and I don't know what to do about it."

"I don't know what to do either. But I know I can't stop. I can't simply walk away from who I am because it's scary."

"Let me walk beside you, then," he whispered.

"But I can't lose you."

"And I can't lose you."

He looked at me then, and I wasn't sure what else to say.

I didn't think there was anything else *to* say.

"I truly hope I'm not interrupting anything," a familiar, deep voice said from behind us. Easton and I whirled, our Wielding at the ready.

Slavik sauntered from the tree line, his palms outstretched, not ready to Wield but to show that he was unthreatening.

There was nothing innocent about the pirate king.

"Slavik," I said, a smile playing on my face.

I could feel Easton's glare.

He was quite good at that.

"I knew you couldn't stay away for long," Slavik said, taunting Easton.

I rolled my eyes. I might not have had the best interactions with Slavik before—after all, his second in command had kidnapped me and threatened to kill me as well as many other people. But Slavik had made good decisions in the end, and I knew that he was protecting his people, even if I didn't always agree with the ways he went about it.

"We're here to ask you for your help," I said, knowing that someone with a better pedigree or more training would probably have been able to get past all of the hidden meanings and tangled words to stroke his ego. They probably would have let things evolve slowly, making Slavik beg to help *us* rather than the other way around.

But I was not that person. And frankly, we didn't have that kind of time.

"You know, I was expecting a bit of flattery or at least some groveling before you asked," Slavik said, mirroring my thoughts.

"You are a member of the Obscurité Kingdom. I shouldn't have to ask you," Easton growled.

"Oh, yes, my king. Should I have gone down on my knees in a show of fealty for you? Or just thanked you again for letting me live all this time and not making me follow all of your pesky little rules."

"Slavik."

"Don't chide me," Slavik said, narrowing his eyes at me before glaring at Easton again.

"I know what you need, and I understand why you need it. But some within this kingdom, one that doesn't quite exist anymore if there are no wards, need help beyond putting their bodies on the front lines in a war that was already lost, long before the Spirit Priestess took her first steps into our kingdom. Whatever that may be."

"The war isn't lost. *Hope* isn't lost."

"Those are some mighty ideals for a girl who has died how many times now?"

"And yet, I always come back," I spat. My hands fisted at my sides.

Slavik looked down at them, at the Water and Fire swirling around each of my hands. I couldn't help it. My Wielding was sometimes far too strong for me, but it wasn't hurting anybody else. If anything, I was showing my force. At least, I hoped I was.

"My mother let you do whatever you needed to do because you were protecting others, even if you pretended that you were some pirate without law and order," Easton said.

"I don't know if I liked the word *let* just then," Slavik drawled.

Easton narrowed his eyes. "The truth is that she let you. And we both know it. You might pretend that you don't care about anyone but yourself and the people you've chosen to protect, but we both know that's not the case. You fancy yourself the Maison realm's version of the humans' Robin Hood—stealing from the rich and giving to the poor. But have you ever truly done that? No. For the most part, you've hidden when things got scary and dark. And while I understand that, there's no more time to hide. No place to retreat."

"Easton's right, though I probably would have said it a little nicer," I said, looking over at my soulmate.

"Slavik doesn't need nice."

"I could use a little nice," Slavik countered, grinning at me.

"Don't look at her," Easton snapped, and I held back a groan, rolling my eyes. Oh, good. Just as Rhodes and Easton had become friends and stopped sniping at each other, Slavik was here to make it all bad again. I hoped it was just stress and not that Easton actually thought I had any interest in Slavik. Honestly, that hadn't even crossed my mind, even if the pirate king did have a whiff of danger about him that was intriguing. And he *was* quite attractive, but I would never tell Easton that.

"You need to stop fighting," I interrupted.

"No, I think we need to get a few things off our chests," Slavik said, ignoring me.

"Fine, but make it quick. We have a realm to fix and to save. So, once you're done fighting to see who's bigger, we can make some decisions."

At that, I threw my hands up into the air and stomped away. Easton just grinned at me.

"I like her," Slavik said.

"She's mine.

"I'm my own person first," I called out.

"Yeah, I like her," Slavik said. Suddenly, all levity vanished from his face. "Your mother might've let me live, but she didn't do anything for the Danes."

"We both tried. We didn't know The Gray and Lore were trying to kill us. I didn't know The Gray had a foothold in our kingdoms for as long as he did. Nor did I know the true depths of Lore's wickedness."

"Maybe you should have known. How the hell were you supposed to keep all of us safe? Your people that you supposedly care about. You didn't even know who was killing them."

"We thought the realm was shattering because of the Fall itself. We had no idea that it was being helped along by the knight of the realm."

"Now you know."

"And we're trying to honor the lives that were lost. We're attempting to make up for the time that we squandered."

"Maybe. Or perhaps that's just what you want us to think." The pirate king shrugged. "I don't know anymore."

"Know this. You have always been on the outskirts of the law, even before the Danes. You've never been perfect. But neither have I," Easton continued. "And you saved many of our people over the years, Slavik. But you didn't see the rot within our world. Your second in command killed hundreds. Just like Lore did. We were both blind to the machinations of those who were supposed to protect our people when we were trying to save the realm. So, get off your high horse and help us. We need help."

"Please," I added, and Eason shot me a look.

Slavik's face was a mask of uncertainty and calculation. He had to help us. We needed many more. Because while those already against The Gray were strong, I was afraid we wouldn't be strong enough. We had found dozens of strong Wielders along the way, including the Unkindness of Fire. But we needed more. So many more. I knew that our other scouts were also finding people. Soon, there would be no rock left unturned.

But we needed Slavik. We needed everyone he was connected to.

Because we still didn't know what The Gray had in store for us, or when he would come. Or how we might go to him. Because we needed to make a stand. Soon.

"It's not just me, you know," Slavik said. "It will never be just me."

"That's sort of the point," I said, shrugging. "I keep calling you the Underkings, but that's not really the title, is it?"

"It wasn't before, but it sure as hell will be now," Slavik said, grinning.

I watched as Easton rolled his eyes, his mouth tugging into a smile.

"Well then, it seems I should talk with those other Underkings to figure out exactly what our plans will be."

"Please stop calling yourselves that," Easton said, a growl in his voice.

I snorted, trying not to laugh. When the love of my life glared at me, I just shrugged. "Excuse me. But you also called him that."

"He did, really? A king of the Underkings? I truly like that."

"Slavik," I chided.

"Okay, okay. I will continue using that term because I can't help it. It is pretty amazing. However, you're right. We need to take a stand against The Gray out in the open. Although I don't know as much about him as I'd like."

"We'll tell you all we can. But who can you get to fight on our side?"

"There are a few who, like me, have been hiding the weakest of us. Those that can't help themselves."

"And those who have always broken the law," Easton added.

"It's true. I mean, why is a rule even there if we can't break it?"

"However," I put in, "I will have the final say. I might not be a queen, and I will never be, but I am the Spirit Priestess. I'm the one the fates say will take down The Gray. So, you will listen to me and those I put in command with me. We need your help, but if you become a hindrance, then I don't want you here."

Easton just grinned at me. Oddly enough, so did Slavik.

"You have my sword, my lady," Slavik said, bowing deeply.

"That sword had better be your actual sword, or I will hurt you," Easton snapped. I threw my head back and laughed, feeling lighter than I had in weeks.

Perhaps it was the absurdity of it all, but I couldn't help the amusement that burst free.

"We need to defeat The Gray," Slavik said softly. "Rebuilding what's left of the realm isn't going to be my job. That will be of the true kings and queens or whoever's left in the end. But I fear The Gray has already unleashed far more than we know."

"The monsters?" I asked.

"They're everywhere. The realm is breaking, shattering and seeping into the other realms around us. It's not just the human realm we could destroy in the end."

"So, all of the dormant monsters *are* coming back?" I swallowed hard.

"And some from the other realms are coming here."

"Speaking of, why are you out here?" Easton asked suddenly, his hands outstretched, ready to Wield.

"I was hunting. And I still am. And given that the trees are now silent? I have a feeling we are now the ones being hunted."

And on that prophetic announcement, a scream echoed from the trees around us.

CHAPTER SIXTEEN

EASTON

I RESISTED THE URGE TO PUSH LYRIC BEHIND ME SINCE I KNEW SHE wouldn't appreciate the protection. Slavik was at her other side in an instant and gave me a look over her head. I lifted my chin and knew that though Lyric could take care of herself, she wouldn't have to. The pirate king and I would keep her safe.

And if she heard those thoughts, she'd probably hit me with her Wielding herself.

A few other Earth Wielders came up behind us, while Slavik barked out orders to his team.

Our crew came up on our other side.

"They were hunting something, and it's coming at us now," I informed our group.

"It's a gorgon," Slavik snapped.

I closed my eyes and let out a breath. "You're serious?"

"Why would I joke about a giant gorgon trying to kill us?"

"Isn't a gorgon like Medusa?" Lyric asked, confusion in her tone.

The trees in front of us swayed as if something substantial moved through them, coming after us.

Rhodes answered. "In the human realm, the stories of the Greek being with the head of snakes was a gorgon, yes, but the gorgons here? It's sort of a mix of that and the worst terror you could ever think of."

"So, it's not one of the good guys, then," Lyric said with sarcasm, but I knew she was just trying to relieve the tension since all of us were running on no sleep and constant fear.

"You'll just have to wait and see what it looks like as it tries to strip the meat from our bones," Wyn answered, her Earth Wielding rumbling beneath her feet. Slavik looked over at her and gave her an appreciative glance. Teagan and Rhodes both glared at him, and I pushed that observation back.

I'd have to deal with whatever was happening with my seconds in command later. For now, I needed to keep Lyric alive because none of us had been expecting a gorgon.

Finally, it came through the trees, and I sucked in a breath.

It was almost the size of the hundred-year-old trees, its body made of stone. It had the head of a bull with horns longer than seven feet.

Its body was that of a bull's, as well, though it had scales running down its back and what looked like what once might've been wings etched into the stone.

It had snakes around its head, the one nod to the human realm's version of Medusa—that and the fact that it was stone itself.

The problem was that, much like the basilisk Lyric had told me they fought, if it looked you in the eyes for too long, you were dead —turned to stone with no way to come back.

"Don't look it directly in the eyes."

Lyric looked down and cursed. "How are we supposed to fight it, then?"

"You drown it, burn it, bury it, or slam it to the ground repeatedly with your Air," the pirate king said simply, even though there was nothing simple about what he'd said.

"Okay, then. Let's do this." Lyric paused. "Is it just one of them, or do they travel in packs? Or herds. What do you call a group of gorgons?"

"I'd say your death, but that seems a little too on the nose," Slavik said, and I forced myself not to smile. I might not particularly like the pirate king for many reasons, but he was entertaining.

I leaned closer to Lyric. "They don't travel in packs, and they don't even raise their children. They give birth and let the baby survive on its own. At least, that's how it was millennia ago."

"Okay, then."

The gorgon made its way through the trees, and I looked up at the meters-tall beast and hoped to hell we made it through this. Because this gorgon was only the first step in our new quest. The Gray would be much harder to kill.

The gorgon slammed its front hoof into the ground, shaking the earth beneath our feet. Fire erupted from its nostrils, its eyes narrowing in calculation. I let out a curse as one of the Earth Wielders, a younger one from what I could see, screamed, and Slavik cursed, as well. The young Earth Wielder had looked into the eyes of the gorgon and now stood as a stone statue behind us all.

Slavik shook for a moment, and I almost moved forward with Lyric in case the man did something stupid in the heat of the moment.

"For Travis!" the pirate king screamed. We moved, Lyric by my side, Rhodes on my other. We surged, my Fire Wielding seeping out of my fingertips as I slammed it into the gorgon. The flames lashed amber against its stone hide, but it wasn't enough. "Keep hitting that same mark," I ordered the others. "Whatever you can do. Do it."

Teagan nodded, and then he and Wyn moved together as one, with Rhodes aiding, using all of their Wielding against the spot I had hit. Luken worked with the Earth Wielders and Brae, using their Wielding and her fire to get at the gorgon's ankles.

"We need to blind it," Lyric said, and I nodded, looking up.

"Think you can take us both up there?" I asked.

"We've barely practiced that," Lyric said, and I grinned, adrenaline coursing through my body.

"No time like the present to see if we can make it happen in the heat of the moment," I said, and she nodded, putting her hands out to either side of her, gusting Air Wielding beneath her. She hovered above the ground a foot or so and then angled her right arm so she could do the same beneath me. I sucked in a breath as I moved next to her. The pirate king laughed.

"That's a new trick, Priestess. I like it."

I didn't bother to look back, mostly because I didn't want to fall and die, but I was glad the pirate king sounded surprised. We had all trained and were far more powerful than we were before. Lyric more so than any of us.

She gripped my hand suddenly, the Air Wielding cascading over my body, and I let out a breath, the buffeting wind almost too much. Suddenly, we were flying, hovering in front of the gorgon. It spewed more flame at us, but Slavik and Wyn were there, pushing Earth Wielding at it and dousing its flames.

"Fire," I whispered, trying not to look down. I wasn't afraid of heights, but it was a little disconcerting with nothing beneath my feet.

Lyric gave me a tight nod, unable to speak because she was focused on using her Wielding. I understood.

We both threw out our free hand and lashed Fire into each of the gorgon's eyes. It stomped the ground below us, and people screamed, moving out of the way. I hoped to hell that nobody got hurt.

Then the gorgon staggered back, screeching in pain at the loss of its eyes.

It couldn't blind us anymore. We had successfully blinded it.

It stomped again, lowering its head to try and ram whoever it could. Its horn smashed into the ground, leveling trees in the process, all the while thrashing and screaming and trying to kill us all.

Not all monsters were evil. Some had roamed our world long ago in peace and harmony. But those like the gorgon were born evil, only made to create chaos and kill.

So, while I wouldn't harm every animal and mythical being that came into our realm, the gorgon trying to kill those I loved needed to go.

And, thankfully, the others understood that and agreed.

We fought together, breaking through the beast's stone hide until the smell of burnt flesh beneath stone singed my nostrils. Lyric lowered us both to the ground, and I let out a shaky breath when I landed.

"Okay, then," she whispered as the stone gorgon slammed to the ground again, the earth shuddering beneath its weight.

"That wasn't something I expected to do today," Wyn said,

rolling her shoulders back. She had dirt smeared all over her face, and someone's Fire had singed her shirt.

"Did one of us get you with Fire, or was that the gorgon?" Lyric asked, and Wyn just rolled her eyes. "No, that was the gorgon. It got a little too close. But my new Water Wielding's coming in handy," she said, and the pirate king's eyes narrowed.

"You're a Water and Earth?"

"Yes, what of it?" she asked. I knew she hadn't meant to mention that. Sure, the others would have noticed if they had seen her fight, but with the commotion and chaos of the battle surrounding us, they wouldn't have been made aware of it so quickly. But now that she had said it out in the open, there was no hiding it anymore. She was an enigma now, just like the Spirit Priestess. And I knew that Wyn wasn't completely happy about it.

"None of our people or those I have seen have Water and Earth. But I have seen former Danes become filled with unexpected Wieldings lately. And now they need to be trained."

"That's why we're here," Lyric said. Not only for your help but also to see who else we can help. Who we can train."

"They're not all going to want to join an army," Slavik said. Then he looked into my eyes.

"There's a reason they didn't fight for the queen and then you later. They don't want to be conscripted."

"We have never conscripted anyone."

"No, that was my father and uncle," Rhodes said. "The Lumière did that. They forced their people to fight and die for them. And they did it under the guise of training. And though I fought for them to stop, no one listened to their Seer, my sister, or to me. But it was never the Obscurité."

"Sure could've fooled me," Slavik said, looking directly at me.

"Well, maybe you should've spoken to us instead of hiding."

"Is this helping anyone?" Lyric asked, and I looked down at her and shrugged. "No, maybe not. But there are a lot of old battles without closure and connections between all of us. We're hundreds of years old, Priestess."

"Maybe, but it's time to look towards the future. I know the past is paved with darkness and pain, but we can't defeat The Gray if we're constantly fighting amongst ourselves." She let out a breath, and I nodded. "Slavik, we're not going to force you to fight with or for us. We're not going to force any of the Danes either. But they do need to be trained. You know that as well as I do. If people hadn't helped me with my Wielding, I'd be dead. And we all know that. They need help. And we can send them places so they can get it. If they don't want to fight in the battle, we have other places for them. Places where they can be safe—or as safe as possible with The Gray out there. But if they want to help, if they want to defeat The Gray alongside us, then we will welcome them."

"I understand," Slavik said after a moment. I held back a breath of relief. I might not like the guy, but I knew if I had been born in another world, I would've ended up just like him. On the outside looking in but fighting for something I thought was important. I didn't like that I could see myself in him—both who I used to be and the man I wanted to be.

"Well, killing the gorgon probably alerted everybody to where we are. In case you wanted to hide," Slavik said.

"I guess we'd better get back to the Fire Estate."

"Not your court?" Slavik asked.

"The court is gone. Burned to ash."

Slavik's brows rose. "I've been out of the loop for far too long, it seems. Tell me more."

"On the way," Lyric said, pushing through. "We need you to find any others who will fight with us. But we've been gone from the Fire Estate for too long. I think we need to head back."

I looked at Lyric and nodded. "Yes, we need to go back. Our people need us. And I think The Gray has been quiet for far too long."

"You're right, and that scares me."

I nodded and met Slavik's gaze, then looked at the others.

The Gray *had* been silent for far too long. And when The Gray got quiet, that meant he was planning.

And whatever he had planned for us might mean the end of us all.

While we had defeated a gorgon and had taken down countless others who had come for us, we had lost people along the way. And though we also gained new members for our army, I had a feeling it wouldn't be enough.

I knew what would be enough, though. *Who* would be enough?

And that was the woman standing beside me, the one who had claimed my heart.

Because the prophecy surrounded us, smothered us with its deceptions and secrets.

In the end, it would be army against army, Wielder against Wielder.

But The Gray would only have one person to fight.

And it wouldn't be me. It wouldn't be the other princes or kings or those with titles.

No, it would be the Spirit Priestess, the woman I loved.

Even though I had all the confidence in the world that she could defeat him, I didn't have faith in the prophecy.

For in order to defeat The Gray, I wasn't sure she would survive.

She would likely sacrifice everything to protect the people she loved.

Even herself. And her soul.

I didn't think I was strong enough to hold her back, or perhaps I was terrified that I was so weak that I wouldn't try.

CHAPTER SEVENTEEN

LYRIC

"NOT LIKE THAT," JUSTISE SNAPPED BEFORE GOING OVER TO ONE OF the newly made Wielders and showing him how to use his Fire Wielding.

I gave Easton a look, and he gave me a firm shake of his head.

Justise's temper was far shorter than it used to be. He used to growl more than anyone else I knew, including Easton and Luken, so that was saying something. It made me sad that I couldn't find a way to reach him—that nobody could. He had to learn to Wield with one arm, something he could do but it hadn't come easily. After all, he had lived for centuries, Wielding and battle planning with both arms, moving his body with a kind of grace that not many warriors possessed.

Now I knew he felt off-kilter, and there was nothing I could do about it but support him and not get in his way.

However, he was scaring the young Wielders, the former Danes, and even the Maisons who hadn't been born with Wielding.

Now, they were using all four types of Wielding, trying to figure out how to fight in this war we all felt as if we were two steps behind in.

It wasn't lost on me that there wasn't another Spirit Wielder yet.

At least not one out in the open. Maybe they didn't know they had Wielding, or perhaps didn't know how to use the power.

Perhaps there weren't any left.

As a thought far more sinister than I wanted to think filtered through my mind, I wondered if maybe they were on the side of The Gray now.

After all, The Gray was a Spirit Wielder, as well. One who used shadow and death rather than using his Wielding to protect souls.

Not that I was any good at using my Spirit Wielding. But it buffered the others within me so I could fight. And that was fine with me for now. My people needed my help, and I would fight alongside them and figure out how to use the rest of my Wielding as I did. I had once been like the people Justise and Slavik were training in front of me. I had been lost, unable to use my Wielding, feeling as if I were breaking.

My body had almost shattered, my soul along with it as the power became too much. I didn't want to see that for the others.

Thankfully, it seemed as if everybody was okay.

Either I was far weaker than they were, or my power had just been too much. Wielding more than one element at a time wasn't easy, and most had been born with at least their original magic, able to grow into their powers as they grew into themselves.

But Wyn and I were a little different.

I looked over at my friend as she stood next to Rhodes, her arms outstretched. She had a sphere of Water in her hands, and she spun it as if playing with a ball, even though she wasn't technically touching the liquid. Rhodes had his arms folded over his chest, a scowl on his face as he watched her work.

We had many Water Wielders with us now, some from the former kingdom, some new. However, Rhodes was still the strongest, even stronger than Delphine, the former queen. Which was why he taught those around him as much as he could, even though everybody was beyond exhausted.

Wyn and Rhodes butted heads more than not, but Wyn was becoming stronger under Rhodes' tutelage, and I had to believe that we were all here for a reason. I didn't want to think about what the outcome might be if that weren't the case.

Easton joined me, sliding his arm around my waist, squeezing my hip for an instant before he let go.

I looked up at him and smiled. "Hi there," I said.

"Hey."

"So, what's the plan?" I asked.

"We keep training. And when we feel the army is ready, we go to the Shadow realm."

"I meant for the day, I was there when we came up with the major plan," I said, my voice a little hollow.

"I don't have plans for the day other than training and then going to sleep next to you."

I smiled at him and leaned into his hold, needing his touch.

Others looked at us, glancing our way as if they didn't know whether they were intruding or not. It didn't matter. I kissed Easton's chin and went back to training.

"The people need a leader," Slavik said as he came over.

I raised a brow at the pirate king. "And are you trying to step into that role?"

Slavik threw his head back and laughed, his hair falling over his face. "No, not even a little. I like the spaces where I live. I used to call them the shadows, but I guess The Gray has taken that word from me, hasn't he?"

"He's taken many things."

"But, as I said, the people need a leader. And we all know that it's not me, it's not someone from the Lumière, and it's not you," Slavik said softly.

"No, it'll never be me. I'm their sacrificial lamb, and they all know it."

"You don't sound bitter about that," he said softly.

"How can I be when I know it's the truth."

"I don't think of you as a sacrificial lamb," Slavik said softly. I looked over and frowned.

"No?"

"I think of you as the one to bring us together, the one who gives us a fighting chance. But during battle, and especially once this is all over, they'll need more than hope. They'll need a leader they can blame if things go south. That's what leaders are for, after all. To make the hard decisions. To accept things even if they make mistakes. And to be a pawn and a scapegoat if the people aren't happy."

"That's not the best way to think of royalty. Or any leader for that matter."

"Call me bitter, but that's why I've not always been on the side of the law." Rhodes walked up and looked at Slavik.

"You told her?"

"Told me what?" I looked between them. "Since when are you friends?"

"We're not," they said simultaneously, and I held back a laugh.

Easton glared at my little group, and I tried to smile at him in reassurance, but I honestly had no idea what was going on.

"I was getting to it," Slavik said, grinning.

"Well, since we're all out here, we should make it happen."

"Make *what* happen?" I asked, exasperated now.

"When this is all over, we can decide if there is succession of royalty or voting or if there's anything left for someone to rule over. But for now, we need someone to lead."

"It's not me," I said.

"No, but it's someone you're close to." Both men looked at Easton. He glared at us, and I froze.

"He doesn't want that mantle."

"He already has it. These are his people. He's already making decisions. We need a ruler. The people need someone to listen to, to issue the call of battle. And not just because they think they know who they're following."

I looked at Slavik, confused. "What do you mean?"

"Everyone's following him as it is. Even us. But nobody knows who's in charge of all of this. Is it Justise? The king's bastard?"

"Watch your tone," Rhodes said softly.

"I know you don't like the word *bastard*, and for that, I'm sorry. But it's the truth. Just like Luken."

I froze, trying not to look like I knew anything about that. The truth of Luken's father wasn't something I was going to mention. Possibly ever.

"It's not going to be me. It's not going to be the pirate over here," Rhodes said with a glare. "But morale is at a crucial point, at the precipice where it could lead to an army that prevails or one that goes into the shadows. The people might know who they're following, but they need to see it. They need to see all of us over the weak that are The Gray's forces."

"And what does Easton have to say about this?" I asked.

"That's the best part," Slavik said. "We're not going to tell him."

"I don't like this," I said.

"I knew you wouldn't, but you don't have a choice."

"Rhodes."

"I'm just saying. The people need this, they need us, and that's what we're going to do."

"Okay, here we go," Slavik said. He puffed up his chest and sauntered towards Easton.

Easton gave me a look, and I winced, not knowing what would happen. Regardless of the outcome, I had a feeling that Easton wasn't going to like it.

"Easton, you know there is something I forgot to do when I joined this little band of merry men."

Easton frowned at Slavik.

"Shower?"

"Very funny," Slavik said amidst the soft laughter filtering in the air around us.

As if they knew something important was going on, people had stopped what they were doing to watch the exchange.

Suddenly, Rosamond was at my side, her eyes unfocused as she saw into the future. Then, a smile played on her lips.

A smile had to be good, right?

Emory joined Rosamond, ready to catch her if the Seer fell, and I had to wonder what was going on between the two of them—though it wasn't my place to ask. Especially not right now.

Rhodes moved to Easton's side, standing a little behind Slavik, and just smiled.

"What is this about?" Easton asked again.

"It's about what I should have done a long time ago," Slavik said, his voice suddenly serious. He went down on one knee and bowed his head. "To my king. the King of the Maisons."

Shock rippled through the armies, and my heart rate sped up, tears pricking the backs of my eyes.

Easton didn't want this. Only, nobody else could lead right now. Perhaps Rhodes, but with so much going against him given what'd happened within the Lumière Kingdom, I didn't think anyone would follow him in this moment.

I had hoped we would have time before we needed to make decisions, but perhaps Slavik was right. Maybe we would make other decisions once the war was over. Still, I didn't know who would be left to call on when that time came.

"Slavik," Easton whispered, just a bare breath on the wind that I wasn't sure anyone but me had heard.

"To my king, the one who will lead us by the Spirit Priestess's side as we fight The Gray. You have my loyalty, my Wielding, and my life."

As if they had all orchestrated it, Rhodes came to Slavik's side and knelt in front of Easton, as well.

"My king," Rhodes said, not a hint of mockery or irony in his tone.

The others came up then. Wyn, Justise, and Ridley. Rosamond and Delphine. Lanya, Griffin, and everybody that had followed us knelt. Even those who had not fought yet knelt.

"To our king. And to our Spirit Priestess."

I stood in front of Easton, and he held out his hand as if we had prepared for this, but there was no readying yourself for something like this.

"You will never bow to me," Easton said, as I slid my hand into his.

"Nor you to me."

He leaned forward and kissed me softly on the mouth before looking out at the others.

He held up his free arm. "Rise. We will fight. We will fight for the Maisons, for our realm, and for any other realms that touch ours. Any that are in danger because of the corrupt depravity that existed beneath our noses, shrouded in deceit for so long. We will fight, and we will win."

Cheers ricocheted through the crowd, and I looked at him, wondering if we knew what we were doing.

When our friends finally stood up, Easton glared at them.

"A little warning next time?" he snapped under his breath.

"If we had warned you, you would have put someone else in your place," Slavik said.

"Are you saying I wouldn't die for my people?" Easton asked.

Rhodes shook his head. "No, that's not it. But you don't believe you deserve to be at the helm."

"You might be right, Rhodes. But when this is over, we'll find out who the true king is."

The two former princes looked at each other, something passing between them that I didn't understand before they nodded and turned away.

I opened my mouth to say something, but a screech in the air made me wince.

I whirled, my arms outstretched, the others doing the same. And then I cursed.

"It's Zia," Easton snapped. "Lady of Earth."

The Lady of Earth. Wyn's mother. Justise's sister. And Easton's aunt.

Our enemy.

"How did she get so close?"

"Perhaps because she has the shadows near her," Easton whispered, and I looked around, noticing the shadows dispersing from behind her.

So, The Gray had pushed her here, but it appeared she was alone.

There was nobody else with her. Right?

"You've made a poor decision in your choice for king," Zia said.

"You're the one who made the wrong move," Easton said.

"Because I chose the side of loyalty and winning? No. You're going to die, and you're going to hurt before you do, but then you'll finally be with your dear old mother. The perfect queen with the perfect life."

"Mother," Wyn gasped, anger clear on her face. Her hands tightened at her sides, but Teagan didn't go to her and try to calm her. No, it was Rhodes. He put his hand on her shoulder and squeezed it, and she relaxed marginally as if not quite ready to jump and fight and possibly lose everything so early.

"Oh, daughter. You were always such a disappointment. But that's fine. I haven't needed you for a long time. Soon, I will find a new path. One that has nothing to do with an offspring made of nothing. A Dane with no power and no future."

The Lady of Earth snapped her fingers, and the rocks behind her lifted, hiding an army that none of us had seen.

"Kill them," she snapped, and Wielders from the other side came at us, screaming.

"Man your stations!" Justise yelled.

"Find your Wielding partner!" Slavik added.

In a blink, we were off, fighting the smaller army in front of us.

I didn't know if this was a distraction, or just the Lady of Earth trying to find one last way to hurt us.

She only had maybe forty people in her army. We had hundreds.

But her troops were trained, and ours were only learning.

However, the only reason she had gotten so close was because of the shadows themselves.

That reminded me that we didn't have a strong enough army when it came to the shadows. My Spirit Wielding couldn't protect us, not when I didn't know how to fight against the darkness.

I pushed those thoughts from my mind, knowing they weren't helping anybody, and ran towards the fight. I pushed out my Fire Wielding, cutting off one of the Earth Wielders before they came at Delphine.

Delphine, however, was much stronger than I gave her credit for. She stood firm, her feet planted hip-width apart, her hands outstretched. Her hair blew in a breeze I couldn't feel, as if she had Air Wielding. She might not be able to see, but she could feel. She threw her hands up into the air and pushed Water towards the army. People screamed, drowning, but Delphine didn't budge. She only moved her arms faster and faster until wave after wave of Water formed, stripping the army down to three.

Everybody froze, staring at the former queen of the Lumière.

"You chose the wrong side," Delphine whispered. Only it wasn't a whisper for most. No, it carried on the wind. I looked at Lanya, who also had her arms out, buffeting the former queen of the Lumière.

It seemed the two had learned to fight together, something so graceful and strong that it left me staggered.

"You always were weak. You married your little king because you were good at getting down on your knees. And yet, he's dead. And you can't see."

"You let your husband die, lied that he was your soulmate."

"Your king wasn't your soulmate, either."

"Nobody ever assumed he was. I did my duty, and I was wrong

for so long because I was too weak to fight his control over me. But I'm no longer weak."

"No, just dumb and blind."

Zia threw up her arms again, but then she screamed, her eyes going wide and bulging. I moved forward, tried to understand what was happening. The others were taking care of Zia's small army, staying alert in case The Gray sent anyone else. But I wasn't paying as much attention to them.

No, I was focused on the tableau in front of me.

Rosamond stood before Zia, her hair flowing in the air much like Delphine's and Lanya's, and she shook her head sadly.

"You shouldn't have angered your daughter. Shouldn't have killed and taken things that were not yours."

"You are nothing, Seer. Weak."

"No, you are."

I tripped at the sound of Emory's voice from behind Zia. Now I knew why the other woman had screamed and was screaming again.

The cuffs were off Emory's wrists. Now, they were in Rosamond's hands.

Emory was a siphon. She could take Wielding. And it seemed the Seer wanted that to happen.

We would have a chat about this later.

I was sure Emory knew that, but she didn't care.

"Your family did this to me, and now I'll make sure you understand exactly why that was a mistake," Emory said, her voice lashing like a deadly blade.

She put her hands on Zia's face, and the former Lady of Earth fell to her knees, screaming in agony.

Magic filled the air all around us, colors and swirls of mist and auras mixing.

Everybody froze, looked at the siphon, my friend, the girl I had once thought I loved, and I couldn't breathe. I couldn't do anything.

Because Emory had taken Zia's Wielding. She took it all and then dispersed it amongst the people around her. Others' shoulders straightened as power flooded into them.

Zia crumpled to the ground, her chest heaving as she fought for breath, but she wasn't dead.

No, she was just a Dane now, or perhaps something even lower in power.

When Emory staggered a bit, Rosamond was there, snapping the cuffs around her wrists again and leading Emory away from the fray.

I wasn't sure why Rosamond had wanted this to happen, but as Rhodes and Wyn moved closer to the former Lady of Earth, I tensed.

"She's powerless," Wyn said as we moved closer to her.

"But still dangerous," Rhodes added.

"Always dangerous," Wyn said.

Before I could open my mouth to say anything, to wonder exactly how I could make this better, Zia screamed and began to convulse. We all moved back. Shadows encircled Zia, pouring out of the ground like mist. They wrapped around her, sucking her into the dirt itself. Wyn screamed, moving towards her mother as if trying to save her, but one of the ropes of smoke and shadow lashed out, snapping at her face. If Rhodes hadn't moved her back at that exact instant, it likely would have killed her. And that was the only thing I knew for sure.

We all stood back in horror as The Gray took his revenge on Zia for not doing what she had been told.

For failing.

That was the cost of failure: death and agony.

Other screams sounded around us, and those left of Zia's army began to yell before their shouts were cut off in a snap, the earth taking them back to wherever they had come from.

I peered around, my hands shaking as I looked at my mate, my king, and wondered what on earth we could do to fight this.

The Gray had amassed so much power. Yet, somehow, we were supposed to win.

Despite the losses, regardless of the unknown, we had to be stronger than this.

Though I had no idea how we were going to do that.

CHAPTER EIGHTEEN

EASTON

I OPENED MY EYES AT THE SOUND OF SILENCE. I LET OUT A LONG breath. Lyric was still sleeping in my arms, finally in a deep sleep after an entire night of restless tossing and turning.

She had to be exhausted. I was, and I was grateful that she was finally sleeping and able to rest.

The day hadn't gone quite as any of us had expected, although none of the days from now on would.

I had slept for perhaps an hour, but I didn't really need much rest these days. It was as if my wellbeing were on edge, pushing me through with adrenaline better than sleep ever would. I knew me going along with that wasn't the safest thing for us, but I just couldn't close my eyes. I worried if I did, someone would come and hurt Lyric. Destroy my people.

I didn't want to be king. But it wasn't as if I could tell anybody other than Lyric what I wanted. Saying that I didn't want to be king of the people, that I was afraid others would die because of my choices sounded as if I didn't understand what needed to be done. They needed a leader, one they could trust, and I worried that if I weren't careful, I wouldn't be strong enough for them.

I needed to be stronger than I was now and gain a sense of purpose, self—and anything else a king required.

My mother had been a true queen. She had made mistakes, but she had started her royal line on the losing end. When her father died during the Fall, with the two old men fighting for power that didn't make any sense—possibly orchestrated by The Gray and anyone else on the Obscurité side—my mother hadn't had a choice in the matter.

She had fought against the Lumière her entire life because that was what she had been told to do and what she had learned. And given the Lumière had constantly attacked our kingdom and tried to take our power and hurt our people, she had fought back the only way she knew how.

But the knight of our realm, Lore, seeded deception within our ranks even before we were aware of it.

Lore had cursed me and killed my father. He had taken so much.

But in the end, my mother had died for our future. She had died as the queen the kingdom had known she could be.

I missed her with every breath I took.

I missed my father, too. I missed how we had been a family long before I realized what my duties entailed as a prince.

I hadn't searched for Lyric as Rhodes had because I had been forced to stay behind to protect our people. Lore had hurt our kingdom to the point where my leaving would have led to more deaths. Rhodes had had the option to go because while he might have been a prince, he hadn't been the king's son. So, he had more freedom to find Lyric. I would always be grateful that he had done that because it brought Lyric to me—even if it hadn't been what Rhodes had thought he would be doing to guarantee his future.

In the end, however, Rhodes and I had developed an understanding. We knew what we needed from each other and what we had to do.

And that meant I had a friend I never expected to have.

The time for battle was upon us, and we were losing people left and right. Yet we were gaining them, too.

And they were all my people. I was king, and Lyric was my Priestess. Not my queen, never that. Not because she couldn't be, but because she was already higher than that. I had thought perhaps I would be her consort, and that was a title I would gladly take.

For now, that wasn't an option. For now, I would be a leader who sent my troops into battle, perhaps to their deaths, maybe to victory.

The decision wasn't an easy one.

Lyric mumbled in her sleep. I tightened my hold on her and kissed her softly on the forehead. When I got out of bed, careful not to wake her, I searched for my pants.

I pulled the leather over my hips and made sure Lyric was covered and still sleeping before leaving a note.

I needed to work off my tension, and though Lyric and I had done a good job of that before we went to sleep, I needed more. Had to run it off or perhaps use my Wielding to train.

Rhodes and Slavik were outside when I got there, both sitting on the stone wall, staring up at the night sky.

"I see it's a night for restlessness no matter the title," Slavik said, handing me a tankard of mead.

"So, you're getting drunk and looking at the sky, then?" I asked, lifting my chin in thanks before taking a big gulp. The warmth of the alcohol spread through me, and I nearly smiled. I hadn't done much of this recently. Teagan, Arwin, and I had used to carouse back in the day. We'd find random taverns and drink and eat our worries away, if only for the moment.

But now, I didn't think there was enough alcohol or food in the world to make that happen.

We had all suffered losses, and Wyn's were the deepest today.

"I'm surprised you're not with Wyn," I said to Rhodes, raising a brow.

Rhodes gave me a funny look and then shook his head.

"She's grieving."

"No, she's not," Slavik said, taking a sip.

"What do you mean by that?" I asked, curious.

"She went to sleep alone after growling at Teagan and you to leave her be."

"Are you spying now?" Rhodes asked, anger in his tone.

"I don't need to spy when she screams and shouts at us. Lanya went after her, if that helps," Slavik added, his tones hushed. "Delphine at her side."

"The ladies will help her heal as much as possible."

"Wyn and I...we're not like that," Rhodes said suddenly, his voice sounding distant.

I looked at the other man and shrugged. "It would be fine for you to find comfort where you can. Wyn's a good person. And I guess you are, too."

Rhodes' lips twitched at that.

"Thank you for the vote of confidence. However, I don't think now is the right time to wonder what could come of that comment."

Slavik snorted and took a sip of his drink. "If not now, then when? You need to find a good woman or a man and enjoy the fruits of your labor. Because you don't know what's going to come with the sunrise."

"I hate that I'm starting to like you," I said after a minute, and Slavik just beamed.

"It's not time," Rhodes said and shook his head. "Might not ever be. I'm not good at figuring out what my path should be, after all." Rhodes gave me a look, and I shrugged.

"You were meant to be her protector, just like I was. I thought she was yours, as well."

"I take it you're talking about the dear Spirit Priestess." I looked over at Slavik and shrugged. "I thought she was with the Air and Water Wielder, as well. They were a cute couple."

Rhodes just shook his head as I glared. "I'd watch your tongue," Rhodes added. "Our king here seems to be a bit growly."

"Ah, yes, don't want to mess with the king's moods. One minute you're laughing with him, the next it's *off with your heads.'*"

"You know, I just said I was starting to like you. I was wrong. I can't stand you," I said, grinding my teeth together.

"You love me. And you love all of the people I brought to your side."

I gave Rhodes a look, and he just shrugged.

"I'm pretty sure half of the people you brought with you are all wanted for some reason or another. Murderers and thieves."

"Murderers, according to Lore. And that is why you haven't found them yet."

"Perhaps," I said.

"And the thieves? Well, that one's probably true. As king, you can use your power to get rid of us, or you can wait until you use us and then figure out exactly what to do. Decide if you're going to pardon those who helped protect the land or seek justice."

"I don't know what to think of you, Slavik."

"Nobody ever does," the pirate said with a shrug. "But that's fine with me. I like the air of mystery. Makes the ladies swoon."

"If that's what you tell yourself at night," Rhodes said with a laugh.

"I bet I can make Wyn—"

"I wouldn't," Rhodes said tightly.

Interesting.

"What about that Emory? She seems like a firecracker."

"Emory is a siphon and has not made the best choices in the past," I began.

"Neither have I. Nor have any of us. But she fought to protect the kingdom and seems to be turning over a new leaf."

"You're right," I said. "She *has* turned over a new leaf. But we still don't know what her powers can do. We saw what they did to Zia." I added, thinking of my aunt. She had looked so shaken before The Gray killed her. I had watched others lose their powers, but none like Zia had. It was if she had lost a part of herself along the way, and I didn't think I would wish that on my worst enemy. Or perhaps I would, considering that was The Gray.

"Anyway," Rhodes added, "I think Emory is spoken for."

I met Rhodes' gaze. "Lyric and I assumed so," I said carefully.

"Ah, by the Seer? I approve. She's very protective for a human," Slavik added.

"She's not human any longer," I said. "But she doesn't have the power and strength of a Maison either. She's training."

"See? You're adding more and more to your ranks. Beyond just what the perfect Wielders used to be." I looked over at Slavik.

"You're right. We made mistakes in the past. We're probably going to make mistakes in the future. But I hope they are new ones that we can remedy, not a repeat of the old."

"That is what a good king should do," Slavik said.

"I cannot believe you guys did that," I growled.

"Are you going to fight?" Rhodes asked.

"Not now, but when this is over? You and I are going to have a long talk."

I glared at Rhodes, who lifted his chin. Hopefully, he understood the message. I would be king for now because we needed a war king, but once this was over? If what I thought was coming came to pass, I knew I'd want nothing to do with the throne.

I didn't think I would be in any shape to be king, nor would I even be a whole person anymore.

"The idea that you guys can talk about a time after the war gives me a little hope. Marginal at best, though."

I turned to Slavik. "It's not easy figuring out what's going to happen after this. I want to pretend that we can decide what's coming next, but we can't. And we all know that not everyone will make it out of this alive."

We were silent for a moment, just drinking, not needing to fill the void.

If you had asked me what my life would look like just a year ago, it definitely wouldn't have been sitting next to the light prince and the pirate king, drinking mead and staring at the stars while my soulmate slept in my bed, still warm from our lovemaking an hour before. But here we were. And this was the future we had to fight for.

"What's that?" Slavik asked, setting down his drink. Suddenly sober, I leaned forward and swallowed hard.

"That is a Fire Wielder who doesn't know what he's doing," I said, standing up.

"Are we sober enough for this?" Rhodes asked, rolling his shoulders back.

"I hope we are because I don't think anyone else is going to help us."

We were at the far edge of the estate grounds, one where we didn't have as many sentries because the only way to get to this part from the outside of the estate itself was from The Gray's lands. And The Gray wouldn't send an entire army to a small piece of land, so it would only be him or one person at a time. I looked over at the sentries on duty near us. They were still talking amongst themselves.

"We've got this," I said.

One bowed before going back to his post, Wielding at the ready. They would come with us if needed, but for now, I wanted to see exactly who was out there.

The three of us made our way to where the Fire Wielder shot out bursts of flame one after another as if not knowing how to close their hands and steady their palms.

"A former Dane?" Slavik asked, his words slow.

"Perhaps," I said, dread roiling in my stomach.

My jaw tightened as we looked at the man standing in the field, Fire shooting out of his palms and feet, singeing the earth around him.

"A former Dane, who used to be an Earth Wielder," I whispered.

"Who is that?" Rhodes asked.

"Durlan. The Gray's second."

Both Rhodes and Slavik readied themselves, stomping on the ground as they prepared their Wielding.

I stared at The Gray's second in front of me and frowned. "I'd hoped you were dead," I said.

"You tried to kill me. So did your bitch. But you couldn't. And now, I have these new powers thanks to The Gray."

"You should thank your Spirit Priestess," Slavik said. "Your Gray has no power. He just leaches it from the land and others. The Spirit Priestess is the one who gives."

I hadn't wanted to tell anyone outside of certain circles about what was going on, but I didn't think the man in front of us would live long enough to report to The Gray. He deserved to die for what he did to Lyric, let alone all the others he had dared to hurt.

"The Gray always wanted you," Durlan snapped, Fire sparking from his fingertips. He blew on them, his face gaunt, his eyes strained from the power. He couldn't handle it, and no one was here to train him. No one would. Was this what The Gray was doing to his people? Letting them die?

I didn't know, but regardless, Durlan didn't deserve my sympathy. Not after what he had done.

"The Gray always wanted you," Durlan repeated.

"Why?" I asked, truly curious now. "Why would he ever want me to be part of his circle?"

"Because he couldn't have his son there, so he figured he would take you instead."

Both Rhodes and Slavik stiffened beside me, but I didn't turn to them. Luken's secret was his own, but perhaps I should tell the others soon, especially if The Gray and his people were just going to blurt it out.

"You were promised to The Gray as his third because Lore wanted power. You have enough power. You don't need to be with The Gray. You were always nothing, and then you betrayed him by cutting off that curse of yours with your stupid Priestess."

"Watch your tongue," Rhodes snapped, and I grinned.

It was nice to not have to fight on my own, to have people who wanted to battle alongside me. I always had that, but not against Durlan.

"The Gray's fourth is dead. Lyric killed him."

"He was weak. A little Whisperer who thought he could gain secrets and, therefore, power. Favor with The Gray. But he was wrong. He was nothing."

"Whatever you say," I whispered, trying to understand what Durlan wanted.

"I should be enough for The Gray. But no, he wanted his Easton. And his precious son. And now, he wants the Spirit Priestess? Why? I've always been there for him. I've always been loyal. I will be the one who takes you out and kills you. Then I'll take your bitch, too."

"I would watch your tone when it comes to my mate," I said. "So, you're saying that you want all of the power that comes from The Gray?" I asked.

"I want you dead first. After, I'll take whatever The Gray gives me."

"I'm sure The Gray will kill you, but whatever," Slavik said with a shrug, and then Durlan moved. He shot Fire from his hands, but it was unwieldy, too hard, and too fast. Durlan screamed at the pain as his veins bulged in his arms, and Slavik pushed up the rock in front of him, blocking the Fire with ease.

I looked at my friends, and they both shook their heads, not sure what to do. Did they keep Durlan alive? That would be the smart thing so we could question him about The Gray. But I didn't think we were going to hold The Gray's second for long, not with the way his power kept fluctuating, his body shaking from being overloaded. I had only really seen this happen to one other person, and Lyric had somehow survived. Because I had been able to hold her in place, to give her some of my stability so she could find her own.

I couldn't do that for Durlan. Not that I'd want to.

"You took so much!" Durlan screamed.

"I took nothing. The Gray's the one who's done it all."

"Lies!" Durlan screamed and shot Fire towards Rhodes, who flicked his wrist and doused it with his Water.

The casual show of power from the two men at my side enraged Durlan. He threw his hands into the air and then slammed them down, pushing Fire towards me. I used my own Fire Wielding to lock the Fire in the air, something I didn't often do because it took more energy than it was worth. But I needed to show the man my strength. Show him what a true Fire Wielder could do. Durlan screamed and shot flame after flame after flame at us. We blocked his attempts, not even using the full depths of our powers. Durlan's body began to shake, his skin stretching awkwardly as if he had too much flame within him.

"He's going to burn himself out!" Slavik said over the man's screams.

"I don't think we can stop him," I whispered. And I couldn't. None of us could. Not with how Durlan was wasting his soul trying to take us out.

"I deserve everything. You are nothing!" Durlan shouted. The high-pitched scream echoed in the silence around us, and others came to see what was happening. Lyric was suddenly behind me, I could feel her, but she didn't come too close. I knew that if she did, Durlan would focus his attention on her. But it was too late anyway. Durlan screamed, then fell to his knees as the Fire consumed him, taking him body and soul because he couldn't control it.

As Durlan let out his last breath, his eyes wide, I shook my head and tried to douse the flames as much as possible. No one deserved to die like that, not even the truly heinous.

Lyric was at my side in an instant and slid her hand into mine. "That could have been me," she whispered.

"It wasn't," I said, my voice clipped. I didn't want to think about her like that. Didn't want to think about what would've happened if she hadn't been able to control her powers.

"I was able to survive because of you," she said.

I shook my head again. "You were able to survive because you are strong. I just happened to be there for some of it."

"But you were there, and I was never alone. Not really."

"Not like him."

We moved forward, continuing to douse the flames with Earth and Water, attempting to see what we could do for the man who had died for his power.

In the end, we couldn't do much of anything.

Durlan had died at his own hands, from his lack of strength. Because The Gray had been selfish in not teaching Durlan how to defend himself.

There was no coming back from this. No silver lining for the Wielder.

The Gray's second was dead, and sadly we hadn't gotten anything out of him that we didn't already know.

The Gray hadn't come, hadn't tried to save the man who had been by his side for decades.

Suddenly, the injustice of it all, the depravity and the sadness, slid over me. I looked at the people around me, those of our circle, and knew that I wasn't alone. That was the only thing I could promise myself: we would do our best to work as one, even if the soullessness of death was the only thing to comfort us in the end.

CHAPTER NINETEEN

LYRIC

EVERY PART OF ME FELT AS IF A BRICK HAD HIT ME, OR AT LEAST AS IF I had fallen from a tall height, thus bruising every inch of skin I had.

Training for hours on end and then using whatever precious time I had left to battle plan would do that to a person.

"I think my Wielding is going to bed now," Wyn said from my side.

"Can your Wielding go to sleep?" I asked.

"Maybe, it needs a nap. And a good, hearty meal. And wine. Lots and lots of wine."

I snorted, shaking my head. "It would be nice to have a night off and have a drink, even though I don't think I'm old enough to drink yet." I almost laughed at that last part. To think of human laws when I hadn't been human for over a year felt odd.

"You're in the Maison realm. You're old enough. You're fighting wars, and the Spirit Priestess is supposed to save us all and all of that lovely prophecy crap. You're allowed to have a glass of wine."

"Well, thank you for your permission," I said, shaking my head. "Although I really just want a nap. Though I feel bad that I'm so tired. Because we need to be training harder."

"You and I are still learning our new elements, and we're training so hard that our bodies hurt. We're allowed to rest. After all, we're all waiting for the other shoe to drop, and that could happen at any moment."

"Well, thank you for making me think of the next horror that awaits us, rather than what my bed feels like."

"You're just thinking about who's in that bed with you," Wyn said with a wink.

I knew I was blushing a deep red, and I tugged my hair out of its short, stubby ponytail. I missed the long waves I once had and the fact that I could braid it or do a hundred different hairstyles. The sword that had cleaved the ends of it hadn't left me with enough hair to do much with, though it wasn't as if I knew how to style my hair. However, Easton didn't seem to mind it this length. I blushed again.

"So, things seem to be going well for the two of you."

"Perhaps."

"He's the king, and you are his Priestess. I'm pretty sure the two of you are having enough fun at night that it's another reason you're so exhausted in the mornings."

I covered my face with my hands and groaned. "Stop it. Or I'm going to ask why you're so tired."

I lowered my hands as Wyn just blushed and looked away. "I have no idea what you're talking about."

I had just been fishing, but I grinned. "So, tell me? Why *are* you so tired?"

"The new Wielding. That's it."

"Why don't I believe you?" I asked.

"You don't have to believe me. I am sleeping alone. And I probably will for a very long time."

"So, it has nothing to do with the former Lumière prince who looks at you when you pretend you're not looking at him?"

Wyn froze and shook her head, her expression falling. I felt horrible and could have rightly kicked myself just then for prying. We liked teasing each other, and Wyn was a good friend, but I had been fishing, and now I felt terrible.

"There is nothing between Rhodes and me. And there will never be. There's far too much animosity in our past to go forward with anything other than an alliance. Plus, he annoys me to no end."

"He doesn't annoy you that much. Not anymore."

"He is pompous and self-righteous and an asshole most of the time. He thinks he knows what I need to be doing to prove that my Wielding is increasing and improving. So...no, thank you. He's not mine."

"Good to know," Rhodes said from behind her. I looked up, not having realized he, Slavik, and Easton had joined us.

I winced as Easton just shook his head at me and kissed my temple. "Stay out of it," he whispered, his voice barely above a whisper. I was sure that no one else had been able to hear.

Slavik, however, put his hands on his hips and grinned at Wyn. "Well, if you're still looking for someone and this prince over here isn't interested? How about a king?"

He leered, and I knew it was overdone just to make Wyn laugh. Thankfully, she did. She snorted, pushed at Slavik's shoulder, and moved past Rhodes without saying another word.

"Well, that was fun," Slavik said, slamming his hand down on Rhodes' shoulder. Rhodes was big and strong, but Slavik had that Earth Wielding energy that made him slightly bulkier. The fact that Rhodes winced at all told me that Slavik hadn't held back with the motion.

"Okay, then. Are we ready for our next meeting?" Rhodes said, completely ignoring the rest of us and what had just happened.

I shook my head. "I'm too tired right now. I could use some sleep. I'm sorry."

"Don't be sorry," Easton said, looking around. "I honestly think everybody could use a break tonight. We are all fighting with the same goal in mind. Sure, we might not be enough for The Gray at this very moment, but if we don't find a way to relax and increase morale, it's not going to be good for any of us."

I was grateful. I didn't want to have to try to persuade him in front of the others.

"I bet if we talked to Justise and Ridley, they could help us figure out how to make sure everybody has time to relax."

Rosamond walked in, Emory by her side, Luken and Braelynn following.

The Seer smiled. "No worries, I know what must be done. Food is already on its way, the same with mead and other accouterments to make people happy. Tonight will be a night of relaxation and morale-boosting."

"Sometimes being a Seer has its advantages," Emory said.

"And, sometimes, it's scary as hell," I said, giving Rosamond a look.

"You're right. It isn't easy to keep up with everything going on, but I saw that we needed time to relax, so I took it upon myself to do what I could. If that was in error, don't worry, I can take it back."

"Thank you, Seer," Easton said. "Thank you for taking care of our people."

"Always, my king. For as long as I am able."

And on that cryptic note, they walked away as a group, leaving me and Easton standing with Rhodes and Slavik, all of us seemingly confused as hell.

"Has she always been that spooky?" Slavik asked.

"Since I was a little kid," Rhodes answered.

"Really?" I asked, intrigued.

"Yep. My sister's always been a little creepy, a bit different, and she was well into her powers by the time I showed up. However, she was always there for me, even when my mother couldn't always be because, apparently, my father was trying to kill her."

"I'm sorry," I whispered.

"Don't be. We've all been through hell, but we're here. We're together. And we're going to beat The Gray. We beat my family, we won against the Obscurité, who tried to take everything from us. We'll beat this, too. Because that's what we do."

"And on that note, I do believe it's time to drink, make merry, and maybe find a few Wielders who don't mind making a little more." Slavik winked at me, put his arm around Rhodes' shoulder, and nudged him towards where the others were gathering.

"Well, Slavik is sure a boost for morale," I said.

Easton gave me a look.

"What?" I asked.

"Slavik sure is something."

I snorted, and Easton and I moved a few feet towards the group. Suddenly, I heard something behind me. I froze and turned slowly on my heel.

"Did you hear that?" I asked.

"No, but something feels wrong. I miss our wards."

Easton mumbled that last part, and I wasn't even sure he realized he'd said it out loud.

"Let's go see what it is."

"Every time we go over to see what it is, it's always someone or something trying to kill us," Easton said.

"True, but that seems par for the course these days."

"Do you sense him?" Rosamond asked, and I turned to the Seer. My eyes went wide.

"Where is Emory? Didn't you just go the other way?"

"I did. They're making sure the others have their night of peace. But it's time to face someone that should not be here."

"You should go back," I said quickly. "Go get Rhodes."

"No, I will go with you. Rhodes doesn't need to see this. Nor does Delphine."

"What is it, Seer?" Easton asked.

"It is of what should not be. It is of darkness and death." She paused. "It is a perversion."

I gasped. Knowing who it probably was. "Eitri."

The Seer nodded.

"So, when The Gray shadows took him that way, what did it do to him?" Easton asked.

"It is of what should not be," the Seer repeated.

"Okay, then. We need to go," I said, my Wielding at the ready. I was exhausted, the training had taken so much out of me, but it didn't matter. From the way Rosamond was staring into the darkness, I had a feeling it had to be Eitri. And she didn't want her brother to be forced to see another of their family twisted in this way.

"Do you need to be here, Rosamond?" I asked.

"I do. For one of us needs to be near family. And my brother does not need to bear that burden."

She started towards the forest, her dark hair flowing around her, the brown of her skin shining in the moonlight.

I swallowed hard and followed her, Easton right beside me.

"I don't like this," he growled.

"I don't like any of this, but Rosamond wouldn't lead us into danger."

"I want to believe that. So, I'm going to trust her."

I knew that trust didn't come easily when it came to Easton. We had to fight back the fear. We needed to see who was here.

As we made our way through the forest, bile rose up into my throat as I saw what lay in front of us.

Eitri was there, his body gray, large gashes all over his chest and arms as if he had been cut with a sword many times. His eyes were rimmed in red, and drool slid down his face.

As he looked at us, I noticed his neck had an odd angle as he growled.

"This is what happens when dark magic fails. When the Wielding of the shadows enters a body but doesn't quite leave it. This is what The Gray could be if he had not been strong enough to withstand it."

I glanced at Rosamond.

"What do you mean?"

"The Gray accidentally put part of himself into this one. Out of anger, out of spite, out of darkness. The Gray uses his Wielding to put on a face of beauty, of what should not be. He hides from me, from the other Seers. So, I cannot see everything. My cousin here is no more, just a shade of what he once was. Of *who* he once was."

"What do we do?" Easton asked, Fire Wielding in his palms.

"I will take care of this," Rosamond said.

"You don't have to do this."

"I do. My grandmother lives, my brother lives, as do my friends. At least, some. But the line of our family will fade into dust one day soon if we do not prevail. The shade in front of us is not a true Lumière anymore. He is what The Gray would have been without power," she repeated.

I froze. "How do we defeat The Gray, Rosamond?"

"You need to find the power within him and strip it so he is no longer a man."

"How do we do that?" I asked.

"The fates have not let me see. But I'm afraid that there isn't a way." Her voice broke at that, and despair filled me, my hands shaking. "There has to be a way. All of this was for nothing if there isn't."

The Seer looked at me, her eyes full of clouds and mist. "I know that, Priestess. I'm not the one with the power to defeat him. For I cannot see. Eitri here, though he cannot move, though he cannot speak, has come somehow, to show us what should not be."

"Who sent him here?" Easton asked.

"The fates," the Seer whispered. "They show us what we must do, even if it makes no sense."

"Rosamond," I whispered.

"We must find a way. For I cannot see it. And I fear if I cannot see it then it cannot be done."

"We'll find a way," Easton whispered to me.

"Of course, we will. We will not lose."

As I looked at Rosamond, the idea that she had no hope, that a Seer could not see a path to victory, scared me more than anything.

Because I had always trusted Rosamond to help us find our way.

If all she saw was mist and death? The unknown?

Then how would we find our path and know what to fight for?

"Be at peace, Eitri," Rosamond whispered.

The boy who was once the cousin of two of my dearest friends, the true prince of the Lumière, looked up, his eyes wide. Suddenly, he let out a gasp and was no more.

Because the power within him had not been real, it had not been true. And, somehow, the Seer had used her Air Wielding to pull it from him.

But, as she'd said, he was just a shade of The Gray.

And that was not how we were going to defeat the tyrant.

I looked at Easton, worried now beyond anything I'd felt before.

If we couldn't find a way to defeat The Gray, we would lose. And we would perish.

And all would be lost.

CHAPTER TWENTY

LYRIC

I NEEDED TO SPEAK WITH THE SPIRIT WIELDERS.

Throughout my short life—though it sometimes felt far longer than the mere two decades I had lived—the Spirit Wielders had always brought me to them. I had called out to them in pain and begged for help, and they sometimes listened. They'd intervened to save my life, had overheard my words in order to scold. And had listened to me to try to teach.

As the dawn of our battle approached, something I knew deep in my bones, I knew I had to ask them for help. I understood that they wouldn't be able to give me much. They weren't of this world, of this time. So, asking for help in a physical sense would never amount to anything.

They had given up part of themselves to save me the first time I nearly died with Easton bleeding out near me, succumbing to the same mortal wound as I had.

But perhaps they could give me advice or something now. I felt as if I were floundering with my five elements, even though I had mastered them as much as I could in a short period.

I could Wield all of my magic, although Spirit was the element I wasn't sure I would ever understand. I didn't know the intricacy of its power. That would come later, I knew it. For I wouldn't have Spirit within me to match The Gray if it wouldn't be important later.

"Are you going to sit there and ask the Spirit Wielders for help?" Easton asked, his arms crossed over his chest as he leaned against the doorframe. His dark hair slid over his forehead, and his signature smirk was on his face.

I smiled despite myself and shook my head. He looked so much lighter now, like the boy I had met with the firedrake when we used the elements around us to protect our friends.

He had been heart-heavy, weary, and battle-worn.

And yet he had smiled and annoyed me to no end.

Now, here we were, two separate halves of a whole, bound together in a way that only made sense to us.

"Why are you looking at me like that? I'm going to blush."

I smiled then and lifted my chin. He knew what I wanted, so he moved away from the doorway to prowl over to me before pressing his lips to mine.

I moaned, wanting more, yet knowing this wasn't the time and place for this.

"Thank you," I whispered.

He frowned as he straightened, looking down at me where I sat in the middle of the floor, runes sketched on the cement all around me in the empty room and all over my skin. All thanks to Alura's and Rosamond's teachings.

"You're acting funny. Are you sure you haven't already met with the Spirit Wielders?" he asked.

"No. Well, not really. I was just thinking about how we first met."

"And how dashing I was?"

"Dashing is a word for it," I said with a laugh.

He knelt in front of me before sitting down fully, crossing his leg in front of mine. Our knees touched, and he traced my palms with his fingertips, the caress going straight through my knees and up to my hips.

"If this works and you speak to them, you need to come back. You don't get to stay there."

I frowned, looking at him and the pensive look on his face.

"Of course, I'm coming back. There's a battle to fight."

He stared harder, and I knew what he was thinking.

"And I'm coming back to you. Just like you always do to me. It's what we do."

"One day, we'll grow old in a castle somewhere while someone else rules. Perhaps we can even farm. I would like to learn how to farm."

I laughed at that—a full belly laugh that made me shake my head. "I don't see you as a farmer. Although, I could see you with a scythe and some hay, shirtless and sweating under the sun in the Fire territory."

"When we make it through this—and it's not an *if*, Lyric—I will farm shirtless for you."

I wanted a future like that. One where we could laugh and joke and perhaps find what we were meant to be.

Only I saw in his eyes that he didn't believe it.

And it wasn't his soul he was worried about. No, we both knew what would be lost if we won this. But we didn't say it. Didn't speak it. There was no reason to. It would only drive a wedge between us, and we needed to be a strong unit. Now more than ever.

"Okay, you're welcome to be here, but you can't touch me. When you do, I can't think."

"You're giving me the best compliments these days," he practically purred.

I let out a sigh, shook my head, grateful when he let his hands drop. I knew he had his palms outstretched over the tops of his knees like I did, mirroring my pose.

He would pull me out if this went sideways, and I trusted nobody but him.

I knew I should be able to have faith in everybody in my circle, but the idea that there was still a traitor in our midst worried me.

Yet I pushed those thoughts from my mind and did my best to tug on the Spirit Wielding within me. The warmth spread through my chest and ran down my limbs.

"Spirit Wielders, come to me. Speak to me."

I whispered the words, grateful that Easton didn't laugh. I wasn't sure what I was doing or what I should say, but it seemed right.

The runes on my skin warmed, and I cracked open my eyes to

see them glowing, matching the runes on the floor. Easton froze in front of me, but I closed my eyes again and relaxed into the moment.

They were listening.

Hopefully, they would answer.

"Spirit Wielders. Heed my call."

"What can we do for you, darling Lyric?" Seven whispered in front of me. I opened my eyes and found myself sitting cross-legged as I was before, but no longer in the room with the runes and Easton.

Instead, I sat in the same spot I always did during these dreams that were not dreams. Each of the four seasons represented on the corners, as well as the elements—spring, summer, fall, winter. Earth, Air, Fire, Water. All blended together to create a ring of all that was, is, and ever will be.

"Thank you for answering," I said, fearful that they would send me away with no answers at all.

"Of course. We are here. Your young man is waiting for you, as well. You will go to him, as it was always meant to be."

The bond that lay between Easton and I warmed, and I knew she was speaking of my soulmate, the spark that connected us even through curses and death itself.

"Do you know what happens next?" I asked, unsure of where I should begin.

"I only know that it must happen, not what will be," Seven said.

The others mumbled around us, each of the twelve Spirit Wielders present as before.

While One used to speak to me, now, Seven had become the spokeswoman.

Perhaps it was because she reminded me of my mother. Or maybe it was just fate.

There seemed to be a lot of that going on lately.

"The great battle will result in betrayal and loss. But it will also bring hope and union. The skies will fall, and the crystals will rejoice. But we cannot see past the fear of death."

"Am I going to die?" I asked, not knowing I was going to ask the question until it was already out. Cold filtered through me, starting with the Spirit Wielding within me and spreading through the other elements.

Seven gave me a sad smile, one that reached her eyes and made me want to cry.

"Death can be a beginning or an ending. But you know who you are. You are the Spirit Priestess, the mate of the former King of Obscurité, and the one they rally behind. You are the savior of the people."

"And to save them, to defeat The Gray, I know I will die."

The truth settled on me like a second skin, the crystals in my flesh shining like a beacon. They begged to go back to their places, to exist in the realm in truth rather than buried within my skin.

They didn't belong within me, and I would change that. And by doing so, I would fix the Maison realm.

"I can protect everybody," I whispered.

"You can. And you know what must be done. You are so close, Lyric. You have made us all so proud."

Tears filled her eyes, but she blinked them away and reached out to cup my face.

Warmth spread through me, and I felt acceptance.

I was going to die.

But I understood it.

I had to be the sacrifice.

If I didn't perish, The Gray would come back.

I had always known this was the way.

I just hadn't known that I would be as okay with it as I was.

As I let out a breath and opened my eyes again to find Easton in front of me, curiosity in his gaze, I knew I could never tell him what I knew.

I couldn't tell anyone.

They would go into battle, knowing we fought for our kingdom, for our realm. But they couldn't know that it would be my last fight.

I leaned forward and brushed my lips against Easton's, sinking into him, craving more.

"Did you talk to them?" he asked, clearing his throat as I leaned back.

"I did. Riddles and such as always, but I think we'll win. I have to believe it."

He searched my face, and I did my best to steel myself for what he might see.

But he didn't see my death, at least I didn't think so. He saw something, though, that much was clear in his expression, but I didn't let it break me.

Instead, I leaned forward, crawled into his lap, and let him hold me.

Later, I would be strong. Later, I would fight and do what I could for those I loved. I would sacrifice all, and I would do it willingly. Gladly.

Nobody would know that I was breaking inside all the while, that I was afraid to lose everything I had just found.

They didn't need to. They needed to see strength. And I would give it to them.

But for now, I let Easton hold me, the truth between us loud in the spaces between us.

Deafening in the silence.

Because Easton knew. How could he not? He could touch my soul.

But he didn't say the words. Nor did I.

I simply let him hold me and thought about a future on a farm that would never be.

CHAPTER TWENTY-ONE

LYRIC

BRAELYNN MEOWED AT ME, AND I LOOKED DOWN AT HER LITTLE furry face, her bat wings outstretched. I rubbed my temples.

"We have battle plans to pore over. I can't follow you on a trek tonight."

She purped, this time growling low, as well, something that had nothing to do with being a cat.

No, that was a dragon growl coming from a cat's mouth.

I blinked and set down the book I had been reading and scrambled off the bed.

"Okay, okay. Please don't turn into a dragon inside the castle."

We were still at the Fire Estate, training our troops and getting ready for the next battle to come. If I had anything to say about it, it would be the final. And because it wasn't our place, I didn't want to add any unnecessary damage.

Namely from a dragon who wanted me to come and play.

Braelynn looked at me again, and smoke slithered out of her nostrils. I rolled my shoulders back.

"Okay, let's go," I said, knowing she'd turn into a dragon and pick me up with her claws if I didn't concede.

Either that or send one of the other girls in.

I'd spoken with the Spirit Wielders only yesterday, and while everything had changed within me since, it still felt as if nothing had shifted.

I would be fighting alongside my friends. My family.

And I would do my best to keep everybody I loved alive.

Even if that meant sacrificing myself to do it.

I knew what I had to do.

I just hoped nobody else figured it out along the way.

I followed Braelynn's little furry butt to the other end of the estate where Rosamond and Emory had apparently set up a girls' night.

"Okay, we don't exactly have a microwave here, so no popcorn. Though I could have tried to use an open flame and a pan with some corn. Only that seemed a little outrageous," Emory said.

I smiled despite myself and hugged her close. It was the first time I had touched her willingly in a while. Her nullifying bracelets clinked behind me, and I sighed, hugging her tightly.

"Thank you. I guess I needed a night off."

"We all do," Emory said. "And I at least got us some snacks and drinks and big fluffy pillows to hang out on."

"I have a feeling Rhodes and the others will show up to see what we're doing at some point," Rosamond said, setting a plate of cheeses and fruits and various kinds of honey on the table in the middle of the room. "However, this is clearly a boys-not-allowed event."

I grinned. "Well, it will be nice to have time for us. There is a lot of testosterone in this castle."

"Tell me about it," Wyn said, pulling her hair out of her braid as she strode into the room. Her tresses flowed around her in luscious brown waves as she threw herself onto one of the pillows.

"This is decadent. I could get used to this."

"I'm sure you could," Rosamond said, her gaze going hazy for a moment as if she saw a vision. She didn't let us know what it was, though, and I let it be.

She would tell us if it was necessary. Or if it was time.

We were all learning what those times meant.

Alura walked in a moment later, her hair still blowing in a

breeze that wasn't there, a small smile on her face. "Hello there. Thank you for inviting me," she said softly.

"It's good to have you here. You've been in the human realm for so long. It's nice to have you back."

My gaze sharpened at those words, not knowing much about Alura's past. But I did remember that it seemed as if she and Rosamond had known each other back in the human realm.

Lanya came in next, Delphine on her arm, and I moved out of the way so the two women could walk inside.

Thanks to how slowly the Maisons aged, the women looked the same age as Rosamond, not like grandmothers beyond their fifth century of life. Rosamond was four hundred, and Lanya and Delphine had both been alive during the Fall, and that was over five hundred years ago.

And yet, they didn't look a day over thirty.

Maybe even twenty-five.

Delphine's eyes were open, no longer covered in bandages, but they had gone opaque, The Gray's magic having taken her sight but not her resolve.

She had lost her son just a few nights before. Though, in reality, she had lost him long before then.

Every single woman in this room had lost someone dear, but we were all still fighting.

And we would continue to fight.

"I invited some of the other warriors," Rosamond said, and Wyn nodded.

"Me, too. They might show up a little bit later, though, as they are just finishing cleaning up from training."

I smiled at that. "It would be good to get to know more people outside of my inner circle."

"You've already been speaking to so many," Rosamond said. "You've been wonderful with your duties and responsibilities. The people see it."

"You're doing a good job, darling."

"You are," Lanya said, coming over to me and cupping my face in her hands before kissing my brow.

"You're doing so wonderfully. It seems as if you've been in this realm your entire life, centuries even, rather than these last two short years."

"Has it been two years?" I asked, shaking my head. "It seems like so much longer."

"And yet, yesterday," Emory said, petting Braelynn between the ears.

I nodded, looking at my ex-girlfriend, my former enemy who was now my friend.

What had been done to her was barbaric, and I had no idea what would happen to her once this was all over, and the Maison realm had been put back together again.

Would we be able to change her powers? She was a siphon, and it wouldn't be safe for her to be near anybody in this realm without the bands on her wrists.

And those cuffs needed to be changed every few weeks or so, with Justise the only one skilled enough to do it.

With him now nearly out of commission, he was much slower at his craft than he used to be. He was still working on them for us, and Emory was willing to help wherever and however she could. Yet it seemed like so much was out of our hands, out of our control, and I refused to let it be.

"This is not a time for sadness," Rosamond said, and Alura nodded beside her.

"Exactly. Tonight is girls' night," Alura said, saying the words as if she had never said them before.

Maybe she hadn't.

She was far older than most of the people in this room, that much I knew. Maybe she'd never had something like this since she'd been apart from everybody for so many years.

Hell, I hadn't had girls' night since the human realm. Though, sometimes, I hung out with Wyn on the trail from estate to estate.

But even then, those times were few and far between.

There was always testosterone around, men growling and wanting to be in our space.

I didn't mind it, usually. But I hadn't realized how much I needed time with just the women in my life.

That thought made my belly clench as I remembered my mother—and the look on her face before she died.

She was gone now, and there was no bringing her back. No amount of Spirit Wielding would ever do that.

Besides, I knew better than to taint myself with that distorted magic.

The Gray had done worse, and now our realm was breaking because of it.

Perhaps it was already broken.

"Okay, where's the mead?" Wyn asked, her legs draped over another pillow as she sprawled.

I laughed, shaking my head, and went with Rosamond to help her gather the drinks.

We lay there and laughed, and it was almost as if I were back home in the human realm, enjoying myself without a care in the world.

I'd had cares, worries, and uncertainties.

But it had never been anything like this.

I hadn't found my purpose until I came here.

Now, we were ready to fight to save our world.

And we would.

I just didn't want to lose the women at my side as we did. I didn't want to lose anybody.

"Has your Familiar found her third?" Alura asked, and Rosamond shook her head.

I leaned forward, confused.

"What do you mean?" I asked, reaching out so Braelynn would come to me. She plopped onto my lap, and I scratched her behind the ears, once more missing my best friend.

"Her third," Alura said again.

Rosamond answered. "She hasn't yet. She's found two, her cat form, and her dragon form, but not her third. Soon, I believe. I can see it."

"What are you talking about?" I asked.

"Familiars are special," Rosamond said.

"I know that. But you have all been so mysterious about her. What aren't you telling us?"

"Please, tell us," Emory added, and I reached out and gripped her hand.

Wyn noticed the gesture, and I shrugged it off.

None of us were the same people we were back in the human realm. And I didn't want to go back to that place. But Braelynn was ours, and if there was something wrong, I needed to know.

"Most Familiars only ever find one form. It's a blessing for them to find two. However, Familiars born of Danes in the time of sorrow and who sacrifice for those they love can come back from the brink of death to find their third form." Rosamond paused, looking directly into my eyes and then at Braelynn. "Their human form."

My heart pounded in my ears, and I swallowed hard before looking at the cat in my lap. "Braelynn...she can find her human form again?"

"I've seen it," Rosamond whispered. "But true Familiars are no longer only human or Maison. They must live their lives in thirds. A third of the time in their feline form, a third in their warrior form, a third in their new skin."

"You're saying Braelynn can one day become the girl we lost? She can talk and hug and be with Luken?" I gasped. "Oh my goddess. Luken. Does he know?"

Rosamond shook her head, and my heart fell. "When she turns, she will have a third of her life to be who she was, though never fully that. None of us were who we were once. Luken does not know. I couldn't give him hope in case the years or centuries passed, and my visions changed. Yet...I don't think we will have to wait for long."

Excitement filled me as I looked down at Braelynn. She wiggled off my lap and ran towards Alura. Alura leaned down and brushed her hand along Braelynn's back.

"It's time," the other woman whispered. "Come back."

I stood with the others then as Alura danced away. Rosamond came forward, her arms outstretched. Magic slid over us, and my body shook, the Spirit Wielding inside me reaching out.

"Let it free, Lyric," the Seer whispered.

I looked up at her, not understanding what she meant until the Spirit within me pushed.

I placed my palms together before pushing my hands out, palms facing Braelynn. The warmth within me surged as if I had been holding it in place for just this moment, then it burst from my body and raced towards Braelynn in her cat form.

Others spoke, but I couldn't focus on anything but the cat in front of me.

A blinding light shook the room, and I staggered back, my

hands falling to my sides. Suddenly, I inhaled and caught a familiar scent.

Easton gripped my hips to keep me steady as the men filed into the room, all of us staring at the woman in front of us.

The woman who now wore a blanket Lanya had procured out of seemingly nowhere. Her long, dark hair covered her face, and her pale skin glowed in the candlelight.

Her entire body shook, but as she turned to look at me with those familiar eyes I loved so much, I blinked away tears before nearly falling to my knees.

"Braelynn!" I screamed before nearly tackling her to the floor. I held her close, aware that the others were speaking, explaining what had happened. But I couldn't talk. I could only hold my friend as Emory drew nearer, hugging us as one.

Then I moved away, cupped Braelynn's face, and knew that we would have time to chat later. I would make time.

Now was not the time. Because Luken was there in an instant, plucking Braelynn off her feet and holding her close. Tears slid down the warrior's face, and I moved away, Easton kissing my temple as his arms wrapped around me.

It was such a private moment as the soulmates held one another as if they'd never done so before...as if this were a precious gift.

It was beyond that.

It *was* a gift. One of fate. Of truth. Of sacrifice.

We all stood there, knowing this had to be a sign.

Braelynn was back.

She was alive.

She was whole.

She was a symbol of what we could have.

We moved away to give the couple privacy, and the others spoke of prophecy and futures, but I could only think one thing.

I had my best friend back.

And now I was going to leave her.

Again.

CHAPTER TWENTY-TWO

EASTON

No AMOUNT OF SCOUTING WAS GETTING US ANYWHERE CLOSE TO THE Shadow realm. Lyric nearly killing herself to reach the Spirit Wielders had done nothing but give her the look of conviction in her eyes that worried the hell out of me. But we didn't talk about it. Why would we? If we did, we'd have to discuss the possibility that neither of us would make it out of this battle alive.

If Lyric died, then so would I. I wouldn't live in this realm without her—even if I survived the loss of our bond.

I had already survived for hundreds of years beneath a curse I hadn't even known I had wrapped around my heart. I wouldn't do it again.

However, it would be for naught if we couldn't discover whatever it was the damn Gray was hiding.

We stood in the training area in front of the estate, Wielders all around us acting as sentries while others trained, using their new powers or learning how to fight as Danes. Or to fight for the first time, as it was in the case of the Wielders who'd had magic their entire lives but had never been soldiers.

To be part of the realm didn't mean you were forced to fight for it. There were other ways to fight other than with blood and possible death. Our bakers and teachers and scholars...all of them fought in their own ways.

But now, many of them were coming with us wherever we went. To fight The Gray.

They were battling for their people, too. And that meant we had taken this time in the lull between skirmishes and pain to train them.

They would be some of our last resorts because I would not let them become cannon fodder.

But everybody needed to know how to use their Wielding to protect themselves and the person next to them who may be weaker.

That meant long nights of training for my uncle, and even longer nights for those watching.

"Is the sentry back yet?" Teagan asked from my side, rolling his shoulders back.

"Should be soon. I hate sending out so many scouts at once, but we need to determine how to get to The Gray."

"You know that it may all be for nothing if he attacks us first."

"That's why we've been fortifying the Fire Estate while training and readying to travel if it comes to that. It won't be easy, no matter what, but we can do this."

"It's not like we have a choice," Teagan rumbled, playing with the Fire at his fingertips.

"Are the women and the others okay?" I asked casually, searching for the sentry. He should be here soon, but I wasn't going to hold out too much hope.

I was running out of it as it was.

"They're doing fine. Why do you ask?" Teagan asked.

"Because you've been growling at Wyn every chance you get. More so than usual." I turned to my best friend.

Teagan was silent for so long that I wasn't sure he would answer. "After we lost Arwin, I wasn't sure how we would make it."

"He wouldn't have wanted us to give up," Teagan said, shrugging, even though I knew the loss of our trainee had done something to him. It had broken something in all of us.

We had lost Arwin because we hadn't been strong enough to save him.

I just hoped we were better now.

"Wyn is learning how to use her new powers, so she's spending more time growling at Rhodes than letting me work with her. It's fine," he added quickly when I raised a brow.

"Really?"

"She's not my soulmate. We've known that for a long time. And, in the end, that's not going to matter, is it? Not if we can't find The Gray and end him. Not if we can't find a way to mend our realm."

I nodded, tension taking root in my shoulders.

"I think Lyric has a way," I whispered.

"What do you mean?" Teagan asked.

"When the time comes, and the battle finds us, I think my soulmate is going to sacrifice herself. I think she'll somehow use all five elements, and that will be how she protects and heals the realm."

I hadn't even meant to say the words out loud. But as Teagan took a staggering step back and looked at my face as if he couldn't quite believe I had so casually said the words aloud, I knew I had to let it out, or it would be too much.

"And you're just going to let her?" Teagan shouted.

"I do not *let* Lyric do anything," I said.

"So she dies, and the realm is safe. And you're fine with that?" Teagan asked, his voice rising even more.

I gave him a sharp look, and he quieted down a bit. I knew that nobody had heard our exact words because we were far enough away from the group, searching for the sentry, but I didn't want others to overhear.

"I'll be damned if I let her die alone for us."

I didn't need to say anything else because Teagan shook his head, sighing.

"Because you're planning to go right along with her to protect everyone."

"She's going to do what she has to, and I'm willing to make sure she doesn't have to do it alone."

"You sound insane," Teagan said, and I knew he was trying to lighten the mood a bit, but that wasn't going to happen, not at this time of war.

"I don't know what we're going to do, but I do know I'm going to protect her. I'm going to protect our people. And I'm going to kill The Gray."

"Unless Lyric has to do it," Teagan countered.

"If that's true, then I'll stand by her side and help her wipe off the blade," I vowed.

"I like the sound of that."

I narrowed my eyes as I spotted something in the distance. "Scout's on his way."

"Is that Heath?" Teagan asked, and the sentries moved around as if sensing Heath was coming, as well.

Heath was an Earth Wielder, and he was special.

He could use the Earth around him to create compressed stone that was crystallized and could reflect light. He could also breathe through soil somehow. Meaning, he could burrow beneath the topsoil of the earth around him, and travel long distances that way, conserving energy and making it so most people couldn't even sense he was there.

That we could see the plume of dirt above him now, told me that he was letting us see him.

There was a reason he was our best scout.

Teagan and I ran forward to meet him, eager to hear the news. I took one look at him and fell to my knees in front of Heath as he collapsed in front of us.

Jagged claw marks marred his shoulder, split his abdomen, and blood poured from his mouth.

"Dear goddess. Heath," I muttered.

"I'll go get Ridley," Teagan said and ran back towards the castle.

I knew others were shouting, things were getting done, but I just looked at the man I had sent to his death and felt the blood drained out of me.

"Heath,"

"He's at the Lumière Court," Heath whispered, blood bubbling from his mouth.

"Don't speak," I growled. "Save your energy."

"We both know I'm dead."

"No," I gritted out.

Suddenly, Lyric was at my side, Ridley next to her. "Heath," she whispered and reached out to grab his hand.

She had only met him twice in her time here, yet the tears that flowed down her cheeks were real.

She was everything. She had cracked my ice, even though I had flames running through my veins.

And now a man I had called a friend, someone I constantly sent out on dangerous missions, was dying in my arms.

"Lumière Court. Army there. And The Gray. Attack soon. They're...coming."

"Heath," I growled. "I'm sorry," I whispered.

The people near me would understand the pain in my words, and what I needed to do. I would be the king in a moment, but for now, I needed to be the man who was losing someone he had sent to his death.

And when the light faded from Heath's gaze, and Ridley slowly closed his eyes, I shut my own, my whole body shuddering. Suddenly, Lyric was there, wrapping her arm around my waist, leaning her cheek on my shoulder.

"The Lumière Court?" she whispered.

"The Lumière Court," I said softly.

We wouldn't need to find the Shadow realm because it seemed The Gray wanted us to find him.

Or maybe it was just easier to gather his forces at one of the castles we hadn't yet destroyed.

I didn't know The Gray's motivations beyond power, but this only meant we would have to fight him on our turf. Lands that many of our fighters knew well.

And that would count in this battle.

At least, I hoped to hell it would.

I stood up with Heath in my arms, while Lyric stood with me, helping me carry the fallen scout back to the estate.

Some stared with wide eyes, others with determination.

Heath had gotten us the information we needed, and he would not die in vain. Not like so many of the other Wielders, both Lumière and Obscurité, had died.

Sadly, as I lay Heath down in the infirmary so Ridley could clean him up, I knew that Heath wouldn't be the last.

Far from it.

"The Lumière?" Rhodes asked, walking towards us shirtless, covered in dirt and sweat and grime. He had been training the others, Wyn at his side, mud covering her face, her pants wet from probably learning how to Wield with Water.

They looked exhausted, all of us were tired, but we were ready. Because we had to be.

"The Lumière Kingdom."

"I guess it's where it all began for some of us," Rhodes said, shaking his head. "The Gray will have changed some things to make it work for him. We may not have the upper hand that we need," Rhodes countered.

"I know more of the castle's secrets than most," Delphine said as she walked towards us from the other side of the infirmary, soft blankets in her hands. Lanya stood beside her, guiding her way.

"I will help with the plans now that we know where the battle will be held. Now, go. Make your battle plans while we lay this son of the realm to rest."

I looked at the woman who had been the wife of my mortal enemy and knew she was just as broken as the rest of us.

She hadn't had a choice in her destiny, and when she had been able to do so, she had fought on our side.

And she still was.

Would she be one of those who fell? I didn't know. Because so many were going to die. I didn't have to be a Seer to know that.

"Okay, let's make some plans," Justise said as he walked towards the others of my royal cabinet—or so they called themselves.

Lyric slid her hand into mine and squeezed.

"This is what we've been training for. We can do this."

I nodded, then leaned down and took her lips in a soft kiss so I could center myself. I was the king, someone who would lead his people beside the Spirit Priestess to fight The Gray and save the realm.

I just hoped to hell I was enough.

The plans took hours to finalize, but we were used to this. We knew what we needed to do, where we would start.

We would go to The Gray and try to gain the element of surprise.

If we didn't? Then it would be on the traitor—the one The Gray had warned us about.

Only Lyric and I knew of his or her existence, and I was afraid that if we told anyone else, then the spy would know what we had planned.

But what if the traitor was in the room with us?

No. I had to trust my friends, the ones that had been on my side for centuries, who fought and bled with us.

If I didn't, then what was I fighting for?

When all was finally done, I stood in my room, stripped off my sweaty shirt, and wiped my face with it.

I was exhausted, but we had less than two days before we left for the former Lumière Court.

Less than two days before we began what could be the end.

I didn't want this to end.

I wanted the realm to be safe, sure. I wanted our people to be safe.

But if this was truly the end, then these were my last moments with the woman I hadn't known I'd have.

"When you look at me like that, I can see your fear," Lyric said and rose to her tiptoes to kiss my chin.

I looked down at her and frowned. "You shouldn't see my fear," I whispered.

"I can see all the same."

"Don't worry. We have this. We are strong. The prophecy is on our side."

The prophecy was going to kill her, but I didn't say the words aloud. She already knew. And that's why we weren't speaking about them.

I was going to lose her. The realm was going to take her from me, and I couldn't stand in her way. If I did, I was doing her a disservice, and I would be killing millions.

"I love you," I whispered.

"I love you, too."

"If I could hide you away, I would," I blurted.

"If you could hide me away, you wouldn't be Easton, and I wouldn't be Lyric."

"Maybe, or perhaps I *will* become all caveman and lock you in a dungeon so nobody can hurt you."

"I wouldn't let you," she whispered.

I knew that, but I didn't want to think about the future. Didn't want to think about anything but this moment, right now. So I lowered my head and brushed my lips against hers. She moaned and wrapped her arms around me. I leaned into the kiss.

We were slow if a bit eager. It was as if we knew this would be the last time we would be with each other, touching and feeling.

And when we lay together after, and I held her close, her breaths finally easing into slumber, I knew I would give up anything to keep this if I could.

Just as I knew there would be nothing left of me to give for that to happen.

CHAPTER TWENTY-THREE

LYRIC

THIS WAS IT. AFTER MONTHS OF TRAINING, SEARCHING, AND TRYING to unravel the prophecy, we were here.

We were going to fight The Gray today.

This was the day I would die.

I wasn't sure how I was supposed to feel about that, but there wasn't much time to think.

"We have another twenty minutes," Easton said, while Rhodes walked on the other side of me, a scowl on his face.

We were going back to the place where he should have grown up, though I knew he rarely visited. He had spent more time with his grandmother and on the road searching for me. Or out helping his people.

But now, the court was nothing like it had once been.

Nothing was.

"We have two battalions coming in from the side, another two moving up from behind. We're as ready as we're going to be," Teagan said from behind us.

I looked forward, knowing the court was coming up and that we had to say something.

"Okay, let's do this," I said before turning to look at the Wielders and warriors we had brought with us.

I did not want to lose a single person today, but none of these people were fighting for me. They were fighting for their realm and their futures. For their children.

I might be a symbol, but I wasn't the reason they were fighting today. I was only the domino that helped things fall, and it had happened as soon as I had been found and pulled into the Maison realm.

I understood that, but I was still sending these people to their deaths if we weren't careful.

"The time has come," I said, my voice echoing. We had sentries stationed all around us, scouts letting us know if The Gray and his people came forward or anyone could hear.

We were safe for now, but we wouldn't be as soon as we crossed the barrier.

"You have all fought bravely up until now. You have trained, and you have sacrificed so much. You have all *lost* so much."

The murmurs in the crowd sent shivers up my spine, but my friends stood near me—Easton on one side, Rhodes on the other.

The two people I had been pulled to the most during this journey, and they were here. Ready to fight with me.

We would all fight today, and we might die.

But we would not do so in vain.

"We will bring this realm together. We are doing so now. Most of you are standing side by side with those who used to be your enemy. Those whose Wielding is not yours. And yet, you are all fighting for a common goal. We have made friends between us, created allies of those we thought we should fight against. But it's not the common goal of death and destruction that brings us together today. It is protecting a realm that has been lost to hate and power for centuries."

They shouted, throwing their fists up in agreement. Nobody used their Wielding. Nobody screamed too loudly. We did not want the Lumière to hear us.

We did not want The Gray to overhear.

"We are ready. We will fight The Gray and his people. We will seal the realm and protect our futures. Your children will be raised in a realm of love, solidified by the sacrifice of those who came before them. They will not know the fear we have. They will not know the heartache you have felt. But we will be there to tell them what we fought for. And let them know why they can live in a world of peace. Because we *will* bring that peace."

Others murmured in agreement, and I could see my friends nodding.

"The Gray would have us divided. Would have this realm turned into his prison. He wants us to break and blend into the other realms, shattering all of them.

"But we are not The Gray. We are Maisons. We are Water and Fire, Earth and Air. We are Spirit, and we are Dane. We are those with Wielding, and those who fight by our sides without. We are those who stand on the side of right. Of good. There is no light or dark. We are beyond that now.

"We are Maisons. And we will fight. We will win."

I lifted up my hand and let out all four of my Wielding elements.

The others shouted. We were ready.

"So, did you practice that speech in the mirror?" Teagan asked.

I scowled.

"No, and I'm pretty sure winging it might not have been the best idea," I said.

But then there was no more time to worry about what I had said. We were past that.

We had spent so long preparing for this moment, time that felt like my entire life, even though it'd been only two short years.

Now, this was the end.

We made our way over the crest towards the court of the Lumière. I froze.

"They knew," Easton growled, the utter betrayal in his voice sending shockwaves through me.

The Gray's army stood in front of us, ready, willing, and dressed in battle leathers equal to ours.

We had not come upon them in secret. We had not surprised them. We did not have the upper hand.

The Gray had known.

Someone had told him.

This was most definitely our end.

"Who told?" Wyn asked, her voice shaking.

"There are so many of them. We're not enough," she added.

"We have to be," I said, shock slamming into me as I looked at The Gray. His robes still covered his body, his hood over his head so no one could truly see his face, but I knew the evil that lay behind that cowl.

But it wasn't him that shocked me the most.

No, it was the person at his side.

The one we had been warned about.

The one Rosamond had not been able to see.

I couldn't see," Rosamond said, her battle leathers marked with the emblem of a Seer. It was so others didn't harm her, much like the symbols the healers wore.

That had been the rule of war here for centuries, but I wasn't sure it was going to help now.

All of those thoughts ran through my head in an instant as I stared at the woman in front of me, with the long, honey-brown hair that seemed to flow in a breeze that wasn't there.

Alura stood by The Gray, her chin held high, but her eyes filled with fear. Was she afraid of the man at her side? Did she once love him? Did she still?

Or maybe what I saw was just fear of us and what we would do.

She would know.

"She's the traitor," Easton whispered.

"I didn't see this. Why didn't I see this?" Rosamond said, her hands shaking.

"Sometimes, we don't see the traitor in our midst until it's too late," Emory whispered, and I swallowed hard, then looked at my friends, wondering what we were going to do.

"She's his mother," I whispered, looking at Luken. Easton reached out and grabbed my hand.

We needed to tell the warrior, but there was no time.

We were too late for so many things. We'd been so focused on devising a battle plan and ending this once and for all that I had missed the most important pieces—the people we were fighting for.

I would never forgive myself for that.

We were close enough now we could see each other clearly, as well as hear each other if the wind permitted.

"Why?" I asked, not even realizing I was saying the word aloud until it was too late.

"You know why," Alura said, her voice still soft, airy, and lyrical, a tone that had always confused me.

But I didn't know her.

Nobody did.

And that would be our downfall.

We trusted her, and we shouldn't have.

"What is she talking about?" Emory asked, the only one of my friends able to speak at that moment. Perhaps because she had been here the shortest time, or maybe because she was the only one with enough power *to* speak at that moment.

"She's talking about who she's fighting for," The Gray began, holding his arms out as if he were preaching a sermon rather than waging war.

"Our realm was shattered long before the idea of a Spirit Priestess. We've all known that. We had the Fall for a reason, after all."

"And yet you're perpetuating it," Easton snapped.

"Am I? Or was I the unwilling participant in a war that was not my own. I stand on the precipice of what started it all."

"The old king might have begun the war, but you embraced it," Rosamond said, her eyes that of a Seer, not the granddaughter of the old king.

"Am I? Or am I the only one who saw the truth. I worked for the old king, but he was the one who decided the Spirit Wielders needed to be used."

"Lie. He wouldn't have done that if you hadn't whispered in his ear," I shouted.

"Perhaps. But he did use their magic. That and the magic of the bones. It wasn't me. I was just a bystander."

"Notice he didn't say '*innocent*,'" Rhodes grumbled.

"Oh, my hands are not clean. But neither are yours. You gained from the deaths of others, young Rhodes. You were the prince of the kingdom that began the Fall. Without you, perhaps there would've been peace."

"Don't listen to him. He's lying," I said.

"Maybe, but others are listening," Rhodes said quietly, and I nodded.

Our army could hear this. Hopefully, they would understand and see what the true enemy was. But we couldn't explain what was happening because we were still figuring that out. And if we weren't careful, our army could turn against us because The Gray lied. He was so good at that.

"The old kings fought for their right to control their kingdoms. Before they came together, the land had been only the territories. Then the kings wanted more land, more power, and created the kingdoms under the Obscurité and the Lumière."

"Are we just going to let him blather on?" Slavik said as he came up to us. The other Underkings of the Maison realm were behind him, everyone who led the underground armies were now fighting on our side.

Members of the League, the Creed, and the Unkindness of Fire were there.

Each of the representatives who stood beside us listened to The Gray explain why he was doing this, even though he wasn't really saying anything.

And throughout it all, I could only look at the woman in front of us.

Alura.

Our betrayer.

She had told The Gray that we were coming.

And now, we wouldn't have the element of surprise.

"Why don't you tell them, my dearest? Tell them exactly why you're fighting at my side."

"Gray," she whispered.

He slapped her hard, and I took an involuntary step forward. Both Rhodes and Easton each grabbed an arm, holding me back.

"I think she should go out and kill him right now," Slavik said. "It would make things easier."

"Would it?" I whispered.

"Maybe. Now, why is she fighting? It seems that she knows that somebody here knows. So, why?" Slavik continued.

I looked over at Luken, who stared at me, Braelynn in dragon form behind him.

She knew just as I did, and I had to wonder if she had told him.

Luken gave me a tight nod, a knowing, pain-filled look, and relief spread over me.

He knew. His soulmate had told him exactly what we had learned, and I was grateful for that.

I hadn't been able to find the words to tell my friend what I knew, but Braelynn had.

"He knows, Alura," I shouted.

"What?" Alura gasped, as the others murmured around us, asking questions. But I wasn't paying attention to them. No, I was looking at The Gray.

The Gray smiled and shook his head, but I had seen the look of surprise cross his face.

He hadn't been expecting that. Good. He should underestimate us. That was how we were going to win this. He thought he knew everything and that he could win this without truly fighting.

He was wrong.

"The Gray is wrong," Alura said, taking steps forward, her hands shaking.

I looked at her then, trying to understand why she had betrayed us. I just couldn't figure it out.

"Why?" I asked. "Why would you do this?"

"I was born during the Fall. The one meant to watch over the Spirit Priestess when she came to us. I have watched others over time, but you were the first."

"Are you going to tell your whole story now?" The Gray asked snidely. "Go for it. They're going to want to kill you anyway."

She raised her chin again. "I have always been the one out searching for you, Lyric. I am not a Spirit Wielder, but I was destined to find our Priestess. I've always been an Air Wielder. Like my son." She looked at Luken then, and the gasp behind us told me that not everybody had figured it out.

She raised her hands, small bursts of Air punching through her palms. "I fell for a man, but not my soulmate. The man that I loved, the one I *truly loved* was killed at the hands of the man behind me."

"He was in my way," The Gray said, shrugging as if none of it mattered.

"I was born at the age of the Fall to protect you, Lyric. But I fell, too." She looked at Luken then, her eyes pleading with her son.

"The Gray is not your father. He tells others that he is because that is who he wants to be. He wants you in his court, but that was never the case. Your father was a good man. Someone who died because of The Gray. And I was given in to his service because of a promise I made. A promise to keep you safe. I'm sorry. I'm so sorry for telling him everything. I'm sorry." She looked at me then, and I could only stand there, my mind whirling with her revelations. Luken wasn't The Gray's son? Alura had betrayed us, but she had done so to save her child, not because she loved The Gray.

It didn't make any sense, but it didn't really matter. Because regardless, Alura had betrayed us, and we were still going to fight. This pause in the battle only gave enough time for our other armies to come around and get into position.

The battalion in front of us was vast and seemingly the whole of The Gray's forces.

He didn't know we had others.

This was our distraction, one we hadn't counted on but would use to our advantage.

"I told you, Alura. I said I would keep him alive for my own uses. However, if you no longer want to go by our bargain, I understand."

The Gray moved so fast that none of us had time to move or prepare. Except for the woman who danced on Air and had the grace and power we all underestimated.

The woman whose name meant elf peace.

The betrayer.

The mother.

The one none of us truly understood.

When The Gray shot out his shadow magic, filled to the brim with Spirit Wielding, and sent it straight towards Luken's chest, I screamed. Fire erupted from Braelynn's mouth, my best friend trying to singe the twisted Spirit Wielding coming her way.

But none of that was going to help.

The Gray planned to use his Spirit Wielding to take Luken's soul.

I didn't know what he could do with that soul, but whatever it was wouldn't be good.

However, before I could use my own Spirit Wielding to try and negate his power, Alura moved. She threw herself in front of The Gray, stopping the Wielding from hitting Luken.

Tears filled my eyes as Alura's mouth opened in a silent scream, and she leveled such a look of love and loss at her son. A child she had never been able to hold. One she had never been able to claim.

I knew I was the only person who could see what was

happening beneath the surface. As Alura fell to her knees, the life fading out of her, I saw her soul.

It screamed in agony, but then The Gray held it in his fist and grinned.

When he squeezed, the soul splintered before melting into shadow.

Suddenly, I understood.

The Shadow realm and magic wasn't a new form of Wielding. It was a bastardized form of Spirit Wielding.

He used the stolen souls of the enslaved to bolster his power.

He was a true Spirit Wielder, and yet...not.

Luken shouted, and The Gray simply grinned and shot both hands out to the sides, shadow and Spirit Wielding erupting from his palms.

The time of peace and quiet was over.

The battle had just begun.

CHAPTER TWENTY-FOUR

Lyric

Luken's sword whooshed, and I ducked out of the way before the blade bit into my flesh. It clanged against the sword of the Air Wielder wearing the enemy's colors, and I rolled out of the way. I gave Luken and nod of thanks before pushing my hands into the ground, letting the Earth Wielding within me scuttle out a path before me. A wall of Earth shot up into the air, pillar after pillar, the sound deafening as I moved forward, slicing through the enemies in my way.

The Gray had struck first, sent shadow towards us after he killed Alura, using her soul to create more shadow magic.

As soon as he shouted her name, he had shot the shadow magic towards us, and the battle was waged.

Our armies fought, the front line at its strongest. Additional regiments from the other two sides of the court were coming in fast, flanking the enemy. However, our numbers were still too few. The Gray had killed off so many over time, but we would continue fighting, and we would win.

The crystals within me started to hum, and I knew their time was coming.

The Gray was in the middle of it all, using his League and Creed members from the Lumièrs side to block any magic from coming at him.

Nobody could get to him, but that was fine. For now. We would get to him soon.

The crystals within me pushed against my skin. I knew they wanted out, to reform somehow, and I knew I would need to get there. But as The Gray used his shadow to dampen sound, somehow able to alter our perception of reality, I staggered but rolled my shoulders back as I threw Fire at the Wielder sending an ice shard towards me.

"Watch out for the ones holding bone markers!" Rhodes shouted over the din, and I looked over to see at least one hundred bone magic Wielders. I held back a shocked breath. They were holding the bones of the dead. Bones they had taken and desecrated. They had used artifacts and death to force magic into them, to sacrifice and murder.

I could barely catch my breath.

We had thought we'd gotten all of the bones off the seafloor in the Water territory. Either we had been horribly wrong, or these murderers had made more of their twisted and tragic weapons. I honestly wouldn't be surprised if it was the latter.

"We're on it!" Emory shouted as she and Rosamond came close, Delphine and Lanya at her sides.

Lanya and Delphine held hands, raised them up into the sky, and began chanting something I couldn't understand. Whatever it was, I knew it was important. All of this was important.

Rosamond did the same, while Emory touched the cuffs on her wrists. They fell into her hands.

I sucked in a breath and stepped forward, my eyes wide.

"It's fine, Rosamond won't let me hurt anybody."

I looked over at Easton, who fought beside me. He nodded, though he still had worry on his face.

"What is going on?" Rhodes said.

"I think Emory is learning to use her powers."

On the battlefield.

Dear goddess.

Emory wasn't siphoning the Wielding from the Wielders

around her. Instead, she pushed out her hands towards those with the bone magic. My eyes widened at what I saw.

As the three former Lumière royals chanted, their magic filling the air over the dampening spell The Gray had produced, I could see the bone magic Wielders start to scream, clutching at the bones they had stolen from the dead—or created with their murder.

Emory pushed out her hands, and purple waves shot through them, the color mixed with red and blue and white. My eyes widened as the Wielders screamed, the bone magic murderers falling onto their faces and writhing in agony as their Wielding was stripped from them, the power rendered inert.

"I'm going to have to talk to my sister about what she's teaching her friend," Rhodes said, his voice breathy.

I blinked, nodding.

"I was not expecting that," I whispered. I didn't have time to focus on Emory and the others anymore, though. However, I did look over as she slid the cuffs back onto her wrists and walked beside Rosamond once more as they battled. She seemed to be here to help Rosamond stay upright, her Seer visions seeming to come one after another, all of them hitting her hard.

I saw the strain in Rhodes' face as he fought the desire to reach out and help his sister. But we were all fighting for a purpose, and that meant we had to leave her be. She seemed to have it under control.

At least, I hoped to the goddess she did.

Teagan and Wyn fought side by side, beaded brown bracelets on their wrists, a prayer for Arwin who was no longer with us. We were all fighting in his name.

I had a similar strap of leather braided into my hair, the same as Easton and others.

We were fighting for those we had lost, but I knew we would lose even more before the day was over.

Still, this was our last dance, and we would win. We would not let tyranny and dictatorship win.

We would not let evil rule.

"He's coming for us!" Teagan shouted and looked over at The Gray, who had begun to move. We watched him fall back behind his people. They didn't even realize they were being used as cannon fodder to protect him.

I looked up to see Luken on Braelynn, her dragon form large and beautiful as she flew down towards The Gray. Luken had somehow climbed on top of his dragon mate and was now fighting with the man who had claimed him as his son.

Even if it had all been a lie.

Yes, Alura had betrayed us, but the world had betrayed her long before that.

I didn't have time to think about that, though. Didn't have time to blame her. Because in the end, we would have ended up here regardless.

With so many warriors on The Gray's side, no amount of forewarning about Alura's betrayal would have helped. Not in the long run. But we were still going to win.

Luken lowered his sword and shot Air at The Gray and the people blocking him at the same time Braelynn spewed fire. The two elements whirled into a cataclysmic funnel, but the League members in front of The Gray raised their hands, and a wave of Water shot towards the dragon.

I shouted, even as I sent Air to knock out the Water Wielders and tried to keep Braelynn aloft.

I knew it was going to be too late.

Because The Gray had Fire Wielders, as well.

They were not the Unkindness of Fire, I didn't know who they were, but they wore uniform robes and seemed to be strong, far stronger than many other Fire Wielders I knew.

They had to be the other half of the Unkindness of Fire, but it didn't matter who they were.

Because they were shooting flames at my best friend.

I needn't have worried because the skies were not just for a single dragon.

Slavik shouted as he shot boulders, one after another, towards the enemy. He laughed like a maniac as he rode a Domovoi through the air.

We hadn't known until it was almost too late that Slavik could speak to the creatures.

I was pretty sure he could also speak to Braelynn in her dragon form, but I didn't have time to think about that.

All I knew was that the Domovoi and other winged creatures were in the air, coming after The Gray and his ilk.

Only they weren't the only things in the sky with Braelynn. The Gray had creatures of his own. Perhaps he couldn't control them or speak to them as Slavik could, but he used the rip in the fabric of our realm to set the creatures free.

So, above us, the Domovoi and wyverin flew.

The sea by the court that had once held dolphins and other creatures now held Kraken, their tentacles clashing as they fought light versus dark.

Gorgons and basilisks and other monsters fought against one another.

The Gray's dragon came at Braelynn, but she was faster, and Luken was there for her.

It was all of the Maison realm at once, fighting for what they had.

The creatures of the past were now in the present, and not all of them wanted chaos. They followed Slavik, each under his control to a certain extent. And since Slavik was on our side, I counted that as a win.

I pulled my attention from the skies back to Easton as we shot Fire towards another battalion. They had Fire Wielders on their side, as well, and our flames met as one, blue and red and purple and orange all mixed together in a fiery blaze that nearly singed. I stomped my foot on the ground, sending Earth towards the enemy, but their Earth Wielders did the same to us.

And on and on it went.

Water against Water, Air against Air.

We all had the same powers, though we used them in different ways.

But we were still fighting, still trying our best to survive.

We were not gaining any ground, however. We weren't losing any, but we were not making headway either.

The Lord of Fire came forward, his arms outstretched, his eyes narrowed. He slammed his hands together, the Unkindness of Fire beside him doing the same. A wall of Fire erupted in front of him and pushed out towards the enemy.

The screams of agony were deafening in my ears, but I ignored them.

There was no peace. There would never be peace until The

Gray was gone for good. Until those who fought for him understood that there were other ways.

But right now, they were dying, and so were we.

Emory fought using the blades that Justise must have given her.

He fought alongside his mate, his husband, Ridley using Water Wielding to keep his husband safe while Justise used Fire Wielding to protect his people.

My heart broke for them, but even injured, Justise was Wielding. He wasn't standing back, he wasn't retreating into himself and grieving over what he had lost. He was fighting.

And Ridley was healing when he wasn't fighting, but they were doing what they could.

All of them were.

Delphine and Lanya continued fighting together, moving their arms in intricate motions that I had never seen before. Still, their practice was one of peace, of an ancient magic I had never heard of.

They mixed their Water and their Air together, calmly defending their people. Delphine could not see what was in front of her, but Lanya was there to protect and guide her.

Delphine had been a prisoner, much like Lanya's daughter had once been.

But now, we would be free. We had to be.

My Wielding sang within me, and I knew it was time.

My Spirit Wielding ached, and I wanted to have it sing to the remaining souls, to help them find their way into the next life. But that wasn't my place. At least, not yet.

I was the Spirit Priestess, and I would soothe the souls we lost today. I would not bastardize them as The Gray did. But that wasn't enough.

Not yet.

Rhodes stood beside me, his arms outstretched as he hovered just above the ground, using his Air Wielding to slice into his opponent.

Blood splattered on us as one of the gorgons went through the enemy. But we were alive. And we would remain so. I just didn't want to utter the phrase *no matter the cost.*

Easton was on my other side, and the three of us moved together as if we had practiced this for eons instead of mere months.

I pushed my foot into the ground, the mud a mix of the blood and Water and Earth of our enemies and ourselves. Earth shot up into sharp discs again, and I sliced at the basilisk in front of me.

This one was not under Slavik's control.

I shouted. "Close your eyes. Let me finish this."

Rhodes and Easton did as I commanded, at least I hoped, and I shoved my Fire Wielding onto the disc of Earth I had made and beheaded the basilisk with one quick slice.

The creature let out a shocked screech, and its head thudded to the ground. I let out a sigh, my Wielding buzzing within me, needing more.

"Well, then. That was a basilisk?" Easton said, shaking his head. "Good thing your Spirit Wielding can protect you."

"It'll protect Braelynn, as well, but I don't know about you. I don't know if the bond works that way."

"Let's not try to find out, shall we?" Easton said, pressing a quick kiss to my lips before we went back to the battle.

We kept fighting, our Wielding not enough against the others at times because they had the same strengths that we did.

But we had a cause that was just, and I had to hope that would be enough.

"We're getting closer to him," Easton shouted, and I nodded, moving forward.

We were gaining ground, but not enough. The Gray hadn't moved from where he'd started, but more of his members threw themselves in front of him. Dying for him as if his word were law and he was worth their lives.

I didn't understand it. I didn't want anyone to die for me. And they weren't, thankfully. This war was not about the Spirit Priestess. I was here to help, but this war was about the realm.

And The Gray was taking it from us.

Never again. Not anymore.

Slavik jumped off a Domovoi as it flew back into the air. He landed on the ground, pushing Earth towards The Gray's fighters. The other Underkings went with him, Wielders from all walks of life, those who did not want to be in the limelight but ruled their small territories with an iron fist regardless.

They were the ones we had gone to before. Now, they were fighting for us.

None of them was fighting for The Gray.

Luken was off Braelynn's back in an instant and moved to fight next to Emory and Rosamond. Braelynn had reverted to her cat form, probably exhausted from her fight as a dragon, but she was still spewing fire, her bat wings pressed back so she wouldn't hurt Luken.

They were fighting as a unit and making headway.

The League members on our side stood near the sea and moved as one, a graceful dance of footwork and arm movements to push Water against the League on The Gray's side. They walked silently, one step in front of the other as they pushed wave after wave into the enemy League, making headway. I only hoped it was enough.

The Creed of Wings did the same, though they were braced against wind currents, moving in the middle of the melee, fighting against the former members of their group.

The Unkindness of Fire fought against their counterparts, as well, flame against flame, blue hitting red. The Unkindness was so powerful, they could use blue flame and shocking lightning to push the others back.

We were doing this. We could win.

A scream echoed in my ear, and I turned, a sword slicing into my arm.

But I didn't feel pain. I didn't even hear Easton shout as he came towards me, killing the man who dared to cut me.

It was Wyn who'd screamed. Water and Earth poured from her, and I looked down at the body on the ground. I couldn't hold back; I screamed with her.

Teagan lay there, burns from Fire along his side, a bloody gash near his heart.

His eyes were open, and there was a smile on his face, but he was gone.

Teagan was dead.

The world shook.

CHAPTER TWENTY-FIVE

LYRIC

I KEPT MOVING. I COULDN'T STOP. JUST BECAUSE ONE OF OURS WAS dead, Teagan's eyes now unseeing, Easton standing stiffly at my back as he tried to work through his rage, didn't mean the war was over.

I lashed out, four of my Wieldings moving as one, pushing towards the enemy. Fire, Water, Earth, and Air, as much as I could gather, pulsated from me in an eruption of anger and grief and horror.

I could hear the screams penetrating the magical wall of silence around me, but I didn't let it be the only thing I focused on. I couldn't.

Teagan was dead. And so was Heath, and Arwin, and Lance, and Megan, and Moran, and the man who'd helped to bake bread for our people. The man who had picked up my sword when I tripped and was still learning how to use a blade.

The woman who had helped me sew myself into my battle leathers so they were a good enough fit and could protect me and not shift while fighting.

The woman who had sold flowers when I first entered the realm.

The family that had sold food on the territory between Fire and Earth.

They were all gone. Dead.

So many names that I did not know, all erased in an instant because of a war we were still losing.

So many names, too many faces. But they would not die in vain.

I would mourn when this was over.

For now, I had to fight. We all had to fight.

Wyn stepped over Teagan's body as our healers took him away, doing their best to take care of the dead as well as the living. Water gushed from Wyn's hands, a tidal wave of fury as it crashed over The Gray's men in front of us.

My heart shuddered at the amount of power my friend was using. I wasn't even sure I could do what she was doing now. But there was so much anger in her, so much pain, and it was propelling outwards, agony and grief all wrapped in power and death.

Rhodes was at her side then, using his Air and Water to push her tidal wave towards The Gray's forces. I heard shouts and screams, and then there was nothing, a swath of their army gone by the anger of loss.

Wyn glared at Rhodes and moved forward, slicing her hand through the air as Earth lifted from the ground and pelted the enemy in front of us.

Slavik moved to her side, using his Earth Wielding to add to hers.

The three of them worked as one, no words needed between them.

I looked over at the others, trying to find the people I knew, those of my heart, but it was too hard to see.

People bled and cried, and it seemed Ridley and his team couldn't get to everybody who needed them.

But they were trying. We all were.

"We need to get Teagan's father," Easton called as he joined me, Fire flying from his hands as he fended off another League member who got too close.

I wiped the blood and grime from my face and nodded.

"He's going to hurt somebody if we don't get to him fast."

But we were too late.

I knew we were.

The Lord of Fire, the one who had stayed in our realm after losing his soulmate, stood near The Gray, Fire in his outstretched hands.

He had separated from the Unkindness of Fire, so he had no backup. Somehow, he had made it through the melee and was now surrounded by the enemy.

He had lost his wife, had somehow survived the mortal wound that killed her.

I knew it was likely sheer force of will and a need to be here for his son that had let him remain in our realm and not go where the Spirits roamed.

But now his son was gone, and there was nothing left for the Lord of Fire to fight for.

"Face me, Gray."

The Lord of Fire's words might have been quiet, but I could hear them as if he were screaming in my head.

Was that because of the crystals?

Or was I just hearing what I needed to?

"Ah, Griffin. Do you think you can defeat me? You are but a shade of the man you once were. The blood on your hands is even darker than mine."

The Gray wasn't shouting, but we were close enough that I could hear.

I kept fighting, focusing on saving as many as I could. Unfortunately, I couldn't get close enough to the Lord of Fire. We were going to be too late.

Griffin was so wrapped up in his grief and his rage that he wasn't going to get out of this.

I did not want to watch another friend die.

But I knew my choices were limited.

"We should have ended you a long time ago." The Gray threw back his head and laughed, his hood falling away from his face.

His skin was so pale it looked like marble. His cheekbones were prominent, yet he had an effervescent kind of beauty. Still, he was almost...put together wrong.

It didn't make any sense.

Perhaps holding all of those souls within him was so intense, that after corrupting the world as he had, had only created death and agony within beauty.

"You couldn't take me out when I was a mere aide to the king. Why do you think you can do so now?" The Gray asked mockingly.

"We tried to kill you back before the Fall, and you did nothing. We will take care of you now."

"No, you won't. You never will. We both know you are worthless. That you were weak before in the Obscurité, and that it was the Lumière who were the strongest. We both know that you are nothing. You couldn't even protect your own mate and son."

I shouted, trying to get Griffin's attention, to convince him to come back to us where we could fight as one.

But nobody could hear me.

I could barely hear myself over the battle and the dampening spell.

Griffin growled. "You brought the Fall with the old kings. You took everything from me. And now, you'll pay." The Lord of Fire raged, Fire bursting from his body, from every pore in his skin as if he had been waiting for this moment forever. The power was unlike anything I had ever seen before.

It wasn't mayhem, wasn't a casual display of strength. No, it was targeted. He knew exactly who he was aiming at. The Gray ducked, but he didn't fight back, not right away.

However, he did look a little scared.

I would relish that look for the rest of my days.

For as long as I had them anyway.

Griffin and The Gray circled each other, shadow against flame as they fought. Finally, The Gray was using his powers and not hiding behind others.

No one seemed to want to get in the middle of this skirmish, but nobody was helping them either.

Red against purple, light versus dark, I could barely see what was happening as I was still fighting off other foes in front of me, sweat dripping from my brow, my body aching as I lost strength.

But I kept fighting—my eye on The Gray and Griffin the entire time.

You created the Fall," Griffin shouted again, flinging more Fire.

"And you didn't stop me."

Everything that happened next did so in a cacophony of silence, the vacuum created by the shadow magic. By the screaming of souls that had been silenced long ago. The ones he'd twisted into his own kind of strength and malice and mist.

I screamed, but still, nobody could hear.

There was nothing left to do.

We had been silent for too long.

The Gray let out some smoke, the long tendrils of death he wielded, and wrapped them around Griffin's neck. Griffin let his arms spread out wider, his Fire filling the area, burning those on The Gray's side but not touching a single hair on any of ours.

He looked directly into The Gray's eyes, then turned to me and nodded.

I held back tears, knowing they wouldn't help anybody.

Instead, I slammed my foot into the ground and did my best to let the Spirit Wielding within me try to stop the ropes of smoke and death The Gray had let loose.

But it wasn't enough.

I wasn't strong enough yet.

But I would be.

I had to be.

Griffin turned back to The Gray and...exploded.

His entire body erupted in flames that shot out as if a bomb had been placed there, the flames burning through the masses.

I ducked, but the Fire didn't even touch me.

"My goddess," Easton whispered beside me. I looked up to see The Gray staggering back, his people holding him as they doused the flames that covered his body.

The Gray had a single singe mark on his face, angry and red and bleeding.

It wasn't enough, yet still, I smiled.

I smiled despite the death and the pain.

Because this proved that The Gray could be hurt.

And I knew that Griffin had done what he needed to do.

He was no longer in pain.

But we were still here.

We moved forward, all of us pushing through the enemy ranks to get at The Gray. Once he was gone, it would be the beginning of the end.

Because the realm was still fracturing, and I needed to piece it back together.

Yet I knew the crystals within me were what would get that done. They were scratching at my skin even now, bursting to get through. But they were not ready yet.

It felt as if there were knives under my flesh, trying to burrow out.

Maybe I wasn't in the right position yet, or perhaps this wasn't the right time.

Either way, I knew that once the crystals emerged from my skin, it would bring the Maison realm together as it should be.

At least, that is what I hoped.

I wasn't sure what else I could do, so I kept moving, kept fighting.

And hoped to hell we got out of this.

Because we needed to.

"You're out of lords, aren't you?" The Gray spat. "No more territories, no more leaders. Just a lost king, and a prince who never got his title."

"And you are megalomaniac who isn't long for this world," I shouted back.

"Look at you with the big words. But it's not enough. *You* will never be enough."

The crystals shimmered beneath my skin, and I moved forward, one arm outstretched, the other pushing Water towards those who might come against me.

I could feel my people surrounding me. Delphine and Lanya moving next to Rosamond and Emory, taking out our enemies one by one. The ladies were covered in blood and soot, but they were still moving. Emory limped, but she was still fighting.

Wyn and Rhodes and Slavik came around the other side, all of them covered in blood and bruised and bleeding themselves.

But they were still fighting, as well.

Justise fought with Fire, burning through the enemy as he covered his husband. Ridley was on his knees by a member of the Creed, who was bleeding out.

Ridley was saving him. Saving as many as he could.

And Easton was by my side, fighting, a warm presence that I

knew would always be at my back. He would always be there to help me.

I refused to let any more of my friends and the people I cared for die for a man who believed he was *owed* the power of a realm.

The Spirit Wielders beckoned me from beyond. I could feel their presence around me.

We were going to win.

I would take out The Gray.

Suddenly, the prophecy came back to me, and I knew my sacrifice was coming.

I knew what I had to do. But first, I needed to get closer.

I moved in front of The Gray, and he smiled.

"Tired of letting the innocent die for you?" The Gray asked.

"You're the one hiding behind the lines, barely fighting. But I see you still have a mark on your skin. You weren't strong enough once you finally raised your hands to try to save your measly life."

His hands moved to his face reflexively, but he didn't touch the scar. Instead, he narrowed his eyes before smiling at me again.

The cruelty in that smile was like an effervescent lullaby leading to nightmares. It slid over my body, but I ignored it.

He was malice wrapped in a package of beauty.

But he would not defeat me. Not today. Not ever.

Because I was the Spirit Priestess.

And we would win.

"I created the Fall. The kings died because they were weak. And now, the King of Lumière and the Queen of Obscurité are gone, taken out as a result of their own failures. Every knight and chess piece I put on the board has brought us here. And you were always two steps behind, falling because you weren't good enough. You call yourself a savior? You can't even save your friends. They will die knowing you were weak. Knowing that they put their faith in the wrong Priestess.

"You don't even know how to use your Spirit Wielding. You are weak, and you have always been. No amount of training and leather will pull you from the path I have set for you and me. The path of death. At least for you. You will die by my hand."

"No, I don't think I will."

He shot out his arms, shadow magic and Spirit Wielding blending into a rope as it wrapped around my chest. I threw out my arms, my Spirit Wielding pushing against the shadow. It sliced through the rope easily, and The Gray eyed me for just a moment before he smiled. Fear slid through me.

I had figured out how to stop the shadow magic.

But I didn't think it was enough...

No, not yet. This wasn't the end.

I was proven right as The Gray moved forward in an instant, the deafening cacophony of his dampening spell making my ears ring. I felt a trickle of blood as an eardrum burst, and others screamed, falling to their knees—even those on The Gray's side.

He was killing everybody.

Easton appeared, staggering forward with his Fire Wielding at the ready, but The Gray moved his shadow, slamming Easton to the ground, burying him in earth.

I screamed, using all of my elements—Fire to slash across his face, Water to drown him, Air to pull the oxygen from his lungs, Earth to bury him.

He took each in stride, never even moving.

I wasn't strong enough.

I couldn't use all five together. At least, not yet. But I was trying.

I could do this.

The Gray finally moved, and I barely felt the pinpricking sensation that assaulted me.

I couldn't hear the screaming anymore, but I looked down at the rope of shadow penetrating my chest, piercing my heart. I blinked up at him, wondering how he had done it.

This couldn't be the end.

No. I was the Spirit Priestess, and I hadn't yet pulled the realm back together.

At that thought, the crystals erupted from me, shards of pain slicing my skin like a million pieces of glass erupting from my body. I looked into The Gray's eyes and knew he thought he'd won.

And then there was nothing more.

This was death.

CHAPTER TWENTY-SIX

EASTON

I FELL TO MY KNEES, MY ENTIRE BODY SHAKING AS I CAUGHT LYRIC.

Blood poured from an open wound in my chest, one that had not come from a blade. My flesh was broken, but as a result of the smoke that had pierced my mate's heart.

I heard others shouting around me, some clearly not understanding what was happening. I couldn't either.

Lyric's eyes were open, but I couldn't see her pupil or iris. Instead, smoke billowed beneath a glassy film as if she were being possessed by the shadow magic.

I had seen firsthand how the shadow magic and The Gray's Wielding increased once he killed Alura. So, I could only guess that perhaps he was twisting his Spirit Wielding now.

I hadn't had a chance to ask Lyric how it all worked.

There would be no more chances for anything if I didn't fix this.

"What?" Rhodes asked, sliding through the mud and blood on his knees to kneel beside me. He raked his gaze over Lyric's prone body, his silver eyes going wide.

"No. This isn't how it's supposed to happen."

"And it's not. Keep everybody on task. We're going to fix this."

"The Gray is gone," Rhodes shouted.

How were we supposed to do this?

The Gray had disappeared in a puff of smoke and shadow as if he had been waiting for that moment to do so.

"I don't know how we're going to do this. But I need to save her."

"You're bleeding, from the same place Lyric is. The wound's mortal, Easton."

I looked up at the man who had been my rival, my enemy, the man I thought loved Lyric, someone who might still love her, and let out a breath.

"This can't be the end," I whispered, my entire body shaking.

"It's not going to be."

But then the earth shuddered beneath us, and Lyric's eyes opened impossibly wide, smoke billowing from her mouth.

Suddenly, she was gone.

I was left holding nothing but air and faint tendrils of smoke.

"What the hell?" I asked, surging to my feet as I searched for her. Rhodes held me up, my knees shaking.

"She's gone. Where did she go?"

"The Gray has her," he said, his voice just as shaky as my legs.

"But I have to get to her."

"We have to find her," Rhodes agreed.

"I'll find her. I have to find her."

I slid my hand over the gaping wound in my chest, blood still trickling out, and saw the horror. "Where did she go?" I shouted, but then Rosamond was there, her eyes glowing, her skin radiant. "You must go to where The Gray has shattered. You must find the one that matters."

"Where? How?" I asked, swallowing hard as Rhodes kept me steady.

I wasn't even sure the rest of the army had realized what had happened. They were still fighting, trying to save our realm despite the cost. I would let them because the battle was not just about Lyric or me. It was not only about The Gray. It was about so much more.

Our people could not know that Lyric had been taken by The Gray.

"I will help. I can do this."

"Not alone!" Lanya shouted, Delphine by her side. Both were covered in soot and blood, both bleeding from wounds on their faces and arms.

But they were far stronger than most of the people on this battlefield.

"How?" I asked, blood trickling from my mouth. I wiped it away, ignoring the fact that I was going numb.

"We'll open a portal to the Shadow realm. We can only do it because its tendrils are still here. That is why we could not do it before," Lanya said, looking directly into my eyes. I nodded.

If she had been able to do it before, we would have found The Gray, though not on the battlefield. We could have ended things long before this. And where it might have been safe.

I understood. I wasn't raging.

I barely had enough energy to stay standing.

"I'm going with you," Rhodes said, and I shook my head.

"No, you need to fight with Justise and the rest of them. You need to keep Wyn from killing herself."

"I can help more by your side," Rhodes said.

"No, stay here. The people need you. In case, Lyric and I don't come back."

I met the other man's gaze, the man I knew would make a far better king than I ever would or had been. He nodded tightly before I stumbled towards the women. They each put a hand on me, against the blood on my chest, and started to chant.

I didn't know what they were doing. It was old magic. Maybe one day they would teach Lyric and me. In the back of my mind, I vaguely remembered my mother whispering these kinds of chants before everything changed. Even when my father was still alive. Before Lore had ruined our realm, rotted it to the core.

"Find her. Save her."

The women continued chanting as the fight raged around us, the rope of light from the spell wrapping itself around me. I felt a sudden tug on my chest until I was falling.

Falling and falling and falling.

When I landed, it didn't hurt.

Instead, I looked up and thought I recognized where I was.

This had to be the Shadow realm.

They had sent me here. Now, I needed to find Lyric.

I ran my hand over my chest and blinked, noticing that I was still covered in blood, but the wound had healed.

Did that mean that Lyric was okay?

It had to.

I wouldn't allow for any other thoughts to cross my mind.

I made my way down the hall, the sound of my footsteps on the stone loud in my ears.

I had no Wielding here, not with the dampening properties of the Shadow realm itself.

It had taken much sacrifice and dark magic for The Gray to use his Wielding here.

This had been meant as a prison for him. Instead, it had turned into a refuge of evil. A retreat where he could plan his attacks.

I turned the corner and tripped over my feet.

Lyric hung in front of me, her arms pulled tight above her head, secured with ropes of shadow magic. Her feet barely touched the floor.

She was unconscious but alive. I could see her chest rising and falling as she took deep breaths. But she wasn't the only one in the room.

The Gray stood before her, his back to me. I wasn't even sure he was aware of my presence.

Yet it was the other man who lay there that surprised me.

Teagan?

Dear goddess, Teagan was here.

And that was when I looked around and realized we weren't in the Shadow realm at all. These walls were not the gray, dingy concrete of the prison I had been in before.

This was not where I had nearly died. The place I had escaped to get back to Lyric.

Where the hell were we?

"I think we're in the Spirit realm," Teagan said as he came near me.

I blinked at him, reached out to touch him, and then dropped my hands.

"You're....how...?" I whispered, afraid that Lyric and The Gray would hear.

"They can't hear us. See that line?" Teagan asked, pointing to a line of white dust. "They're in a magical circle. We can get in, but twelve hooded men and women who were the Spirit Wielders, I think, told me to wait for you."

"You're...are you alive?"

Teagan looked at me then, but I realized there wasn't a speck of dirt on him. No blood, no wounds. He looked whole...and healthy.

"What's going on?" I asked, trying to formulate words.

"When I died, I came here. The twelve Spirit Wielders that Lyric always talks about made sure I was safe—at least as safe as I could be given I'm dead. They said I was brought here to lead another person and tell you what they need you to do."

"But you're dead. I'm so sorry, Teagan. I need to get to Lyric. I'm so sorry."

"You never have to apologize to me. You have always been there for me. You have always been my brother. I'm only sorry you have to see me this way."

"What do I do now?"

"You're going to cross that line." He pointed at the white line again. "You're going to cut her bonds, and the two of you will bring The Gray back to the Maison realm. When you do, you'll be able to defeat him."

"You're sure of that?" I asked, my heart thumping.

"Well, the Spirit Wielders with their hoods and creepy voices didn't actually say that last part, but I'm going to believe that you two can beat anything. Look at you. You've both had mortal wounds, more than once now, and you survived. You were meant to save the world."

"Lyric. She's dead, though."

I said the words I hadn't meant to say aloud—the ones I had been ignoring this whole time.

Teagan gave me a sad smile.

"Yes. She is. But I think there might be a loophole."

"How so?"

"Well, she still has the crystals within her skin. Use them. Get her home."

"And you?"

I didn't know if I wanted the answer.

I needed to get to Lyric. I had to save my people.

But I couldn't leave Teagan here.

Wyn would never forgive me.

I would never forgive myself.

"I don't know," my best friend said with a shrug as if his death didn't mean anything.

But it had. Though his life meant so much more.

"Come with us," I whispered.

"Not quite sure how that will work." Teagan looked around, confusion in his gaze.

"I'm not sure how any of this works—" I began, but my best friend shook his head.

"Save her so she can save the rest of us. I guess that's the rest of *you* now, huh?"

He smiled again, the sun shielding his eyes. I reached out, blinked when I found he was solid, and then pulled him in to hold him close.

"I love you, brother."

"I love you, too, my king." Teagan pulled away and looked at Lyric.

She was awake now, her gaze locked on mine. I still wasn't sure The Gray had realized I was here.

Good.

I didn't have my Wielding, but I had never been in the Spirit realm before. For all I knew, this was how it usually worked.

The Gray still had his shadow magic or whatever the hell he wanted to call it. I] have to be smart.

Far smarter than I had been before.

I looked to where Teagan was and blinked when I realized that he wasn't there anymore. Instead, there was a sword in his place. A blade that looked remarkably like Luken's.

Interesting.

I picked it up, the heft in my hand solid.

I let out a breath and took a step over the white line.

The Gray turned to me in an instant, surprise in his gaze.

"You."

"Me. Now, let me go," I shouted and charged.

But I didn't go towards The Gray.

Killing him wasn't my destiny. As it was, we were in the Spirit realm, and I didn't think killing him here would work out the way I wanted.

A thousand voices filled my head, and I knew it was the Spirit

Wielders and the lost souls of old. They urged me on, giving me a sense of purpose far greater than I had ever thought possible.

I kept moving. I jumped, moved out of the way of The Gray's swipe, and sliced the sword through the shadow rope.

Lyric landed on her feet, if a bit shakily, then stood, her chin held high as she grinned.

"Thank you," she whispered.

"You can't kill me yet," she snapped at The Gray.

"You might not ever. There are more forces at work than you could ever dream."

"You are nothing. I killed you once. I can kill you again."

The desperation in The Gray's tone didn't warm me.

Because desperate people did horrible things.

"We will fight this out in the Maison realm. The place that will never be yours."

Lyric held out her hand, and the crystals in her skin shone brightly.

I had never seen her look like this, so radiant. Like a queen. No, a Priestess.

She knew exactly what she was doing.

And I would follow.

Always.

I gripped her hand and barely registered that someone else was holding her other hand.

I blinked, but I could only see The Gray's shocked face as he grabbed for us.

He couldn't reach us.

Hopefully, he never would.

CHAPTER TWENTY-SEVEN

LYRIC

THE CRYSTALS SHONE BENEATH MY SKIN, AND I RAISED MY ARMS, finally understanding what I was meant to do.

Death had come, but not for me.

It had come for the past, and now, we would face the future.

"Lyric!"

I dropped my arms and looked off to the side where Rhodes and the others stood, their chests heaving as they fought the enemy.

I would go to them, I would fight with them, but I had other things to do first.

I raised my hands again, the crystals embedded beneath my skin pulsating.

"Shine. Heal our realm. Become who you were meant to be. I hear you."

The crystals sang in my ears, even as the Wielders below me, near where I stood on top of a hill, still fought.

This was what I was meant to do.

I saw The Gray standing on the other side of the battlefield, having followed us through the portal from the Spirit realm. It was the same portal the Spirit Wielders used in my dreams.

This was the first time Easton had followed me, though. The first time I had seen another there, other than the Spirit Wielders.

But Teagan had been there, as well.

Now, he stood next to me, waiting.

I would get to The Gray, but first, I had to save the realm.

That was why I was the Spirit Priestess. Not to fight the evil that caused the destruction of so much. But to pave a way for peace and to secure our future.

We would get to the evil eventually, but first, we needed to secure a base of hope, peace, and understanding.

A foundation that would create a network to bring our realm to a new sense of wholeness.

"Come on, seal that rift. We're here for you. Always."

I let my head fall back, and the crystals tore from my skin, leaving bloody marks down my arms and legs and the rest of my body as they fled.

The crystals reformed in front of me, shining shards of glass and gems, nothing dark versus light. Simply a kaleidoscope of color, the rainbows bursting.

People on both sides of the battle stopped what they were doing.

Wielders let their hands drop. Water ceased in its struggles. Fire diminished, Air settled, and Earth stopped quaking.

People shouted, looked up. The hope in their voices and eyes gave energy to the crystal. There wasn't an ounce of fear to tarnish the healing.

I could feel all of that, even as I melded my five elements to create this new crystal.

Water encircled the crystal, a single cylinder catching on each end as it moved to create a ring.

Fire came, as did Earth, and Air, and Spirit, each advancing from the Wielders in the area, but mostly from me.

The Spirit Wielders had not been lost. They had only been buried.

But they would come back. I knew this.

Teagan let out a sharp gasp beside me, and I held back a smile.

There would be more Spirit Wielders to come once we defeated The Gray. Because we would.

I had no more doubts about that.

I could feel it within me as the twelve Spirit Wielders of the past and the future moved in behind me, no longer circling me in protection.

Instead, they were here to aid me, to push, to bridge the gap.

But Teagan, the newest Spirit Wielder, held out his hands and smiled.

Fire erupted from him, adding to mine, and the other Spirit Wielders did the same, those with dual powers adding their own elements.

Easton looked at me as he held up his hands, adding Fire and Earth, his magic blending with mine in such a peaceful way that it felt as if this were what we'd been waiting for our whole lives.

Centuries after the Fall, here we were, creating the bridge that would seal the rift in the realm.

This was not the end of it. It was only the beginning.

The beginning of hope.

The Gray screamed.

The crystal above us shone brightly before it rose into the sky. I knew it would come back. We would see it again. But first, it needed to heal. Not itself—we had helped with that. It needed to go to the rifts and seal where the creatures were entering, fix where we had lost so many. Our realm had fractured, but now it was being pieced together by its people and its power.

And I was the conduit.

The people were the battery.

The battle in front of me paused for a second, as if those fighting knew things had changed, that something had happened. Oddly enough, it didn't last for long. It couldn't. Not with The Gray in front of us. Not with those who still followed him and wanted the ending he had orchestrated, desired his new world order.

"We need to get The Gray," I said, and Easton tugged on my hand. I turned to him, looked at his frantic gaze, and rose to my tiptoes. He crushed his mouth to mine. A brief kiss that told me he was here.

Later, I would try to understand everything that had happened. Later, I would think.

My work wasn't done yet, though.

"For the realm!" Rhodes shouted from behind us.

"For the realm!" Teagan echoed.

"For the realm," I whispered to Easton.

And then we were fighting again.

The Gray lifted his hands and shot shadow and lightning into the air.

He was no longer hiding the true malice of his powers from the people who followed him.

I looked up at the sound of a screech and smiled as Slavik came forward riding his Domovoi again, flying next to Braelynn.

Braelynn swooped down, and I jumped, landing on her back with a shocked laugh as we made our way down the hill.

Easton and Teagan followed, each of them taking out Wielders as they did.

The battle raged, but we would persevere.

I could feel the realm healing in my soul and I knew we were close.

We only needed to take out The Gray.

But I would need to control the shadows and disperse them to bring about peace. If we didn't do that, someone else could learn what The Gray had done.

Because there would be more Spirit Wielders in the future. I knew that much. And I had learned the hard way that not every Spirit Wielder was good.

Just like not all Wielders on any side wanted peace.

I rode my dragon, my Familiar, my best friend, as we flew down into the battle.

The Creed and League members on The Gray's side worked together, finally coming out of their daze brought forth by the new crystal. They created a wind and water funnel taller than a skyscraper.

I moved forward and pushed my Wielding at it, doing my best to disperse it.

Wyn and Rhodes and Luken appeared, using their Wielding with our Creed and League members to stop it.

Braelynn opened her mouth and spewed fire, evaporating some of the water, and we worked together to disperse them.

The Creed and the League members fell, our combined powers far too great for them.

Slavik and his Underkings worked together to dispatch the other creatures, hopefully sending them home. Though perhaps we'd figure out how to live in harmony with those that had snuck through.

For now, though, they weren't attacking us. And that was enough.

Only The Gray and his forces were left. He didn't have the power to control the creatures who had escaped anymore. Nor to let them out.

Nobody did.

Not even Slavik.

Delphine and Lanya worked side by side with Emory and Rosamond and Ridley, taking care of the injured and using their Wielding where they could.

But then Emory moved away from the others and came running towards me. I landed near her as Braelynn shifted to her human form, and the three of us stood together, chests heaving as we looked at one another.

"Use your Spirit Priestess Wielding or whatever it is and destroy those ropes. I'll fight with him."

I looked at Emory, my eyes wide. "Are you sure? It's so much power. It could kill you."

"I can do this. I can at least siphon off some of his power so you can do the rest. But we need to go.

"Move faster!" Easton shouted from our other side. I nodded at him, hoping we would make this work.

I had to have hope. It was one of the only things I had left.

And so we fought through the lines.

Brae in her human form fought with a sword I hadn't known she had strapped to her back.

Apparently, she had picked up a few things from Luken along the way and was fighting, protecting me. Rhodes and Rosamond fought as one. Wyn joined in, all of them working together to corral the enemy.

They were clearing a path to The Gray.

But The Gray didn't seem to care. He kept shoving his people in front of him, making them take the brunt of the Wielding.

He was a coward to the core. Only now, some of his people were seeing that.

By the end of this, I hoped all of them would realize the kind of being he was.

We moved, Wyn and Rhodes fighting together again.

Teagan came up from behind me, finally having caught up with Easton.

I would need Teagan and his Spirit Wielding in the end. Thankfully, he seemed to know this.

I knew the others had things they wanted to know, like how we could be here after dying. We would answer all those questions. But first, we needed to fight for our people.

"For our realm," I whispered.

"For our realm," Emory and Braelynn echoed. Suddenly, I knew the three of us would get this done with the help of our people.

We hadn't been born in the Maison realm. But we were here now. This was our home.

We had died already, and would die again to protect it.

Easton had gotten me out of the Spirit realm, and the others were fighting their battles. But now, this was for me and those with the power to defeat The Gray.

"You think you can beat me!" The Gray shouted, as the others continued to fight.

I could see all of them in my periphery, all of my friends and my new family, fighting and protecting us.

I could feel the weight of my parents' souls on my heart, of Arwin and everyone else we had lost to get to this point.

Even Queen Cameo was beside me, aiding me.

We were not alone. But The Gray was.

He just didn't realize it yet.

"And what do you expect to do when you find yourself with that power?" I asked, my voice calm. Too calm.

"I have all the power. Something you've yet to realize. You may have created a new crystal, but I will defile this one just like I did the last. The Maisons don't deserve this realm. I deserve this power. And because I made that known, they put me in a prison. They have cannibalized their own powers and destroyed themselves. And now they will learn what happens when they take from me."

"You're wrong. Now, you will learn what happens when you try to destroy a civilization."

I raised my hands, my four elemental Wieldings surrounding my Spirit Wielding, boosting it.

This was why I was the Spirit Priestess. I might not be the

strongest of everyone in each individual element, but I could use all five to do this. This was my destiny.

It was why I was here.

Easton's eyes were on me, but I knew he would fight to protect me.

Just like Luken fought to protect Braelynn.

And Rosamond with Emory.

But the three of us girls were here, with Teagan behind us, and we *would* do this.

Braelynn raised her chin before lifting her sword and smashing it into the ground.

The Wielding surrounded us, the power within me shuddered and spiraled through the sword as if she'd pulled it out of the ground and handed it to me.

"Do what Luken does, arm yourself."

I grinned.

I hadn't been able to take the sword from the Spirit realm. But I could use this.

The Gray's eyes widened, and I smiled.

Teagan pressed his hands to my back, and his Spirit Wielding slid through me, bolstering mine.

We had no idea what we were doing, but we could hear the twelve Spirit Wielders of our past, the cacophony of so many more voices, those who had died or had hidden to protect their loved ones.

This was what we needed to do.

We were going to win.

"For the realm!"

"For our people."

I sliced through the first rope of shadow.

The Gray screamed and came at me again, but Teagan held up his Fire Wielding and blocked the blast.

Easton was there with Earth, and Wyn with Water. Rhodes with Air.

They were all there, blocking The Gray's Spirit Wielding with Teagan amplifying mine.

Everything went through the sword and towards The Gray.

I looked at the blade for a second and frowned.

This was the one that had killed me. I knew this weapon. But where had Braelynn gotten it?

I didn't have time to think about that, though. I knew that this was the sword that would help me defeat The Gray.

But first, we needed to weaken him.

I gave the woman behind him a tight nod and prayed that she would be okay.

She was far stronger than she had been before, stronger than any one of us had given her credit for.

When The Gray fell to his knees and screamed, I looked up at Emory, her dark hair flowing behind her as she pulsed with power, her skin nearly translucent.

Her veins popped, fluorescent purple with lightning flashes as she siphoned some of the power from The Gray.

"It's too much!" I said. "Let go, I can handle this."

"You don't have to handle everything!" Emory said, her voice cracking.

Her skin was so thin, nearly paper-like. She was going to die if she didn't stop soon.

Braelynn moved forward, shifted to her dragon form in a blink of an eye, and swiped at The Gray.

She couldn't kill him, not with so much power radiating from him and protecting him, but she sliced a jagged tear through him, knocking him down again.

Emory staggered back, and Braelynn swooped forward, then plucked an unconscious Emory from the ground and flew away.

My friends were there to help and had sacrificed so much.

But this was not the end. Not yet.

"You must finish this," Easton said as he came up beside me.

"So much death," I whispered.

"I know. I'll do it if you need me to. But this is your fight."

I didn't need him to do anything for me. I didn't need anyone to save me.

I thought maybe we could imprison The Gray like before, but I knew that wasn't going to work. Not when he staggered forward and reached for a blade left on the ground by a dead soldier.

He would keep coming. He would keep killing. So, I moved forward, ready to stop him.

Only, he was faster.

He picked up the blade and shot the last of his shadow magic through it. But instead of pushing it towards me, he threw it into the air.

Slavik was there, both he and the Domovoi flying forward and blocking Braelynn.

I gasped as I watched the pirate king fall to the ground. He'd saved the Domovoi's life, as well, an innocent creature that hadn't asked for any of this.

We were too slow to stop his fall, and I shuddered at the crunch that sounded as he hit the ground. Rosamond was only able to let out her Air Wielding at the last minute to brace his fall.

The Gray hadn't tried to kill me. Instead, he had tried to kill those who were mine.

He might've succeeded in killing Slavik.

"You do not have to kill," Seven whispered in my ear.

"We can handle this, darling," my mother whispered right after.

Tears stung my eyes, and I raised my hands, knowing that they would help.

The Spirit Wielding within me burst forth, though this time, instead of cutting through the shadow magic, it dispersed it.

The Gray screamed and then gasped as they flew back to wherever souls ended up in the end.

Those he'd used would no longer be prisoners to The Gray. But as I blinked and looked up, I saw I was not alone with my friends on the top of this hill.

No, there were many.

The twelve Spirit Wielders stood around our group in a circle, and given the shocked looks surrounding me, I knew the others could see them.

The Spirit Wielders were able to show themselves now because they were here for the end.

We were all the sacrifice, but not how The Gray expected.

"Your reign of terror has come to an end," I shouted, the battle still raging around me, though those on my side cheered with me.

"You were The Gray, but now you will be forgotten in our histories. We will move forward without you. Together."

I raised my hands, and the Spirit Wielders from the past, the future, and the present, moved as one. The Gray screamed, the Spirit Wielding within us all boosted by the other Wieldings I held.

The Gray shouted and tried to move towards his army, but they were no longer fighting.

Suddenly, The Gray was dust, no longer there. Not even in memory.

Our people shouted as the battle waned, and all I could do was stand there, trying to catch my breath.

I looked at my friends, at those who were still here, fighting, bleeding, and I knew that, somehow, we had made it.

The Gray was gone. The realm would be healed.

We had a future.

And I was a part of it.

CHAPTER TWENTY-EIGHT

EASTON

HOW DOES ONE CLEAN UP AFTER A BATTLE FOR SURVIVAL?

Slowly.

And with the help of many people.

I looked out across the kingdom, the realm, and knew it was mine. As it was for those who stood near me.

The Gray was gone, turned into dust, now only a memory.

Some would fight for him still despite that, but those were being taken care of.

They would not go to the Shadow realm prison, at least not until we figured out exactly what The Gray had done with it while he was contained within those walls for all those centuries.

However, those who still wanted to kill Lyric, and anyone who still wanted to taint the power of the realm would be dealt with.

We weren't handing out executions. We were not The Gray. We were finding a new path.

We would not go down in history as those with blood in our eyes and on our hands.

Yes, I had blood on my hands, I knew that.

But we would rise above and against.

And now, we would rebuild.

And with building came decisions.

Decisions that I had to be part of, even if I wanted to walk away from them.

"Easton," Lyric said as she moved closer, a smile on her face. She had brightness in her eyes that I hadn't seen for far too long. Maybe since that first time at the Fire and Earth territory border when she had been just learning about magic and didn't know about all of the darkness in the world yet.

The realm's destruction was no longer a burden she had to carry, at least not alone.

We all had responsibilities, and we would do whatever we could to find our footing in the future. But Lyric was the Spirit Priestess, and she had saved us all. As foretold.

I moved forward and cupped her face with my hands.

"Hello, Priestess."

She smiled at me, the cuts on her forehead, her chest, and everywhere else now gone, healed thanks to Ridley and the other healers.

She was whole. Had all of her elements, and was stunningly beautiful.

"I see you're letting your hair grow," she said, tugging at the leather tie at the back of my neck.

I shrugged and shook my hair out when she took off the tie.

"I think I like it," she said, teasing.

I grinned. "It's getting a little bothersome. I just haven't had time to cut it."

"Well, at least when you do decide, you're not going to use a sword on it."

She tugged on her shoulder-length hair, and I held back a scowl.

"Hey, none of that. I was only teasing."

"Let's not bring back the memory of you almost getting your head lopped off by the former King of Lumière."

"I'm sorry, I'm sorry. We can also forget all of the other stabbings and burdens and everything else that has happened if you'd like. Although they still happened. If we talk it through, maybe we will heal faster. Or perhaps a little easier."

"I don't like it when you start making sense."

She raised her brows. "Would you rather I be nonsensical and act like a damsel in distress?"

"You know, my life *would* probably be a lot easier if you were a damsel. But, no, you constantly have to throw yourself into situations where you have to save the world."

"The crystal is back. Whole. Not calling out for its mate. I don't think I'll have to die to save the world again."

My blood ran cold at that, and I swallowed hard.

"Let's not have that happen."

"I'll do my best for you, but you're going to have to do it, too. And no jumping through random portals to save me."

"Okay, I can make that promise."

She snorted, shaking her head. "The crystal is waiting for us," Lyric said.

I nodded. "I think we'll have to build a court around it."

She smiled. "Let's go meet our friends and formulate the plan."

"Let's see if they like what we came up with."

She tangled her fingers with mine, and we made our way to the center of the field where we had set up tents and other structures as our court for now.

We were not going to use the broken-down and nearly burnt-to-a-crisp former court of the Lumière.

The Obscurité Court was gone, but now that the wards were no longer separating the lands, we could potentially build something new here. From the grounds of our sacrifices spring our hopes.

I just had to see if the others would agree.

"So, Spirit Wielder?" I asked Teagan as I made my way towards the others.

He shrugged, looking as confused as the rest of us.

"I'm still not sure exactly what happened," my best friend said, looking at Lyric.

"I'm not a hundred percent sure either. I just knew you had to come with me. I had to die to get to where you were, but you had to be there, as well. It was never solely about my sacrifice. It was the sacrifice of all of us, even if that meant giving up something other than our lives."

Lyric looked at Emory and Justise, and then the rest of us. I nodded, understanding what she meant.

"The prophecy was about all of us."

"It was about the Spirit Priestess and the family she made," Ridley countered.

"It would have been nice if we understood that beforehand," Emory said, and Rosamond shook her head, her hand softly closing over Emory's.

"Wow, did you start the party without me?" Slavik asked, limping his way towards us.

He had nearly died saving Braelynn, Emory, and the rest of us.

I hadn't thought the pirate king had it in him, but I had been wrong.

Slavik grinned, leaned against one of the other people under his command, and slowly slumped to the ground near us.

Ridley got up to look the other man over, but Slavik waved him off.

"Nothing you can do for me now. All of my insides are where they're supposed to be. At least, somewhat."

I held back a grimace at that but nodded at the other man.

"I'm glad you're here. That means we can have this discussion."

"Discussion?" Rhodes asked.

"Is this where he decides he's going to be king and tells us where we're supposed to be?" Slavik asked, winking.

Some of the other Underkings snorted, shaking their heads.

"Not exactly," I said, looking at Lyric.

"Oh. So is this where you tell me exactly what you've been thinking? Oh, wait, I know. We're on the same page."

I felt the pulse of her love and support through our bond and ignored the gagging sounds coming from Slavik and Teagan and even my Uncle Justise.

"Okay, tell us what you've decided."

"First, I think this needs to be where we settle."

I looked at the others. They all nodded.

"I agree," Delphine said, leaning in next to Lanya. The two had become close during this time, and I was grateful for it. They both had a lot of healing to do, they had lost so much, but we would need them in the days to come and beyond.

"So, a new court?" Wyn asked. "And we just decide who it's to be?"

"I think we should take some time to make that decision. After a certain time period, then we can make the next one," I said carefully.

"So, we set up a court under one banner and make a loophole in case something needs to change in the next...what? Ten years?"

"Or fifty, or a hundred. But whoever we put on the throne needs to understand what we're doing here."

"I think everybody in this circle right now understands what you mean," Luken said, Brae in her cat form curled up in his lap.

She had exhausted her human and dragon selves during the battle and the cleanup, so now, she was spending her latest third of time in her cat form.

They would have a long future together, one that might be a little different than others' idea of a future, but they would make it work for them.

"I have already seen what you've decided," Rosamond said with a grin. "And I completely agree."

"I don't know if I'm going to like this," Emory said with a laugh, looking into Rosamond's eyes with an understanding that made me laugh.

"It's not going to be me," Lyric said.

"Who else should it be?" Wyn asked. "You're the Spirit Priestess. Who better to rule a kingdom than the one who saved it?"

I looked at the person I loved more than anything and knew that if she wanted to take the throne, I would follow her to the ends of the earth and beyond. I had already done so once. I would do it again in a heartbeat.

"I am not meant to rule. I'm meant to oversee the Wielding of the realm. I am here to help the crystal and make sure that it is ready and cared for. I'm not meant to rule the realm's people or to govern. I need to make sure the magic and the Wielding within the realm is safe, just, and useful."

"And I was meant to stand by your side as your consort," I said firmly, only a few people gasping at my comment.

"Well then, should I be king?" Slavik asked with a laugh.

"No, I think if you were king, we'd end up in another war, this time with a different realm that we haven't even heard of yet," Wyn said dryly.

"Why? Did you like my dragon?" Slavik asked, winking, and the Underkings laughed.

"We all know who the king needs to be," I said, breaking through Teagan's laughter.

"Yes, we do," Lyric said.

We all looked at Rhodes, who blinked.

"Me? I wasn't ever in line for a throne to begin with."

"You were ten times the prince Eitri was," Wyn grumbled, and I laughed outright.

"What?" she demanded.

"You. Saying that. It's just hilarious."

Wyn smiled. "It did take a lot out of me."

"Thanks," Rhodes bit out. "But I'm not meant to be king."

"No, and that's why you need to be," Lyric said.

"You will be the High King of the Maison realm. Our court will be that of the lords and ladies of each of the territories, as well as the Underkings."

She gave Slavik a pointed look.

"And I a lord, then?" Slavik asked. "I kind of like it."

"We'll give you a title later," I said, laughing. "But we need all of us. Not just those of noble birth. There needs to be more," I agreed.

"And that is where Lanya and Delphine come in," Lyric said. "You can work with me. As part of the Council of Wielders."

Lanya smiled, and Delphine just shook her head.

"I was the queen of cruelty. I don't deserve to be part of any governing body."

I shook my head. "No, you were married to a cruel king who tortured and silenced you. We need all viewpoints of all people who understand why we can't be murdered in our beds."

"We need you, Delphine. If you feel you can do it."

"Teagan, Wyn, we'll need you, as well."

"I don't want to be the Lady of Dirt," Wyn growled.

"You could always be Water," Rosamond said with a smile. "I could take up Air. I think I would like that."

"And I guess I'm Fire," Teagan said.

"If that's what we decide. We will figure out our courts, and we will talk with the people and see what they want and need." Lyric smiled, and I tugged at her hands, pulling her towards me so I could hold her.

The others rolled their eyes, but I just kissed her temple and looked at Rhodes. "You will be our king. The one who takes us into the next century. We've had our Fall. We've shattered. Now, we can rise."

"I'm not the man for this," Rhodes said.

"You're the man we need," Lyric said. "I don't want to rule, but I do want to heal. And to do that, I need to be with the magic and with the crystal."

"So, the king with the Priestess as his aide?"

"Or maybe a Priestess with a king as her aide," I whispered.

"We work together to create a new realm."

I nodded at Rhodes. "Together. We survived the Fall, we survived the war, but our people still need us. And so, we'll do this as we should have before. As one."

I held my Priestess, my Lyric, and I knew we would succeed.

There were dangers out there, unknowns that we hadn't uncovered as yet. But The Gray was gone, and the rot had been unearthed.

We would prevail.

We would have a king, a Priestess, and a healthy realm.

And I knew we could face whatever came at us next.

THE REALM

LYRIC

I WAS THE PROTECTOR. NOT THE RULER.

For that, I would shine.

I never wanted a crown, neither did Easton.

And we would protect the realm with every ounce of Wielding and soul we had within us.

In the month since the great battle, we had rebuilt. With the power of Wielding, we'd built a castle that was a home and a symbol of healing. It had taken far less time than it would have in the human realm.

It was odd to think of the human realm now, a place I wasn't sure I would ever go back to. I wasn't human any longer, and I had no ties to that place anymore.

All the ties that I had were here, and in the Spirit realm I knew I would return to someday.

We were not only building a castle that we called home. We were also building a place in the northern Spirit territory for the newly found Spirit Wielders to train, find peace, and feel at home.

It was much of the same in each of the territories, but instead of a long, torturous journey to get to each of them, we were finding ways to make roads more passable, and for every single person who needed a home to find one.

We were not building a symbol of royalty, or power and corruption.

We were being rebirthed from the ashes, building on the remnants of pain that had once been, to morph into what we needed to be now.

Hope.

And healing.

It wouldn't be easy. And not everybody agreed on everything. But not one person went hungry. Nobody without the power to Wield felt as if they weren't enough.

Rhodes and I worked hand in hand to ensure that others would understand and be able to heal.

And in ten years, we would come back and see if we needed to change how we'd set up the new Maison realm.

That was the promise we had made to the people, and they seemed to understand.

Perhaps not everybody would find peace in that, but we were trying. And learning.

We would not make our forebearers' mistakes.

And we would not let The Gray's shadow be cast upon us any longer.

"Are you ready for this?" Rhodes asked, his gaze raking down my body.

I looked down at the white and lavender robes I wore and grinned. "I've never felt like a princess before. But I guess I'm not one, so I suppose I should say that I've never felt like such a Priestess." I said.

"Would you prefer battle leathers or jeans?"

I remembered my lost hoodie that I had loved so much that I wore every time I went jogging. I had worn it the first time I had found the Negs. I held back a sigh at the memory. I didn't miss much of my old life. There was too much in my life now that I could hold onto.

The Negs hadn't been seen since the day The Gray died.

The other creatures had, those that had slipped through the cracks in the foundation of our realm. But Slavik and others who were able to speak to them were helping us corral them and keep the peace.

I wanted them to remain free if they wished, so long as they were safe and no danger to our people.

We were finding ways to make that happen.

Nobody and nothing deserved to be caged any longer.

Well, perhaps those who kept trying to kill me could be caged for a bit longer.

But that was something we were working on.

"You were about to put a crown on Rhodes' head. Much different than standing beside him as his queen," Easton said, and I saw the laughter in his eyes. Still, I pushed at him.

He looked regal and hot as hell in his royal robes and leather pants.

I just shook my head at him.

"Rhodes was never for me, even if we might have thought so at one point."

"I can't begrudge him for that. I love you too much. Of course, others would see who you are and fall for you."

"Or maybe we always knew that I would be connected to him in some way. A Priestess to the king."

"Perhaps. But a king is going to need his queen."

I thought of who that could be and shook my head.

"There's time for that."

"If he's quick about it. If not, she'll slip right through his fingers. And you already saw what our other so-called king wants."

"He's a council member now. Are they still calling themselves the Underkings?" I asked with a laugh.

"They are. They even have an emblem."

"Is that going to be a problem?" I asked, worried.

"Probably not. Slavik has them under control. Which is something I never thought I'd say, but...here we are."

"Yes, here we are."

"Did we do the right thing? With Rhodes as the king and the council of our friends?"

"There are others on the council that you didn't know before. Ones with pure hearts and brilliant minds. They'll lead us into this new world."

"And we'll protect it."

He tucked my hair behind my ear and smiled. "Always, my Priestess. I'll protect you and our realm."

"You know it should probably be the other way around," I whispered.

"Probably, but I've never been much for rules."

He kissed me softly, and I leaned into him, barely noticing the person clearing their throat beside me.

"You know, we are going to be late to this whole shindig," Emory said, her bracelets glittering in the light.

I snorted and moved towards my friend. Braelynn came from behind her, and I hugged both of them at the same time, wondering how on earth we had ended up here.

The three of us had come to this realm not knowing what we were in for, and all of us had been through hell since.

And yet, somehow, we were together.

Perhaps in far different ways than we'd ever thought possible, but here we were.

Emory was a siphon but learning to use her powers for good.

After all, some Wielders had been thrown into their power so violently, they needed help. And Ridley and Rosamond were teaching Emory how to use her magic for good.

We couldn't take them away from her, but we could help her work with them.

And Braelynn was working with Luken in charge of an army and was brilliant at it.

My peaceful, calm best friend was a dragon, a cat with wings, and the wife of one of my dearest friends.

"What are we doing here?" Wyn asked, Teagan on her tail.

"I think we're just watching Easton kiss Lyric for a while," Brae said with a smile.

"I'm really not in the mood for that," Wyn said, brushing her hands down her dress. "Come on, let's go watch the prince get crowned and become a king."

"You don't have to sound so happy about it," Teagan said with a grin.

"I'm not happy about it. I'm going to have to bow and everything."

"You could always curtsy," I said.

"I am a warrior. I do not curtsy."

"You're wearing a dress," Teagan said, and she shoved him.

"Watch it, Teagan. You may be a nice Spirit boy now, but I have Water."

"Ooh, I'm so scared," Teagan said, running away as she snapped her fingers and spritzed him with water.

I shook my head, my shoulders shaking as Easton full-out laughed beside me.

"Well, our family is definitely insane. But at least we're lovable."

"Whatever you say," I said with a laugh.

"Okay, let's get this show on the road."

We all moved into position, and I smiled at the crowd.

They smiled back, waving and cheering. I was happy that we weren't having Rhodes crowned in a court in front of only certain people.

Instead, we were doing it in the courtyard, where every single Maison who wanted to be in attendance could be. And those who were at their estates or their farms or wherever they were around the realm who couldn't be there, were magically allowed to see through special Water and Air made portals, even if they couldn't travel the distance.

The realm would be of the people, for the people. Not of the power.

The crystal was positioned in the center of the courtyard.

We were not hiding it from anyone anymore.

I swore it winked at me as I passed, and I waved, knowing the others likely thought I was a little crazy.

I knew the crystal might not be fully sentient, but it had cried for me, had healed itself within my body. And now, it was two halves of a whole pieced back together in blood but also in harmony.

Anyone who wanted to see it could, although we did have guards and magical wards around it to keep it safe.

Nobody would be allowed to harm it as Lore had. As the Gray had.

But the world could know it existed and feel its warmth.

It would keep our realm healthy, and we would do everything in our power to keep it healthy, as well.

Eventually, the crystal would be moved to the Priestess domain, something everybody had agreed to.

After all, I was the realm's protector.

But for now, it was warded here.

When Easton and I moved to our new place, the crystal would come with us.

And there, everybody would be able to see it.

Just like they could here.

The council surrounded Rhodes, and I nodded at them before moving forward, approaching the man who had brought me to this realm, the man I had thought I loved.

I still did, but as my friend. My family.

"I still think you might be making a mistake," Rhodes whispered.

"And I think you are my king. And I will always protect you."

"Okay, whatever you say," Rhodes said, and Easton chuckled beside me.

Lanya handed me the crown, and I crowned Rhodes High King of the Maison realm.

The people rejoiced and cheered, and I, their Spirit Priestess, vowed to protect them.

The realm had once been shattered, broken.

But now it was whole, its fissures healing more and more with every breath, birth, and hope that sprang up.

We would remember the dead, honor the souls lost.

But we were reborn.

We would never stand in silence again. Nor in shadow.

I was a Spirit Priestess.

A protector.

And the Maison realm was home.

Lyric's journey is over...for now.

But if you're still in the mood for a more mature fantasy romance... try the Dante's Circle series!

A NOTE FROM CARRIE ANN RYAN

Thank you so much for reading FROM SHADOW AND SILENCE!

I loved writing this world. Lyric and her crew took me on a path I wasn't expecting, and I'm honored you've joined them on their journey!

I hope to one day go back and write a few more stories that are begging for me. After all...I already have an idea...

Rhodes is waiting...

As is his queen...

Lyric's journey is over...for now.

But if you're still in the mood for a more mature fantasy romance...try the Dante's Circle series!

If you want to make sure you know what's coming next from me, you can sign up for my newsletter at www. CarrieAnnRyan.com; follow me on twitter at @CarrieAnnRyan, or like my Facebook page. I also have a Facebook Fan Club where we have trivia, chats, and other goodies. You guys are the reason I get to do what I do and I thank you.

Make sure you're signed up for my MAILING LIST so you can know when the next releases are available as well as find giveaways and FREE READS.

Happy Reading!

The Elements of Five Series:

ABOUT THE AUTHOR

Carrie Ann Ryan is the New York Times and USA Today best-selling author of contemporary, paranormal, and young adult romance. Her works include the Montgomery Ink, Redwood Pack, Fractured Connections, and Elements of Five series, which have sold over 3.0 million books worldwide. She started writing while in graduate school for her advanced degree in chemistry and hasn't stopped since. Carrie Ann has written over seventy-five novels and novellas with more in the works. When she's not losing herself in her emotional and action-packed worlds, she's reading as much as she can while wrangling her clowder of cats who have more followers than she does.

www.CarrieAnnRyan.com

ALSO FROM CARRIE ANN RYAN

The Montgomery Ink: Fort Collins Series:
  Book 1: Inked Persuasion
  Book 2: Inked Obsession
  Book 3: Inked Devotion
  Book 4: Inked Craving

The On My Own Series:
  Book 1: My One Night
  Book 2: My Rebound
  Book 3: My Next Play
  Book 4: My Bad Decisions

The Tattered Royals Series:
  Book 1: Royal Line
  Book 2: Enemy Heir

The Ravenwood Coven Series:
  Book 1: Dawn Unearthed
  Book 2: Dusk Unveiled
  Book 3: Evernight Unleashed

Montgomery Ink:
  Book 0.5: Ink Inspired

Book 0.6: Ink Reunited
Book 1: Delicate Ink
Book 1.5: Forever Ink
Book 2: Tempting Boundaries
Book 3: Harder than Words
Book 4: Written in Ink
Book 4.5: Hidden Ink
Book 5: Ink Enduring
Book 6: Ink Exposed
Book 6.5: Adoring Ink
Book 6.6: Love, Honor, & Ink
Book 7: Inked Expressions
Book 7.3: Dropout
Book 7.5: Executive Ink
Book 8: Inked Memories
Book 8.5: Inked Nights
Book 8.7: Second Chance Ink

Montgomery Ink: Colorado Springs
Book 1: Fallen Ink
Book 2: Restless Ink
Book 2.5: Ashes to Ink
Book 3: Jagged Ink
Book 3.5: Ink by Numbers

The Montgomery Ink: Boulder Series:
Book 1: Wrapped in Ink
Book 2: Sated in Ink
Book 3: Embraced in Ink
Book 3.5: Moments in Ink
Book 4: Seduced in Ink
Book 4.5: Captured in Ink

The Gallagher Brothers Series:
Book 1: Love Restored
Book 2: Passion Restored
Book 3: Hope Restored

The Whiskey and Lies Series:

Book 1: Whiskey Secrets
Book 2: Whiskey Reveals
Book 3: Whiskey Undone

The Fractured Connections Series:
Book 1: Breaking Without You
Book 2: Shouldn't Have You
Book 3: Falling With You
Book 4: Taken With You

The Less Than Series:
Book 1: Breathless With Her
Book 2: Reckless With You
Book 3: Shameless With Him

The Promise Me Series:
Book 1: Forever Only Once
Book 2: From That Moment
Book 3: Far From Destined
Book 4: From Our First

Redwood Pack Series:
Book 1: An Alpha's Path
Book 2: A Taste for a Mate
Book 3: Trinity Bound
Book 3.5: A Night Away
Book 4: Enforcer's Redemption
Book 4.5: Blurred Expectations
Book 4.7: Forgiveness
Book 5: Shattered Emotions
Book 6: Hidden Destiny
Book 6.5: A Beta's Haven
Book 7: Fighting Fate
Book 7.5: Loving the Omega
Book 7.7: The Hunted Heart
Book 8: Wicked Wolf

The Talon Pack:
Book 1: Tattered Loyalties

Book 2: An Alpha's Choice
Book 3: Mated in Mist
Book 4: Wolf Betrayed
Book 5: Fractured Silence
Book 6: Destiny Disgraced
Book 7: Eternal Mourning
Book 8: Strength Enduring
Book 9: Forever Broken

The Elements of Five Series:
Book 1: From Breath and Ruin
Book 2: From Flame and Ash
Book 3: From Spirit and Binding
Book 4: From Shadow and Silence

The Branded Pack Series:
(Written with Alexandra Ivy)
Book 1: Stolen and Forgiven
Book 2: Abandoned and Unseen
Book 3: Buried and Shadowed

Dante's Circle Series:
Book 1: Dust of My Wings
Book 2: Her Warriors' Three Wishes
Book 3: An Unlucky Moon
Book 3.5: His Choice
Book 4: Tangled Innocence
Book 5: Fierce Enchantment
Book 6: An Immortal's Song
Book 7: Prowled Darkness
Book 8: Dante's Circle Reborn

Holiday, Montana Series:
Book 1: Charmed Spirits
Book 2: Santa's Executive
Book 3: Finding Abigail
Book 4: Her Lucky Love
Book 5: Dreams of Ivory

The Happy Ever After Series:
   Flame and Ink
   Ink Ever After

Single Title:
   Finally Found You